Mary Higgins Clark, number one international and *New York Times* bestselling author, has written thirty-five suspense novels; three collections of short stories; a historical novel, *Mount Vernon Love Story*; two children's books, including *The Magical Christmas Horse*; and a memoir, *Kitchen Privileges.* With her daughter Carol Higgins Clark, she has coauthored five more suspense novels. Her books have sold more than 100 million copies in the United States alone.

Alafair Burke is the *New York Times* bestselling author of eleven novels, including *Long Gone*, *If You Were Here*, and the latest in the Ellie Hatcher series, *All Day and a Night*. A former prosecutor, she now teaches criminal law and lives in Manhattan.

By Mary Higgins Clark

The Melody Lingers On
Death Wears a Beauty Mask
I've Got You Under My Skin
Daddy's Gone A Hunting
The Magical Christmas Horse (Illustrated by Wendell Minor)
I'll Walk Alone
The Shadow of Your Smile
Just Take My Heart
Where Are You Now?
Ghost Ship (Illustrated by Wendell Minor)
I Heard That Song Before
Two Little Girls in Blue
No Place Like Home
Nighttime Is My Time
The Second Time Around
Kitchen Privileges
Mount Vernon Love Story
Silent Night / All Through the Night
Daddy's Little Girl
On the Street Where You Live
Before I Say Good-Bye
We'll Meet Again
All Through the Night
You Belong to Me
Pretend You Don't See Her
My Gal Sunday
Moonlight Becomes You
Silent Night
Let Me Call You Sweetheart
The Lottery Winner
Remember Me
I'll Be Seeing You
All Around Town
Loves Music, Loves to Dance

The Anastasia Syndrome and Other Stories
While My Pretty One Sleeps
Weep No More, My Lady
Stillwatch
A Cry in the Night
The Cradle Will Fall
A Stranger Is Watching
Where Are the Children?

BY MARY HIGGINS CLARK AND CAROL HIGGINS CLARK

Dashing Through the Snow
Santa Cruise
The Christmas Thief
He Sees You When You're Sleeping
Deck the Halls

BY MARY HIGGINS CLARK AND ALAFAIR BURKE

The Cinderella Murder

BY ALAFAIR BURKE

If You Were Here
Long Gone

THE ELLIE HATCHER SERIES

All Day and a Night
Never Tell
212
Angel's Tip
Dead Connection

THE SAMANTHA KINCAID SERIES

Close Case
Missing Justice
Judgment Calls

MARY HIGGINS CLARK
& ALAFAIR BURKE

ALL DRESSED IN WHITE

SIMON & SCHUSTER

London · New York · Sydney · Toronto · New Delhi

A CBS COMPANY

First published in the US by Simon & Schuster, Inc., 2015
First published in Great Britain by Simon & Schuster UK Ltd, 2015
This paperback edition published in 2016
A CBS COMPANY

1 3 5 7 9 10 8 6 4 2

Simon & Schuster UK Ltd
1st Floor
222 Gray's Inn Road
London WC1X 8HB

www.simonandschuster.co.uk

Simon & Schuster Australia, Sydney
Simon & Schuster India, New Delhi

A CIP catalogue record for this book
is available from the British Library

Paperback B ISBN: 978-1-4711-4870-5
Paperback A ISBN: 978-1-47115-214-6
eBook ISBN: 978-1-47114-871-2

Printed and bound by CPI Group (UK) Ltd, Croydon, CR0 4YY

Simon & Schuster UK Ltd are committed to sourcing paper that is made from wood grown in sustainable forests and support the Forest Stewardship Council, the leading international forest certification organisation. Our books displaying the FSC logo are printed on FSC certified paper.

In memory of

Joan Nye

Dear friend since our days at Villa Maria Academy

With love

—MARY

For Richard and Jon

—ALAFAIR

Acknowledgments

We now know who did it! Others in this tale are no longer "under suspicion."

Once again it has been my joy to cowrite with my fellow novelist, Alafair Burke. When we put our creative brains together we have a lot of fun.

Marysue Rucci, editor-in-chief of Simon & Schuster, is again our mentor on this journey. A thousand thanks for all the help.

Thank you to Dr. Frederick Jaccarino for his helpful expertise on a medical issue in this story.

"Root, root, root" for the home team. In my case it is "my spouse extraordinaire," John Conheeney; my children; and my right-hand assistant, Nadine Petry. They are always with me with words of encouragement and solid advice. *Thank you, merci, gracias, etc. etc. etc.*

And you, my dear readers. You are always in my thoughts as I write. If you choose to read my books, I want you to feel as though you have spent your time well.

Cheers and Blessings,
Mary

Here comes the bride dressed all in light
Radiant and lovely she shines in his sight

ALL DRESSED IN WHITE

Prologue

It was Thursday evening in mid-April at the Grand Victoria Hotel in Palm Beach.

Amanda Pierce, the bride-to-be, was trying on her wedding gown with the help of her longtime friend Kate.

"Pray God it fits," she said, but then the zipper finally glided past that tricky spot above her waistline.

"I can't believe you were the least bit concerned that it wouldn't fit," Kate said matter-of-factly.

"Well, after all the weight loss last year, I was afraid I might have put on just enough to strain at the waistline. I thought better to know now than Saturday. Can't you just see us struggling with the zipper as I'm about to walk down the aisle?"

"We won't," Kate declared emphatically. "I don't know why you were so nervous about it. Look in the mirror. You're gorgeous."

Amanda gazed at her reflection. "It is lovely, isn't it?" She thought of how she had tried on more than a hundred gowns, checking out Manhattan's finest bridal shops, before spotting this one at a tiny store in Brooklyn Heights. Off-white silk with an empire waist and hand-made lace overlay for the bodice—it was everything she had pictured. In forty-three hours, she would be wearing it down the aisle.

"More than lovely," Kate declared. "So why do you look so sad?"

Amanda looked again in the mirror. Blond with a heart-shaped face, wide blue eyes, long lashes, and naturally raspberry-colored lips, she knew she had been blessed with good features. But Kate was right. She did look sad. Not sad, exactly, but worried. The dress fits perfectly, she reminded herself. That must be a sign, right? She forced herself to smile. "I was just wondering how much I could eat tonight and still fit in this on Saturday."

Kate laughed and patted her own, slightly round belly. "Don't talk that way around me, of all people. Seriously, Amanda, are you okay? Are you still thinking about our conversation yesterday?"

Amanda waved a hand. "Not a second thought," she answered, knowing she was not being truthful. "Now, help me get out of this thing. The others must be ready to go down to dinner."

Ten minutes later, alone in her bedroom, now wearing a light blue linen dress, Amanda slipped on an earring and took a final glance at the wedding gown, now carefully spread on the bed. Then she noticed a makeup smear on the lace right beneath the neckline. She had been so cautious, and still the faint smudge was staring back at her. She knew it would come out, but was this perhaps the sign she was waiting for?

She had spent nearly the last two days as an outsider at her own destination wedding, searching for clues to tell her whether this wedding was meant to be. Looking at that spot on her gown, she made a vow, not to her groom, but to herself: we only get one life in this world, and mine will be happy. If I still have a single lingering doubt, I will not be getting married on Saturday.

I'll know soon enough, she told herself.

In that moment, she found a sense of complete control. She had no foreshadowing of the fact that by tomorrow morning, she would have vanished without a trace.

1

Laurie Moran listened as the teenager in front of her practiced her high school French. She was on line at Bouchon, the newly opened French bakery that was around the corner from her Rockefeller Center office.

"Jay voo-dray un pan chocolate. Make that deux."

The cashier smiled patiently as she waited for the young woman to string together her next request. Clearly she was accustomed to these clumsy attempts by customers to practice their French, even though the bakery was in the heart of New York City.

Laurie wasn't feeling quite as patient. She was meeting with her boss, Brett Young, later this morning and still hadn't decided which story to pitch first for her show's next special. She needed as much time as possible to prepare.

After a final "mare sea," the girl left, a box of pastries in hand.

Laurie was next. "I'll be ordering in *anglais, s'il vous plaît*."

"*Merci*," the woman said fervently.

It had become a tradition that on Friday mornings she would stop at the bakery and bring in special treats for her staff—her assistant, Grace Garcia, and her assistant producer, Jerry Klein. They were grateful for the selection of tarts, croissants, and breads. After she placed the order, the cashier asked if she cared for anything else. The *macarons* looked delicious. Maybe just a few for Dad and Timmy after dinner, she promised herself, and as a treat for me if today's meeting with Brett goes well.

As she stepped from the elevator on the sixteenth floor of 15 Rockefeller Center, she realized how the layout of the Fisher Blake Studios offices reflected the success of her work this past year. She used to be in a small windowless office, sharing an assistant with two other producers, but since she had created a true crime–based "news special" focusing on cold cases, Laurie's career had taken off. Now she had a long row of windows in a spacious office filled with sleek, modern furnishings. Jerry had been promoted to assistant producer and occupied a smaller office next door. And Grace kept more than busy in a large open space just outside. The three of them now worked full-time on their show, *Under Suspicion*, freeing them from other run-of-the-mill news programming.

Grace had recently turned twenty-seven but looked even younger. Laurie had been tempted more than once to tell Grace she didn't need to wear all of the makeup she meticulously applied every day, but clearly Grace preferred a personal style quite different from Laurie's classic tastes. Today, she wore a multicolored silk tunic over impossibly slim leggings, with five-inch platform boots. Her long black hair was pulled into an *I Dream of Jeannie* topknot, teased into a perfect fountain.

Usually Grace lunged for the bakery bag, but today she did not. "Laurie," she began slowly.

"Something wrong, Grace?" Laurie knew her assistant well enough to recognize when she was upset.

Just as Grace was about to explain, Jerry stepped out of his office. Standing between Jerry's long, lanky frame and Grace in her sky-high heels always made Laurie feel short, even though she was a slender five-foot-seven.

Jerry held up both palms. "There's a lady sitting in your office. She just showed up. I told Grace to schedule an appointment for her at some other time. For the record, I had nothing to do with this."

2

Sandra Pierce gazed out the window of Laurie Moran's office. Sixteen floors below was the famous Rockefeller Center skating rink. At least, that's what Sandra would always see, even now, in the middle of July, when smooth ice and swaying skaters were temporarily replaced with a summer garden and restaurant.

She pictured her own children skating hand-in-hand at that very spot more than twenty years earlier. Charlotte, the oldest, on one side; Henry, her younger brother, on the other. In the middle was their baby sister Amanda. Her siblings held on to her so tightly that if her skates left the ground, she would still be safely upright.

Sighing, Sandra turned away from the window and looked for something to keep her attention while she waited. She was surprised at the tidiness of the office. She had never been to a television studio but had been picturing one of those huge open floors with rows of desks like you see in the background of news shows. In contrast, Laurie Moran's office felt more like a sleek yet comfortable living room.

Sandra noticed one framed photograph on Laurie's desk. Seeing the office door still closed, she picked it up and studied it. It was Laurie with her husband, Greg, on a beach. She assumed that the little boy in front of them was their son. Sandra did not know the family personally, but she had seen photographs of both Laurie and Greg online. Sandra's curiosity about *Under Suspicion* had been sparked when the show first aired. But when she recently read an article mentioning the producer's own background with an unsolved crime, Sandra knew she needed to come here to meet Laurie Moran in person.

She immediately felt guilty for the invasion of Laurie's privacy. She knew she would not want a stranger looking at photographs of her, Walter, and Amanda. Sandra winced as she realized that the last time she'd been with her ex-husband and youngest daughter was five and a half years ago—the last family Christmas before Amanda's wedding. Or what was *supposed* to be her wedding.

Will I ever get used to thinking of Walter as my ex-husband? she wondered. She met Walter her freshman year at the University of North Carolina. Because of her father's military career, she had lived all over the world, but never in the South. She was having a hard time adjusting, as if the other students who had grown up there lived by an unwritten code she didn't understand. Her roommate took her to the first football game of the season, promising that once she cheered on the Tar Heels, she'd be an authentic North Carolinian. Her roommate's brother brought a friend along. He was a sophomore. His name was Walter, and he was a local boy. He spent more time talking to Sandra than watching the game. By the time they all sang the fight song in the final quarter—"I'm a Tar Heel born, I'm a Tar Heel bred, And when I die, I'm a Tar Heel dead"—Sandra thought to herself, I think I've met the man I'm going to marry. She was right. They were together from that time on. They raised their three children in Raleigh, just a half-hour drive from the stadium where they met.

She thought about how, in the first thirty-two years of their nearly thirty-five-year marriage, they had helped each other in their very different domains. Though Sandra never formally worked for Walter's family company, she was always advising him on new product launches, advertising campaigns, and especially personnel issues at work. Between the two of them, she was the one most attuned to people's emotions and motivations. Walter returned the favor by pitching in whenever he could to help her with the church, school, and community projects she was always overseeing. She almost smiled remembering the sight of her big bear Walter numbering hundreds of tiny rubber duckies with a Sharpie for the annual rotary duck race on the Ol' Bull River, reciting each number aloud as he added a new duck to the pile.

Walter used to tell her that they were partners in everything. Of course, she realized now that was never quite true. As hard as Walter tried, he struggled as a father. He would show up to recitals and baseball games, but the kids could tell that his mind was somewhere else. Usually, his thoughts were on work—a new product line, manufacturing flaws at one of the factories, a retailer insisting on further discounts. For Walter, his best contribution as a father was taking care of the business, creating a legacy and financial security for the family. That left Sandra to make up for his emotional detachment from their three children.

And then, two years ago, she had made a decision. She knew that she could no longer tolerate Walter's extreme discomfort when she mentioned Amanda's name. We had two ways of grieving, she thought, and there was too much grief for any house to hold under one roof.

She straightened the pin affixed to her lapel, Amanda's STILL MISSING pin. She'd lost count of how many she'd had printed over the years. Oh, how Walter despised those pins in boxes all over their house. "I can't stand looking at them," he'd say. "I can't have a single minute in my own home away from imagining what might have happened to Amanda."

Had he really expected her to stop looking for their daughter? Impossible. Sandra remained devoted to her mission, and Walter went back to his regular life. No more partnership.

So now Walter was her "ex-husband," as strange as the word still sounded to her. She had been in Seattle for nearly two years. She had moved there to be closer to Henry and his family. She now lived in a beautiful Dutch Colonial at the top of Queen Anne and her two grandchildren had their own bedrooms when they stayed overnight at Grandma's house. Of course, Walter had remained in Raleigh. He'd said that he had to for the company's sake, at least until he retired, which she knew he never would.

Sandra heard voices outside the office door, and quickly resumed her seat on the long, white leather sofa beneath the windows. Please, Laurie Moran, please be the one I've been praying for.

3

When Laurie walked into her office, the woman waiting for her immediately rose from the sofa to extend her hand.

"Ms. Moran, thank you so much for seeing me. My name is Sandra Pierce." The handshake was firm, and was accompanied by direct eye contact, but Laurie could see that the woman was nervous. Her words sounded rehearsed, and her voice quivered when she spoke.

"Your assistant was very kind to let me wait here. I'm afraid I had a bit of a meltdown. I hope she's not in trouble. She was very kind to me."

Laurie placed one hand gently on the woman's elbow. "Please, Grace already explained that you were quite upset. Is everything okay?"

In a quick scan of her office, Laurie was certain that the picture frame on her desk was at a slightly different angle. She wouldn't have noticed the subtle movement of any other item, but that particular possession was especially important. For five years, her office had been devoid of any family photographs. She didn't want her coworkers at the studio to be faced with a constant reminder that her husband had been murdered, and that the crime was still unsolved. But once the police had identified Greg's killer, she had framed this picture—the last one she, Timmy, and Greg had taken as a family—and kept it on her desk.

The woman nodded, but still seemed as though she might break down at the slightest provocation. Laurie led her back to the sofa, where she might be able to calm down.

"I'm sorry, I'm not usually such a nervous person," Sandra Pierce began. She folded her hands on her lap to keep them from shaking. "It's just, I feel sometimes as though I'm running out of options. The local police, the state police, prosecutors, the FBI. I've lost track of the number of private investigators. I even hired a psychic. He told me Amanda would be reincarnated in South America in the near future. I never tried that again."

The words were flowing so quickly that Laurie was having a hard time following, but she only needed to hear so much to know that Sandra Pierce was yet another person who thought that *Under Suspicion* could solve her problems. Now that the show was a hit, it seemed there was no limit to the number of people who were certain that a reality-based television show could fix every injustice. Every day, the show's Facebook page was filled with intricate tales of woe, each of them claiming to be more tragic than the last—stolen cars, cheating husbands, nightmare landlords. There was no question that some of the people asking for help truly needed it, but few of them seemed to understand that *Under Suspicion* investigated unsolved major crimes, not minor offenses. Even when legitimate crime victims or their families contacted her, Laurie had been forced to turn cases down. She could only produce so many specials.

"Please, Mrs. Pierce, there's no need to rush," Laurie said, even though she was feeling the time before her meeting with Brett ticking away. She went to the door and asked Grace to bring them two coffees. She had been upset with Grace for allowing a random person into her office, but now she understood why she had. There was something about this woman that called for compassion.

When she turned to face Sandra Pierce again, she noticed that the woman was quite attractive. She had a long, narrow face and shoulder-length, ash-blonde hair. Her eyes were clear blue. Laurie might have guessed Sandra was not much older than her own thirty-six years if not for some telltale wrinkles on her neck.

"Grace said you're from Seattle?" Laurie asked.

"Yes. I thought about writing or calling, but realized you hear from hundreds of people every day. I know it probably seems crazy to you to fly across the country uninvited and unannounced, but I had to do it this way. I had to make sure I didn't waste the opportunity. I think you're the one I've been waiting for—not you, I'm not a stalker or anything, but your show."

Laurie was starting to regret the decision to hear this woman out. She needed time to finalize her presentation to Brett. What was it about Sandra Pierce that caused her to drop her guard and listen to her? She was on the verge of explaining she needed to prepare for a meeting when she noticed the button pinned to Sandra's blazer.

On the button was a photograph of an absolutely beautiful young woman. Her resemblance to Sandra was uncanny. A graphic of a yellow ribbon appeared just beneath the girl's face. Something about the photograph seemed familiar.

"You're here about her?" Laurie said, gesturing to the pin.

Sandra glanced down and, as if reminded, sunk a hand into her jacket pocket and retrieved a matching pin. She handed it to Laurie. "Yes, it's my daughter. I've never stopped looking."

Now that Laurie had a closer look, the girl's smile tugged at a distant memory. She hadn't seen this particular photograph, but she recognized the smile. "You said your last name's Pierce." She hoped that saying it aloud would help her remember.

"Yes, Sandra. And my daughter is Amanda Pierce. My daughter is the person the media calls 'the Runaway Bride.' "

4

The Runaway Bride. Laurie remembered the case immediately once she heard that phrase. Amanda Pierce was a beautiful blonde bride, about to marry a handsome lawyer she first met in college. All of the plans were made for a luxury destination wedding in Palm Beach, Florida. And then the morning before the big day, she simply disappeared.

If that story had broken at any other point in Laurie's life, she knew that she would have recognized Amanda Pierce's photograph instantly. She probably would have even recognized Amanda's mother, Sandra. At another time, the story of a young bride who vanished into thin air just before her dream wedding would have been right up her alley. She knew that some people speculated that Amanda developed cold feet and started a new life somewhere else, away from her overbearing family, or perhaps with a secret paramour. Others believed that she and the groom had a late-night fight, leading to a violent outburst—"it's just a matter of time before her body turns up."

But even though the story was the kind of thing that would normally draw her attention, Laurie had not followed the case closely. Amanda Pierce disappeared only weeks after Laurie's own husband, Greg, had been fatally shot in front of their then-three-year-old son, Timmy. While Amanda's face was being broadcast across the country, Laurie was on leave from work, oblivious to events outside of her own home.

She remembered turning off the television thinking that if the bride hadn't gotten cold feet, then something terrible must have happened to her. She remembered that she felt at one with the family and what they must be suffering.

She continued to study the picture, remembering that terrible day. Greg had taken Timmy to the playground. She had given Greg a quick kiss as he left with Timmy on his shoulders. It was the last time she was to feel his lips warm against hers.

Ironically, Amanda Pierce's wedding was to have been at the Grand Victoria Hotel. Laurie remembered being there and Greg pulling her into the ocean despite her laughing protests that the water was too cold.

Her thoughts were interrupted by a tap on the office door, followed by Grace carrying a tray containing two cups of coffee and some of the pastries Laurie had purchased from Bouchon. Laurie smiled at Grace, noticing that she had opted to offer her favorite—the almond croissant—as a choice for Mrs. Pierce.

"Can I get you anything else?" Grace wasn't exactly traditional, but in the ways that mattered, she had good old-fashioned manners.

"No, dear, but thank you." Sandra Pierce managed to smile.

Once Grace left, Laurie turned to Sandra. "I can't say that I've heard anything about your daughter's disappearance any time recently."

"Neither have I and that's the problem. Even when she first went missing we suspected that the police were only going through the motions. There was no sign of a struggle in Amanda's room. No reports of anything unusual happening on the resort property. And the Grand Victoria—that's where the wedding was to take place—couldn't be any safer. I could see the police looking at their watches and their cell phones as though Amanda was bound to turn up back home in New York, confessing to cold feet."

Laurie wondered if Sandra's perceptions about the police investigation might be biased. Even from the limited television snippets she had seen at the time, Laurie recalled seeing teams of volunteers searching the resort property for any sign of the missing bride. "As I remember, there was a considerable effort to find her," she said. "It was on the national news for weeks."

"Oh sure, they checked off all the boxes of what they're supposed to do when someone disappears," Sandra said, her tone bitter. "And we were also out there in front of the cameras every day pleading for the public to help us find her."

"And who was the we?" Laurie walked to her desk to retrieve a notepad. She could already feel herself getting pulled into Sandra's story.

"My husband, Walter. Or ex-husband now, but Amanda's father. And her fiancé, Jeff Hunter. Really the whole wedding party was involved: my other children, Charlotte and Henry; two of Amanda's college friends, Meghan and Kate; and then two of Jeff's college friends, Nick and Austin. We handed out fliers all over the local area. At first, the search was focused on the resort property. Then we moved out from there. It tore my heart to see them searching isolated areas, canals, construction sites, and swamps around the coastline. After a month, they stopped looking entirely."

"Sandra, I don't get it. Why did they call her the Runaway Bride? I could understand the police suspecting cold feet for a few hours or maybe even a day or two. But surely as time passed they must have shared your concern. What made them think your daughter would just take off on her own?"

Laurie could tell Sandra was reluctant to answer, so she pushed further. "You said there was no struggle in her room. Was her suitcase missing? Her purse?" Those were the kinds of facts police used to distinguish between runaways and foul play. It was hard to run without money or identification, she thought.

"No," Sandra said quickly. "There seems to be only one thing missing from her wallet, her driver's license. All of her clothes, her purse, her makeup, her credit cards, her cell phone—all of them were in her room. In the evening she often carried just a tiny purse with her room card, a compact, and lip gloss. That was never found. She could easily have slipped the license into it if she was planning to use the car. She and Jeff had rented a car at the airport. As far as we know, Amanda was the last one to use it when she and the girls went shopping that morning. There is a self-parking section on the grounds of the hotel. And that's where they kept it."

Or, Laurie thought, she took her license and some cash and met somebody. Laurie now understood why so many people had speculated that Amanda had left on her own accord. She did have another question, however. "What happened to the rental car?"

"It was found three days later behind an abandoned gas station about five miles from the hotel."

Laurie could see that Sandra's mouth had tightened and her expression had become fiercely angry.

"The police insisted on believing that she may have met someone at the gas station and gotten into a different car. The next morning, when the news broke that she was missing and they were showing her picture on TV, some woman in Delray Beach claimed that she saw Amanda in a white Mercedes convertible stopped at a traffic light around midnight the night she disappeared. She claims she was at a long light and got a good look at her. Amanda was supposedly in the passenger seat, but the woman remembered nothing about the driver except that he seemed tall and had a cap on. The woman was crazy, I know it. She loved the publicity. She couldn't wait to get in front of a camera."

"Do you think the police believed her?"

"Most of them did," Sandra said bitterly. "One day outside the police station, I overheard two detectives arguing. They were leaning against a squad car, smoking cigarettes and talking about my daughter like she was some character on a TV show. One of them was certain that Amanda had a secret boyfriend—a Russian billionaire and she's off on some island with him now. The other guy was shaking his head, and I thought he was going to defend Amanda. Instead he said—I'll never forget it—'You'll owe me ten bucks when they pull her body from the Atlantic.' "

Sandra swallowed back a sob.

"I'm so sorry," Laurie offered, not knowing what else to say.

"Oh trust me, I gave them an earful. There's a detective still officially assigned to the case. Her name is Marlene Henson. She's a nice woman but I can tell the trail is ice cold. Forgive me for being personal, Ms. Moran, but I came here to you specifically for a reason. You know what it's like to lose a person close to you. And to not know for years why it happened or who was responsible."

Greg was killed by a single shot to the forehead while he pushed Timmy on a playground swing. The shooter had intentionally targeted Greg and even knew Timmy's name. "Timmy, tell your mother that she's next," he had said. "Then it's your turn." For five years the only other thing Laurie knew about her husband's killer was that he had blue eyes. That's what her son had called him when he cried out, "Blue Eyes shot my daddy!"

In response to Sandra's statement, Laurie simply nodded.

"Now imagine, Ms. Moran, knowing even less. To not even know whether the person you love is dead or alive. To not know whether they suffered or are out there, alive and happy. Imagine knowing nothing. I'm sure some part of you thinks I'm lucky. Until they find Amanda's body, she could still be alive. I'll never believe that she left of her own will but maybe she was kidnapped and is trying to get free. Or got hit by a car and developed amnesia. I can still hold out hope. But sometimes I think I'd be relieved to get that awful phone call telling me that it's over. At least I'd know she's at rest. I'd finally know for sure. Until then, I can't stop. I'll never stop looking for my daughter. Please—you might be my last chance."

Laurie set her notebook on the coffee table, leaned back in her chair, and steeled herself to break Sandra Pierce's heart.

5

Laurie tucked a loose strand of hair beneath her ear, always a sign that she was nervous. "Mrs. Pierce—"

"Please, call me Sandra."

"Sandra. I can't imagine how difficult it must be to not know what happened to Amanda. But our program is limited in what we can do. We're not the police or the FBI. We go back to the scene of a crime and try to re-create the events through the eyes of the people who were involved."

Sandra Pierce was leaning forward, ready to defend her position. "That's why Amanda's case would be perfect. The Grand Victoria is one of the most famous hotels in the world. It's a glamorous setting, and people love stories about weddings, and most of them can't resist a mystery. I know I can persuade my family, including my ex-husband Walter, to participate. And I already called one of the bridesmaids, Kate Fulton, and she said she'd do whatever she could. I believe the two groomsmen will also agree. As for Jeff, I don't think he would have the nerve to refuse."

"That's not the issue, Sandra. First, our show is about cold cases. Cold *crimes*. You said yourself that the police have no actual proof that your daughter was a crime victim. Maybe you're right, and she was taken away by force. But there's no hard proof I am hearing that a crime was actually committed."

Now there were tears flowing from Sandra's eyes.

"It's been over five *years*," Sandra said passionately. "My daughter was a successful businesswoman. She adored New York City. There were no unusual cash withdrawals or credit card transactions before her disappearance and absolutely nothing since then. She loved her friends and her family. She would not put us through this kind of misery. If she didn't want to get married, she would have broken the news to Jeff gently, and they would have gone their separate ways. Please, you must believe me on that—Amanda did not run away."

"Okay, but there's still a second problem. Our show is called *Under Suspicion* for a reason. We focus specifically on crimes where the people close to the victim continue to live under the shadow of suspicion, even though they were never formally charged. Because Amanda is technically just missing at this point, no one has really been considered a suspect in any crime committed against her."

"Oh, I think Jeff Hunter would beg to differ."

"The groom? I thought you said he was right there with you and your husband, leading the search."

"He was, at first, and it never dawned on us to think Jeff was in any way involved in whatever happened to Amanda. But within a week of her disappearance, Jeff hired a lawyer and refused to talk to the police without the lawyer being there. Why would he need a lawyer if he hadn't done anything wrong? Not to mention, he's a lawyer himself!"

"That does seem strange." Laurie knew that innocent people hired lawyers for protection, but it had never crossed her mind to do so, even when she saw a few police officers eyeing her warily after Greg was killed.

"And when Jeff went back to New York, some of the prosecutors tried to get him fired from his office because they were certain he was involved in Amanda's disappearance. Even now, if you go online to those amateur cybersleuth websites, you'll find many, many people who think Jeff fits your bill for *Under Suspicion*. They will definitely tune in to watch if you cover Amanda's case."

Turning Sandra down was proving more difficult than Laurie had anticipated. She was now growing apprehensive, feeling her entire morning go to waste when she was supposed to talk to her boss this afternoon about potential new cases. Laurie had a list of three top contenders for the show's next investigation but hadn't committed to a top choice. She needed to pull her thoughts together.

"Realistically, Sandra, boyfriends and husbands are always under the microscope to some degree when women go missing. But you said yourself that you don't actually believe he was involved," she protested.

"No, I said *at first* we didn't believe it. We actually felt terrible for him. But then the facts came rolling in. First, he hired that defense lawyer. Then we found out Jeff had money at stake. You see, Amanda and Jeff had a prenuptial agreement. Thanks to Walter's business, our family—and Amanda, who worked for the company—had substantial means; Jeff, very little."

"I thought you just said your daughter's fiancé was an attorney."

"Yes, and a very bright one at that. He graduated at the top of his class from Fordham Law School. But he didn't have any family money, nor was he the moneymaking type on his own. Working as a public defender in Brooklyn, he made a third of Amanda's salary, not to mention her wealthy family's business. There was no question she would be the one to take the reins if her father ever retired. I hated the idea of a contract preparing for a divorce before you're even married, but Walter insisted."

"What was Jeff's reaction?"

"As a lawyer, he said he completely understood. I was relieved when he happily complied. But then we found out that, in addition to the prenup, Amanda had also drawn up a will a month before the wedding. Walter was so worried about Jeff robbing the family dry if the marriage didn't work out, but of course Amanda was free to write her will as she wanted. I think she was so upset at her father over the prenup that she wrote a will as a way to comfort Jeff. She left her trust fund entirely to him."

"And how much was that?"

"Two million dollars."

Laurie felt her eyes widen. Sandra wasn't kidding when she said the family had money. "So has Jeff collected on that? Or is it seven years until someone's presumed dead?"

"Yes, I understand that is the law. I suppose if her body is found, that jerk of a cop in Florida will win his ten-dollar bet, and Jeff will get two million dollars, plus considerable investment earnings. Or I'm told that he could try to declare Amanda dead at any time and collect that way. If Amanda had canceled the wedding, he would have been left high and dry. No divorce settlement, and no inheritance, because Amanda would have changed her will immediately once she went back to New York."

"If he was engaged to your daughter, you must have known him well. Did Jeff seem like a dangerous person to you?"

"No. We thought he was a wonderful choice for a husband. He seemed very dedicated to Amanda, loyal to a fault, in fact. But in retrospect, maybe we should have seen the signs. His two best friends, Nick and Austin, as far as I know, are still happy bachelors, always with different women. Birds of a feather flock together, as they say."

"You think Jeff was unfaithful?"

"It certainly seems possible, given the timing with Meghan."

Laurie glanced at the notepad on the coffee table. "Meghan is the—"

"Meghan White, the maid of honor. She was Amanda's best friend at Colby. And they stayed very close afterward when they both moved to New York City. She's a lawyer, too. Immigration law, in her case. Amanda and Jeff knew each other in college but never dated. Meghan is the one who actually reintroduced Amanda to Jeff in New York. I can certainly tell you she must have been very sorry that she did."

"What do you mean by that?"

"Well, it turns out that Meghan dated Jeff before Amanda ever did. And once Amanda disappeared, she swooped back in. They waited barely a year before marrying. Meghan White is now Mrs. Jeff Hunter. And I think one or both of them murdered my daughter."

Laurie reached again for her notepad. "Let's start all over again."

6

Laurie and Sandra were still talking two hours later, when Laurie's cell phone let out a little chirp. It was her alarm, alerting her that her meeting with Brett was in ten minutes.

"Sandra, I'm afraid I have an appointment with my boss." Brett was not the type of person who could tolerate being kept waiting. "But I'm very glad you flew all the way across the country to tell me about Amanda."

As she walked her out of the office, Sandra had one last question. "Is there anything else I can tell you to help you decide to feature her case on the show?"

"I don't make these decisions on my own, but I promise I'll get back to you one way or the other soon."

"I guess that's all I can ask for," Sandra said. She turned to Grace, who was sitting at her desk. "Thank you again for your kindness, Grace. I hope I'll be seeing both of you again."

"It was my pleasure," Grace said, her voice sympathetic.

Once Sandra was gone, Jerry immediately joined them. "Why does that woman look so familiar? Is she an actress by chance?"

Laurie shook her head. "No, I'll explain later."

"Well, she was in there forever," Jerry said. "Grace and I kept wondering whether we should interrupt. Our meeting with Brett is in just a few minutes, and we haven't had a chance to run through our list of story ideas."

They had been planning to discuss their three top contenders one last time before Laurie had to pitch the concepts to Brett. She had started including Jerry in some of her planning meetings with Brett as he continued to take on increasing production responsibilities. She tended to focus on the news aspects of the program—the suspects, the witnesses, how to nail down their stories. Jerry's talent was in envisioning scenes for the actual production—scouting locations, re-creating images from the crime, making the show as cinematographic as possible.

"I didn't expect to spend so much time with her either, but I think I've got a plan. Just follow my lead."

They started to walk quickly down the corridor to Brett Young's corner office.

7

Brett's new secretary, Dana Licameli, waved them directly past her station into the inner sanctum. "He'll want an explanation," she warned in a conspiratorial whisper.

Laurie glanced at her watch. They were two minutes late. Oh boy, she thought.

He spun in his chair to face them when they entered. As usual, his expression was filled with disapproval. His wife once was heard to remark that he woke up every day with a scowl on his face.

"Sorry to be a little late, Brett. You'll be pleased to know that I was talking to someone who may be great for the next special."

"People are either late or prompt. Saying you're a little late is like saying you're a little pregnant." Turning from her, he said, "You're looking especially dapper today, Jerry."

Laurie wanted to throw something at Brett, especially for what she recognized as a double-edged comment about Jerry. When Jerry first started working as an intern at the studios, he was a shy, awkward college student trying to hide his lanky frame with baggy clothes and slouching posture. Over the years, she had seen his confidence grow and his appearance change accordingly. Until very recently, he almost always wore turtlenecks and cardigan sweaters, even in warm weather. But since the first show of the *Under Suspicion* series had taken off, he was experimenting with different fashion choices. Today's attire was a fitted plaid jacket, bow tie, and mustard-colored pants. Laurie thought he looked terrific.

Jerry straightened his jacket proudly and took a seat. If he construed Brett's remark as sarcasm, he wasn't showing it.

"I'm excited for our meeting," Brett said. "My wife, she tells me I don't give enough—what does she call it?—*positive reinforcement* to my colleagues. So, Laurie, Jerry, I want to make clear—I'm excited to hear your ideas for the next special."

A couple of years ago, Brett had been anything but excited when Laurie came back to work. She had taken time off when Greg was murdered. Then her first shows were flops, but that may have been because she was still grieving and distracted, or perhaps it was just tough luck. Either way, stars fall quickly in the land of television production, and Laurie knew that her days were numbered when she proposed the idea for *Under Suspicion*. Now that the show was a hit, she realized that she had been toying with the concept even before Greg died.

"You know, Brett, we can't guarantee that we're going to solve every case." So far, they were two for two. In both previous specials, the people involved in the cases had cooperated with the production and let their guards down when host Alex Buckley had questioned them. It wouldn't always happen like that.

Brett tapped his fingers on his desk, a signal that others should be quiet while he was thinking. As Grace irreverently put it, "He thinks with his fingers." A handsome man with sculptured features and a full head of iron-gray hair, at age sixty-one he was biting to the point of cruelty and equally brilliant in his success as a renowned producer.

"Well, as far as I'm concerned, what matters is that viewers think you *might*, and they want to be there when it happens. Tell me what you have for the next case."

Laurie thought of the notes she had prepared in her kitchen

the previous night while Timmy played video games after dinner. Three cases. She suspected that the murdered medical professor would be Brett's top choice. Because of a bitter divorce, both his wife and father-in-law were natural suspects. He'd begun seeing a woman who herself was recently divorced, so the new girlfriend's husband was also on the list. Plus there was an academic colleague who accused him of stealing research. Not to mention a disgruntled student who had flunked his anatomy class. It was a perfect case for their show.

Also on Laurie's list was the case of a little boy who had been murdered in Oregon, whose stepmother was the leading suspect. It was a good case, but whenever Laurie started to think about the violence that had been inflicted against a nine-year-old boy, she thought of her own son, and would find herself looking at other possibilities.

The third case on the list was the killing of two sisters thirty years earlier. Laurie found the case fascinating, but suspected that Brett would think a thirty-year delay would make the case too cold to capture viewers' attention.

Now all those notes remained on a legal pad in her briefcase.

"I know I told you I had a few ideas, but one of them clearly stands out." For her sake, and for Sandra's, she hoped Brett would agree.

8

Walter Pierce stood in his office overlooking a production floor at Ladyform's factory in Raleigh, North Carolina. Most CEOs would have opted by now for a fancy office on a high floor in a skyscraper, far removed from the everyday employees who worked in manufacturing. But Walter prided himself on running Ladyform as a traditional, family-owned business whose products were all designed and made in the United States. He was a large man, tall and burly, with a monk's ring of hair around a jowled face.

When his great-grandfather first started this company, women were still transitioning from corsets to brassieres, a change galvanized by the metal shortage in World War I. As he was proud to say, "The change reportedly saved more than fifty million pounds of metal, enough to build two battleships."

In the beginning Ladyform had one North Carolina factory manned by thirty workers. Now Ladyform maintained not only the original factory here, but also operations in Detroit, San Antonio, Milwaukee, Chicago, and Sacramento, not to mention the offices in New York.

As he looked down at the busy scene below, he thought how Amanda had been the one who pushed for Ladyform to have a New York City presence. At the time she was still in college, but she was a straight-A student with savvy business sense. "Dad, we need to bring the brand into the future," she had told him. "Women my age think of Ladyform as frumpy girdles that their mothers and grandmothers wear. We need women to see us as the company that helps them look and feel better in their own bodies." She had so many ideas about *rebranding*—designing garments that were both fun and comfortable, modernizing the logo, and adding a line of sports clothing so that the brand represented, as she said, the female form instead of "the underwear people," he thought sadly.

Walter knew he would have rejected Amanda's advice had it not been for Sandra. He had come home one night from work to find her waiting for him at the kitchen table. He could tell from her stern expression that it was time for "a talk." She insisted that he sit down across from her so she could tell him something.

"Walter, you're a wonderful husband and, in your own way, a loving father," she had begun briskly. "And because of that, I don't try to change you or tell you what to do. But you have pushed and pushed and pushed our children to share your passion for the family business."

"I've also insisted that all the children were free to do whatever they wanted," he had answered heatedly. But even as he spoke the words, Walter felt a twinge at the thought of Ladyform ever going forward without a Pierce at the helm.

"Good for you," Sandra snapped. "But may I remind you that you've pushed so hard that our son wants nothing to do with it and has moved all the way to Seattle so he can do something all on his own at the other end of the country. On the other hand, Amanda and Charlotte have done everything you've asked. They do it because they love you and desperately want your approval. And let's face it, Amanda's the one who has really poured herself into the company. Her ideas are spot-on, Walter, and if you ignore them outright, you will absolutely crush her. I'm telling you, I won't stand for it."

So without ever telling Amanda about her mother's intervention, he had approved Amanda's request to open and head a New York office handling the design, marketing, and sales divisions of the company, Walter remembered. Amanda and Charlotte worked there, and he stayed put at the main manufacturing facility in Raleigh.

Then, thanks to Amanda, the company was more profitable than ever, and Ladyform was regularly touted in business magazines as an old-fashioned American company that had successfully "repositioned" itself for the twenty-first century. Amanda, Walter wondered to himself, do you know that you saved the company from going over the cliff?

His thoughts were interrupted by the sound of his phone ringing. He took it from his pocket and recognized the incoming number as Sandra's cell. It wasn't the first time she'd happened to call when he was thinking about her. It had been nearly two years since she moved to Seattle, and still, he thought, they were connected.

"Hello, Sandra. I was just thinking about you."

"Not in a bad way, I hope."

Their divorce had been finalized without too much contention. But despite a mutual promise to keep matters cordial, the process of having lawyers negotiate the end of a marriage that had lasted more than a third of a century had led to some tense moments.

"Never," he said, firmly. "I was crediting you with Ladyform's success. We would never have had the New York offices if not for you."

"Well, that is a coincidence then, because I'm in New York now. I'm about to have lunch with Charlotte."

"You're in New York?" Walter asked. "Just to see Charlotte?"

The question caused a pang of guilt. He had made an extraordinarily difficult decision to choose between Amanda and Charlotte as his successor to head the company. Of course, Charlotte as the older sister had been bitter and hurt, and the fact that she got the job after Amanda disappeared still didn't diminish her resentment.

This past November Sandra had invited him to have Thanksgiving dinner with her, Charlotte, and Henry and his family in Seattle. He supposed it was unrealistic to expect Sandra to continue to see him regularly. The visit had left him wistful and sad.

"No, not only to see her," Sandra was saying. "I'm afraid I've done something that might upset you. Have you heard of the television show *Under Suspicion*?"

What's this about? Walter wondered, then listened as Sandra went on and on about the two-hour meeting she'd had with the show's producer about Amanda's disappearance.

"I thought it was a long shot, but I think she may have actually listened." Sandra's voice was excited. "Please, Walter, don't be angry. She said they only choose a case if the family members all approve. Walter, will you please consider it?"

He winced. Did she really think that he wouldn't turn over every stone if that would somehow solve Amanda's disappearance? "Sandra, I'm not angry. And of course I'll cooperate any way I can."

"Really? Walter, that's wonderful. Thank you. One hundred times, thank you."

There was a smile in her voice.

A little more than five hundred miles north, in the Pierre Hotel in Manhattan, Sandra disconnected her cell phone and tucked it in her handbag. Her hand was shaking. She had been prepared for another argument with Walter, like the ones that had eventually led to the end of their marriage. *How long are you going to keep up with this, Sandra? When are you going to face facts? We still have our lives and two other children. We owe it to Henry and Charlotte and our grandchildren to move on. You've become obsessed!*

But they hadn't had any fights like that since Walter came home from work to find her in the bedroom, struggling to close a very full suitcase. Protesting, he had carried it down to the waiting car. As she got into it, she said, "I can't deal with you any longer. Good-bye." Sandra was relieved that today's conversation hadn't led to another confrontation. Still, as she walked down Sixth Avenue, something was bothering her.

Walter had quickly gone along with being involved if Laurie Moran made Amanda's disappearance the next case in the *Under Suspicion* series. But she knew that reliving it moment by moment as the investigation began would tear him apart.

"I'm sorry, Walter," she said aloud. "But if I get the chance to have Amanda's disappearance examined, I'm going to go through with it, come hell or high water."

9

In Brett Young's office at Fisher Blake Studios, Laurie was making her strongest pitch to feature the Runaway Bride case in their next special.

She began by laying the button that Sandra had given her on Brett's desk. Normally, she would have brought eight-by-ten glossies, but today, she was working on the fly. "You might recognize her photograph. Her name is Amanda Pierce. Five years after her disappearance, her mother, Sandra, still wears these buttons."

Raising his eyebrows, Brett inched the button toward him for closer inspection, but said nothing.

"New Yorkers Amanda Pierce and Jeff Hunter had plans for a luxurious destination wedding. The ceremony was planned for Saturday afternoon, to be followed by a lavish reception. The wedding would be fairly intimate—sixty of their closest friends and family. But the wedding never happened," she continued. "On Friday morning before the Saturday afternoon wedding, the bride, Amanda Pierce, did not show up for breakfast. Her fiancé and maid of honor knocked on the door of her room. There was no answer. A security guard let them in. The bed had not been slept in. Her wedding dress was spread across it. The night before, the bridal party had had dinner together. That was the last time they saw Amanda."

Laurie could tell she had Brett's attention now. "They started to worry. They checked the hotel gym, the beach, the restaurant, the lobby—everywhere they could think of to look for her. Jeff went to the front desk to ask if housekeeping had already made up Amanda's room. The clerk checked, and just as he said, 'no,' Amanda's parents arrived in the lobby. They had to hear from Jeff that their daughter was missing. She's never been heard from again." Brett snapped his fingers. "I knew her face looked familiar. This is that Runaway Bride thing, right? Didn't she turn up in Vegas with some other guy?"

Laurie vaguely recalled a similar story a few years back along those lines, but assured him that it wasn't the Amanda Pierce case. "Amanda vanished without a trace. People don't run away for over five years."

"Without a trace? As in, no body? No new clues at all? Doesn't sound promising."

"It's a cold case. That's what we do, Brett."

"But this one is ice cold. We're talking igloo at the North Pole. Let me guess: the person you were talking to before the meeting was the button-wearing mother? I ran into her in the elevator." Before she could answer, he said, "You're a sucker for a sad story, Laurie. I can't green-light a special just so you can give a platform to the sobbing family. We need clues. We need suspects. I'm sure you want to help this mother, but as I recall, the parents weren't even there yet when the girl disappeared, right? And who are the people who have been living under suspicion since then?"

Laurie explained Amanda's decision to leave her trust fund to Jeff, even though they weren't married yet.

Jerry chimed in. "If you go online, there are thousands of people obsessed with this case. Almost everyone thinks the groom did it and it had something to do with the money. And the facts about the will aren't even public. Not long after Amanda disappeared he had the nerve to hook up with her best friend. They're married now, and I bet it won't be long before they spend all the money together."

"Not that we're biased or anything," Laurie added jokingly.

"Of course not," Jerry said.

The mention of money gave Laurie another idea. "The setting would be perfect, Brett. The Grand Victoria Hotel in Palm Beach. It was supposed to be a dream wedding. All travel, lodging, and entertainment paid for by the bride's wealthy family."

Laurie was pleased when she finally saw Brett scribble some notes. She made out the word "resort," followed by dollar signs. Just as she had predicted, Brett relished the idea of a glamorous setting and financially comfortable participants. Sometimes Laurie wondered if Brett would have preferred for her to have created *Lifestyles of the Rich and Famous: Unsolved Murders*.

"But her body was never found," Brett observed. "Up until now, for all we know, Amanda Pierce is happily enjoying a new life under a new name. I would have thought, Laurie, that your journalist ethics would leave you concerned about violating the woman's privacy."

Laurie had lost track of the number of times that her values as a reporter had clashed with Brett's unmitigated quest for ratings. Now that she was pitching a case that was perfect for television, he was finding far too much enjoyment in giving her a hard time.

"Actually, I've given that some thought. Even if Amanda left of her own accord, we do have victims. She walked out on her distraught family, and left behind at least one innocent person suffering under the gaze of public suspicion. I'm perfectly happy if we find out the truth, no matter where that leads us."

"Well, for once, you and I might be on the same page. This is a good mystery, and the story of a disappearing bride is perfect for television—a young, beautiful woman vanished into thin air from a five-star hotel on the most important weekend of her life. I think I've been an excellent influence on you."

"Undoubtedly," Laurie said dryly. She was already running through the other perks of the case. Of course Grace and Jerry would be thrilled with the setting. Laurie's father, Leo, and son, Timmy, could be with them while they were on location, hopefully in August. Depending on the timing she might be able to finish the shoot before Timmy started school again in September. Her mind had wandered to the thought of brainstorming interview sessions with Alex on the beach when Brett asked another question. "Who's on board?"

The biggest challenge for their show was convincing the victim's friends and family members to participate. "So far just her mother, and supposedly the siblings and one of the bridesmaids," Laurie said. She quickly added, "I didn't want to reach out to anyone else until I got your approval." That sounded much better than *This case just fell in my lap this morning.*

"Full speed ahead. The Runaway Bride sounds like a Runaway Hit."

10

Charlotte Pierce told the waiter that she'd like to have the green salad and the salmon. "And some more iced tea," she said, smiling politely as she handed him her menu. What she really wanted, of course, was a bloody mary and the steak frites, but she was dining with her mother, which meant she would remain on her best behavior in every way.

Charlotte was all too conscious of the fifteen extra pounds she was carrying these days. Unlike her siblings, she wasn't naturally slender, and had to "work a little harder," as her mother used to put it, to maintain a "healthy weight." Ironically, Charlotte's recent weight gain was the result of all the long days she was putting in at Ladyform and the all too frequent fast food she ate to keep herself going.

"Well, this certainly is a lovely restaurant," her mother said, once the waiter was gone. Charlotte had chosen this spot because she knew that her mother would appreciate the elegant and spacious dining room, filled with fresh flower arrangements. She had also made a point to pull her long, messy, light brown waves into a knot at the nape of her neck. Her mother always had a way of suggesting that she wear her hair in a more stylish cut. To Charlotte's ear, it sounded like her mother wishing she were more like Amanda. "How is everything going at work?"

As Charlotte spelled out the plans for marketing the new line of yoga wear, including a fashion show on the cable channel New York One, her mother seemed to be only half-listening. "I'm sorry, Mom. I've run on too long. Oh no, I'm not turning into Dad, am I?"

"Don't even suggest it," Sandra said with a smile. "Remember when the three of you set a timer to see how long he could babble about the new convertible bra?"

"That's right. I almost forgot." Some of the Pierce children's biggest laughs had been at their father's expense. Big, manly Walter Pierce had no qualms talking about bras, underwear, and girdles at the dinner table, in front of their friends, or in the checkout line at the grocery store. It was all just work to him, and he loved his work. The particular incident Mom referred to was Thanksgiving, and the bra was the Ladyform "3-in-one," which converted from standard straps to strapless to a racer-back. Ladyform was the first to launch that design.

When it became clear that Dad was conducting yet another one of his "seminars," Henry was the one to retrieve the timer from the kitchen. He, Charlotte, and Amanda had covertly passed it in a circle around the table as their father described every configuration, going so far as to use his napkin in a demonstration. By the time he realized what was going on, his children's faces were close to purple from trying to suppress laughter, and the timer had hit the eight-minute mark.

"You kids always gave your father the hardest time," Sandra said, reminiscing.

"Oh, he loved it. Still does," Charlotte added, reminding herself that her mother and father rarely spoke anymore. "So, Mom, you called yesterday and announced that you were on your way to New York. I love seeing you, but I suspect you didn't fly across the country just to have lunch with me."

"It's about Amanda."

"Of course it is." Everything her parents said or did or thought was always about Amanda. Charlotte felt cruel for her immediate reaction, but the truth was that her parents had always favored Amanda, even before she disappeared. Charlotte had spent most of her life feeling less accomplished, less attractive, and less recognized than her little sister.

Things had gotten even worse once Amanda was out of college and working at Ladyform, Charlotte thought bitterly. She had been at Ladyform four years before Amanda joined the company. But Amanda had come up with the idea of pairing famous female athletes with fashion designers to create high-end sports bras. After that, Dad treated Amanda as though she were Einstein reincarnated. Amanda's idea was a great one, Charlotte thought grudgingly. The fact that I've been more than filling her job these past five years doesn't seem to have been noticed by either of my beloved parents.

She signaled the waiter. When he came over, she said, "A vodka martini, please." Then she looked at her mother. "Okay, Mom, what about Amanda?"

11

As soon as they left Brett's office, Laurie gave Jerry a light squeeze around his shoulders. "You were terrific in there. I can't believe how much you knew about the case!"

"I was in college when Amanda Pierce disappeared. My entire dorm was completely obsessed. I think I missed two days of class, glued to CNN. I knew then that what was supposed to be a little internship here was my true calling."

Harvey from the mailroom passed them, wheeling a cart of mail with one hand, the other occupied by a half-eaten croissant. "You're officially my favorite person at work today, Laurie."

"Happy to hear it, Harvey."

Once Harvey was out of earshot, Jerry said, "His wife wouldn't be so happy. Last I heard, she had him on some gluten-free diet. I'm glad he's cheating a bit. The mail's been messed up all week."

Laurie smiled. Jerry always seemed to know everyone's business. "So how come you never suggested the Runaway Bride for the show if you were that into the case?"

"I don't know. I wasn't sure you'd like it."

"Because of Greg? Jerry, once Greg's murderer was found, I had a sense of peace. Certainly not closure but peace. That's why if our programs give other people that feeling, I'm glad."

It was true. Once she finally got the answers she'd been looking for about Greg's death, she realized that there was something comforting about certainty. A restoring of order. Though she originally created *Under Suspicion* purely to have a successful news program, she now saw it as a way to help other families.

"Honestly, I considered suggesting Amanda's case for the show once I got promoted to assistant producer. But then when we were in Los Angeles on the Cinderella Murder case, we were staying in that enormous house, and you said something about the pool being nearly as big as the one at the Grand Victoria. You looked sad thinking about it. I assumed—" He let the thought go unspoken.

"You assumed right, Jerry. I was there with Greg, but I'll be fine."

12

Huddled in Laurie's office, the three of them—Laurie, Jerry, and Grace—made a list of all the people they would need to contact before they could officially go into production with Amanda's case. Grace had never heard of either Amanda or the Runaway Bride, so it took Laurie a few minutes to explain the case and its connection to their surprise visitor that morning.

"Well, that makes more sense now," Grace said. "Sandra called while you were in your meeting. She said I should tell you that her ex-husband, Walter, is—quote—*all in*."

"Excellent," Laurie said, checking Amanda's father off the list. "Sandra gave me a list of all of the bridal party members who were at the resort when Amanda went missing. The groom, Jeffrey Hunter, is still a public defender in Brooklyn. He's now married to Meghan White, Amanda's best friend, who was also the maid of honor."

Grace let out an "ooooh" in response to the scandalous news. She liked to think that she could spot the culprit on immediate instinct.

"Don't go jumping to conclusions; we're journalists, remember?" Laurie laughed. "On Jeff's side of the party were two of his best friends from college—Nick Young and Austin Pratt. To Sandra's knowledge, both of them are in finance, most recently here in New York, so hopefully they'll be easy to track down. The third groomsman was Amanda's older brother, Henry. I take it he's the nonconformist of the family."

Jerry was scribbling frantically. "And what about Amanda's bridal party?"

"There's the maid of honor, Meghan White—"

"The one who stole the groom," Grace said.

"Is *currently married to* the groom, yes. Amanda's sister, Charlotte, the oldest in the family, was also one of the bridesmaids. She's now the heir apparent to the family company, which is Ladyform, by the way."

"I love that stuff," Grace said in a whisper, as if it were a secret. "You put that on, and you look two sizes smaller."

Now Laurie knew how voluptuous Grace managed to fit inside those tight dresses she favored. "Well, I got the distinct impression that Amanda was the one who was climbing up the corporate ladder before she disappeared. We might want to be on the lookout for some sibling rivalry there. And then, finally, there's Kate Fulton. Sandra didn't tell me much about her, except that she already spoke to her, and Kate seemed willing to appear on the show. With the exception of Amanda's siblings, the others in the bridal party went to school together at Colby College in Maine. Sandra Pierce strongly believes that they would cooperate."

"I can check Facebook and LinkedIn to see if they're connected online," Jerry said. He was an expert at using social networks to gather background material. "I'll also get contact information for everyone. But that's just the wedding party. We're also going to need to call the Grand Victoria. Part of the strength of the case from a television perspective is the location."

"I'm worried about that," Laurie told him. "The hotel may not want the publicity of reminding people that Amanda disappeared."

"Except there was never any indication that there was any fault by the hotel. If anything, I think the case proves that successful people with excellent taste choose it for something as important as a wedding, not to mention all the gorgeous shots of the property that we'll include in the production."

"Nice pitch, Jerry. When the time comes, I think I'll let you handle that phone call. Sandra mentioned a wedding photographer. Unfortunately, she couldn't remember the person's name, but the hotel might remember."

"And of course the groom might, if he decides to sign on."

"*If* he signs on?" Laurie said. "Don't jinx us. He's Sandra's number one suspect. He has to sign on."

13

Sandra gave her daughter one final hug in the building lobby. "I'm so proud of you, love," she said.

"Mom, I'm going to see you for dinner in a few short hours. Marea, eight o'clock. You know where it is, right?"

"You told me: take Central Park South straight across almost to Columbus Circle. I think I can manage not to get lost. It's a joy to see you twice in one day."

Sandra cherished her time with Charlotte. When she lived in Raleigh, she saw Charlotte and Henry equally, two to four times a year, never enough in her view. She made a point to visit Charlotte as least as often once she moved to Seattle, but if anything, the fact that she now saw Henry regularly made her miss Charlotte all the more.

It was sweet of Charlotte to have spent the entire afternoon with her. After a long lunch at La Grenouille, they walked up Fifth Avenue perusing shop windows and then across town until they reached Ladyform's corporate offices next to Carnegie Hall. There, Charlotte had proudly given her mother a preview of the latest designs.

As Sandra walked back to her room at the Pierre, she pictured Charlotte's face at lunch when Sandra first brought up Amanda's name. In retrospect, she thought, I should have told Charlotte yesterday on the phone about my plan to go to the *Under Suspicion* studio. That way, today could have been purely a fun day.

She should have known that any mention of Amanda would put a damper on the visit. Charlotte was always comparing herself to her little sister. Even five years after Amanda disappeared, she was competing with Amanda's memory.

Once I told Charlotte about my meeting this morning with Laurie Moran, she seemed excited, Sandra thought. And she was quick to volunteer her willingness to participate if the show got the go-ahead. "A day never passes that I don't miss Amanda," Charlotte had said. But there was that moment when her face fell at the mention of her sister's name, followed by the urgent request for a martini.

Charlotte is a good, decent person, but why is she so insecure, even jealous? Sandra sighed. Charlotte's envy could bring out the worst in her. In the seventh grade, she had been suspended for tampering with another student's entry in the science fair.

But no matter how jealous she had been of Amanda, Charlotte would never hurt her little sister. Or would she? Sandra, horrified that the thought would even cross her mind, felt a stinging lump in her throat.

14

As the number 6 train lurched to a stop at the 96th Street station, Laurie was replaying the conversation with Jerry in her head. He knew more about Amanda's disappearance from five-year-old news coverage than Laurie had managed to glean during a two-hour conversation with Amanda's own mother. That's how well he knew the case. Yet he had refrained from pitching a show about his own cold-case obsession because of a comment she had made months ago in Los Angeles. *You looked sad,* he had said. *I assumed—*

Jerry hadn't completed the sentence. He didn't need to, because he had assumed correctly. Laurie's only previous visit to the Grand Victoria had been with Greg. It was their second anniversary. New York had suffered an especially bitter winter. More than by the cold, Laurie's mood had been affected by yet another month passing without becoming pregnant. Her doctor told her that these things didn't always happen right away, but she and Greg had been so eager to start a family once they got married.

Sensing her worry, Greg had surprised her on a Thursday night, announcing that he had arranged to take a long weekend off from the Mount Sinai emergency room, where he was a resident. They spent four marvelous days, swimming and reading on the beach during the day, enjoying long dinners in the evening. Timmy was born nine months later.

When Greg died, I had felt so alone, Laurie thought. We had always pictured ourselves having four or five kids. She loved Timmy—he was more than enough all on his very own—but she never thought he'd be an only child.

But now, nearly six years after Greg's death, she realized that she and Timmy had never been at risk of being alone. Her father, Leo, had retired from the NYPD to help raise her son.

And my immediate family didn't stop there, Laurie thought. Grace could read her mind with one look. Jerry had known that she might not be ready to delve into a story about a young couple getting married at a resort where she'd once celebrated with Greg. Jerry and Grace were co-workers, but they were also family.

And then there was Alex. I don't want to go there right now, she thought.

She walked quickly the few blocks to the apartment. As she slipped her key into the front door, she felt the stress of the busy day fade away. She was home.

15

She was greeted by the smell of chicken roasting in the kitchen and the familiar sounds of cartoon fighting from the living room. *Pow! Hah!* Timmy was playing Super Smash Bros. on his Wii, while Leo read the sports section on the sofa. Laurie had tried to restrict Timmy from these types of games for as long as possible, but even she had been forced to cave.

"Mario doesn't stand a chance," Laurie said, recognizing one character on the screen battling her son's virtual self.

Timmy unleashed a lethal kick and then let out a satisfied "Yesss!" He scrambled up to hug her.

"There she is," Leo said as he stood up. "How was your meeting with Brett?"

Laurie smiled, appreciative that her father remembered that today had been the scheduled pitch. "Better than I could have expected."

"What was his reaction to the cases you were torn between?"

"Forget them. Something really terrific came up today." She gave him the short version of the surprise visit from Sandra. "Do you remember the case?"

"Vaguely. I was still on the job back then, so there were enough crimes in New York to keep me busy."

Laurie heard the musical chime of a game coming to an end,

and Timmy set his controller down. Obviously, he had been listening to them. "So does this mean you're going to be leaving again?" he asked, a touch of anxiety in his voice.

Laurie knew that Timmy worried about her schedule. When they filmed the last special, she decided to pull him from school for two weeks while his grandfather watched over him on the set in California. She couldn't possibly do that for every installment.

"You're going to like this one," she told him. "Instead of going somewhere so far away, it's in Florida, and that's only a two- to three-hour flight. If the project is approved, I'm even hoping to schedule it for next month before you go back to school."

"Is there a water park?"

Laurie sent a mental thank-you to Grace, who had already looked up that kind of pertinent information. "Yep. They've got a slide that's forty-feet high in one of the pools."

"Awesome. And will Alex be there?" Timmy asked. "I bet he'd try the slide with me."

Sometimes Laurie worried how excited Timmy was about Alex being part of their lives. She'd made a point of not rushing their relationship, but of course earlier in the day, her mind had leapt to the same place as Timmy's, picturing herself with Alex on the beach.

"Yes," she said, "Alex is an important part of the show. I've checked with him. He's ready to go. And Grace and Jerry will be there, too," she added.

"Grace is probably chartering a private plane for all her shoes," Leo said.

"I wouldn't be surprised."

Two hours later, as Laurie cleared the dishes from the table, a text message from Jerry came in. He was still at the office and had contact information for everyone they wanted for the show. *Can't wait to get started!* he said.

His college-aged obsession was proving handy already. As Laurie thought about the various people she needed for the production, she worried that the groom and his new wife were absolutely essential. No matter what Sandra had promised, they were also both lawyers, which might make them reluctant to cooperate.

Fortunately, Laurie knew an excellent attorney who could be extremely persuasive. She sent a quick text to Alex, who was the guest of honor at a trial skills conference in Boston for the weekend: *Any chance you have some time Monday night? It might take a couple of hours. It's about the show. And please bring your car. I hope we get to meet with one or two of the participants.*

His response was immediate: *I always have time for you.*

She replied, *I'll call Monday morning with details. Good night, Alex.*

Smiling, she plugged her phone into the charger.

16

"Organized chaos" was the term often used by Kate Fulton when she was getting her four kids settled for the evening. The three-year-old twins, Ellen and Jared, had finished their bath and were in their pajamas, watching a Barney video in the family room. Tonight was a good night. Their singing along with one of the jingles meant they weren't fighting.

After several reminders, Jane had finally gone to her room to read before bed. Now that she was ten, she had announced she should be allowed to stay up later than eight o'clock. "All of my friends go to bed later than that," she had protested. Kate had agreed to consider the request.

Eight-year-old Ryan was her easier one. He always had a sweet and sunny disposition. But he was also the most accident prone as the recently applied cast on his arm attested. He had fallen off his new bike while trying to steer with no hands.

Normally the noise of her household before bedtime would have been oddly comforting. Tonight, though, all she wanted was silence. She had too many other sounds in her head.

Three days ago she had been shocked to receive a phone call from Sandra Pierce. Kate hadn't heard from her since the second anniversary of Amanda's disappearance. Then tonight before dinner, Sandra had called again for the third time since, saying that the producer of *Under Suspicion* was excited about the prospect of featuring Amanda's case. And then right on the heels, Laurie Moran, the producer, had called to explain what participation in the program would involve.

Sandra had offered to pay for all the expenses, so Kate could bring Bill and the kids. If that didn't work, she had said, she would pay for a sitter to stay at the house while Kate was away. My mother will be happy to stay with them, Kate had told her, but I'll accept your offer to pay for a sitter to help.

She got up from the table. The twins had begun to bicker. "Upstairs now, all of you," she said firmly.

The Home Depot store was conducting its annual inventory. As the manager, Bill was still there and would be until some ungodly hour.

Twenty minutes later, the dishwasher on and her four children settled, Kate sat quietly in the den over a second cup of coffee. If this production did happen, how would she feel down at the Grand Victoria again?

She remembered how out of place she had felt last time. Amanda and Charlotte and Meghan had seemed so sophisticated. So very New York. She had felt like a dowdy housewife next to them.

I've loved Bill since I was thirteen years old, she thought. But sometimes I wonder how it would have been if I'd given myself a few years after college to live in New York and date other people, have some breathing room.

She took another sip of coffee.

I never thought I'd go back to Palm Beach, she thought. Five years ago, I committed the worst mistake of my entire life there. No one must ever know. Please, God, she pleaded silently, please don't let anyone know.

17

Walter Pierce opened an email from his daughter, Charlotte. *Hope you love these as much as we do!*

We. She meant her team up there in New York City. Ten years ago, any new product would have been presented to him in this office, right here at the factory, overlooking the production floor—pencil sketches on paper. He would have been the one to decide whether it was right for Ladyform.

Now he opened files on a computer. With the click of a mouse, he could review a digitized version from all angles. And a bunch of people whose names he couldn't remember had already expressed their approval.

He clicked through images of what used to be called a sweatshirt but was now known as a "hoodie." This one's sleeves were equipped with built-in mittens that could be slipped off with a flick of the wrist.

The old Walter would have picked up the phone and asked the person proposing such a silly garment to explain why anyone in the world would want mittens dangling from their clothing. But instead, he hit the reply key, typed *Looks great, Charlotte*, and sent the message.

The phone rang. He recognized the number on the screen as Henry's. That was a nice surprise. Normally, Walter was the one to initiate the phone calls.

"I knew I could find you at work," Henry said.

His son's voice was cheerful, but Walter knew it was his devotion to work that explained why Henry, his grandchildren, and now his ex-wife all lived on an opposite coast.

"I'm just about to head out. Your sister sent me a wonderful new design. How are Sandy and Mandy?" Henry's two girls were named Sandra and Amanda, named for their grandmother and aunt.

"They're a handful, both of them."

Walter smiled as he listened to his only son chatter like a proud father. He leaned back in his chair, closed his eyes, and wondered how his life might have been different if he'd been more like his son. Henry spent just as much time with his girls as his wife, Holly, did. He coached their soccer team, filmed their dance recitals, and cooked breakfast with them every Saturday so Holly could sleep in.

I try to tell myself that times were different back when my kids were small, Walter thought, but I know I could have been a more hands-on father. "Tell them Grandpa Walt misses them," he said, then added, "Do you think your mom's still doing okay out there in Seattle?"

As he spoke, he rocked backed and forth in his chair. It was still hard for him to picture Sandra living alone. He had looked the house up on the Internet so he could at least have an image, but he'd only been inside once when she had invited him to Thanksgiving dinner.

Henry was silent for a few seconds. "She's settling in, sure. That's why I was calling. She talked to you about this television show?"

"She was very excited. Has the producer made a decision?"

"Not yet, but Amanda's case is definitely on the radar," Henry said. "I just wanted to make sure you were actually comfortable moving forward. I know how excited Mom can get. You shouldn't feel obligated—"

"I don't. As I told your mom, I'm proud of her for getting someone to revive Amanda's case after all these years. She's worked her heart out for this."

"But do *you* want this?"

"Sure, if Mom thinks it will help."

"Dad, that's what I'm worried about. Don't do this for Mom, out of guilt, or because you think you'll be making something up to her. I know that not knowing what happened to Amanda is what came between you."

Walter swallowed past the lump in his throat. "Your mother's the most fierce and loyal woman I've ever known. Finding Amanda has become her life's work. Trust me, if anyone understands the need to pour yourself into a passion, it's me."

"Dad, I'm not talking about work. I know you're not always comfortable talking about your feelings, but how come we never talk about Amanda?"

"I still think about your sister every day."

"I know you love her and miss her. We all do. But we never *talk* about her. How come you're so sure that Amanda's still out there?"

"I've never been sure. But that's my hope." Every night, Walter pictured his beautiful daughter and the adventures she might be having. She had always loved to draw. Might she be a painter on the Amalfi Coast? Or maybe she runs a quiet little restaurant in Nice?

"I guess anything is possible," Henry said. "Then Mom says that Amanda would never leave us worrying like this, and that sounds absolutely on target, too. How can the two of you have such different opinions about what happened?"

Walter opened his mouth, but no words came out. He couldn't go into it again. Then he said, "I appreciate your call, son. I'm absolutely on board about this. It'll be nice to see you in Florida."

"You can miss work?"

Funny, Walter thought, I agreed to do the show without even thinking about the company. "I'll be out of the office as long as necessary."

He knew it had taken him too long to see the truth, that he had been a terrible father, unable to connect to his children about anything other than work. My son, he thought, moved all the way to the West Coast to escape hearing about Ladyform breakfast, lunch, and dinner. Then I pitted my two daughters against each other, expecting them both to step into the family business, and not giving either sufficient assurances of my approval.

He wanted to tell Henry why he believed that Amanda was out there somewhere, living a new life under a new name. It was the only way, he thought, she could break free of me and be the person she truly wanted to be. But he just could not admit that.

"We'll talk soon," Henry was saying. "Okay, Dad. Bye."

As he hung up the phone, Walter wondered whether Sandra and his children would ever realize how much he really had changed in the last few years.

18

It was Monday morning, which meant that Jerry and Grace were outside Laurie's office, gossiping about their weekend activities. From Laurie's vantage point at her desk, she gathered that Grace had been carrying on about the strikingly good looks of her latest gentleman suitor.

"And where did you find this one?" Jerry asked.

"You say that like there have been thousands," Grace objected. "And to be clear, it's all just flirting, nothing serious. I met Mark—this one, as you called him—at the driving range at Chelsea Piers."

"You? Playing golf?"

"I'm a woman of many talents. The clothes are adorable, and so are the other players; what's not to like? Speaking of surprising attributes, is that a tan I see?"

Laurie found herself paying more attention to their chatter than the memo she was drafting to the studio's marketing team. She had also noticed some color on Jerry's usually pale skin.

"I visited friends on Fire Island. And it's not a tan. Unlike you, I have two settings: pasty or sunburned."

Laurie found herself smiling as she hit the save key on her computer and rose from her desk. "Okay, are we ready for our meeting?"

Once they were settled into their usual spots—Grace and Jerry on the sofa, Laurie in the gray swivel chair—she asked which of them wanted to start.

She was eager to hear their reports. Normally, she was the one calling the shots in the office, but when it came to social media, she was almost oblivious. She barely understood the difference between a Tweet and a status, a like and a follow. But Jerry and Grace, just a decade younger, seemed perfectly at home in the virtual world.

As a convenient way to split the work in half, Laurie had asked Jerry to see what he could find about Jeff and his half of the wedding party, while Grace researched Amanda's friends.

Jerry seemed more than happy to go first. "Jeff has a fairly small social media imprint, just a LinkedIn profile—that's for professional networking," he added for Laurie's benefit—"and a relatively quiet Facebook page. But I have been able to confirm that he is still in close contact with both Nick Young and Austin Pratt, who are both more active online, and still very much BFFs."

Best friends forever. Between Jerry, Grace, and her son, Laurie was fluent in slang.

"Austin and Nick are still happy bachelors on the prowl, while Jeff has settled down in Brooklyn with his wife, Meghan."

Grace looked at Jerry as if surely he must have more to say. "Is that it? I wish my job had been that simple."

"I also called the Grand Victoria. Want me to start in on that?" Jerry interrupted.

"One at a time, guys. Grace?"

"Well, since my people are more complicated," she said with a pleased smile, "I'll take them one by one. Meghan White, as mentioned, is married to Jeff. She has no Facebook, Twitter, nothing. Private. The other college girlfriend was Kate Fulton. She has four kids and lives in Atlanta. Her husband is the store manager at a Home Depot. There are some old pictures on her Facebook page with Meghan and Amanda, but, as far as I can tell, she has no current contact with any of the old gang. We've got Charlotte, Amanda's sister, working at Ladyform here in New York. And her brother, Henry, is in Seattle. He's co-owner of a winery, married with two girls, at least according to his online posts."

Laurie was nodding. The three Colby men, all still in contact. Meghan now married to Jeff. Amanda's family, scattered across the country. Kate the college friend, married with four children in Atlanta.

"Jerry, you heard back from the Grand Victoria?" she asked. Her biggest worry was that the resort might not let them film on the property.

"I spoke to their corporate office today. They're eager to cooperate. Amanda's disappearance was a public relations fiasco, so my impression is that they want to help however they can. They even maintained backups of all the security camera footage they provided to police."

"Really? Is there a way we can see it?"

"They agreed to send it this week."

The pieces were all falling into place. Jeff was still close to two of his groomsmen, and obviously couldn't be any closer to Meghan. If she could just get him on board, they'd be all set. And if he didn't say yes to Sandra, she had a plan to persuade him. Alex.

19

When Laurie walked out of her building at six o'clock, Alex was standing at the curb next to his black Mercedes. Right on time, she thought. I should have known it.

"I've been waiting an hour."

"Sure you have!"

Laurie had known Alex for over a year now but could still feel herself react every time she saw him. A former college basketball player standing six-four, he still had an athlete's build. He had dark, wavy hair, a strong jaw, and blue-green eyes that shone even behind his black-rimmed glasses. There was a reason Alex Buckley had become one of television's most sought-after trial commentators, and it wasn't merely because of his celebrated success in the courtroom.

She gave him a quick kiss. "I can't believe my luck that you could join me."

Alex's official role on *Under Suspicion* was as its host. The skills he had gained at interrogation in courtroom cross-examinations were perfect for the show's format. In previous episodes, his participation had not begun until shortly before the cameras began to roll. But since the show's last production, three months ago, the lines between official and unofficial had become blurred where Laurie and Alex were concerned.

He opened the car door for her, then walked around to the opposite side and got in next to her. Before he could ask, she handed the driver Jeff and Meghan's address in Brooklyn. "I may have mentioned that I always have time for you," he said mildly.

"Oh, come on! I can't remember the last time you left your office before six. I'm really surprised. How come you were available on such short notice?"

"This is what I get for dating a journalist—the third degree." Alex laughed. "I did make a scheduled trial go away by getting most of the evidence suppressed."

Dating. Of course we're dating, she thought. There's no other word for it.

"Well, I'm not surprised you won, and I'm grateful for the help," she said, as he reached over and took her hand. It felt completely natural.

"Okay, Laurie, what's going on in Brooklyn?"

"Do you remember the Runaway Bride case?"

Alex looked up briefly, scanning his memory. "Somewhere warm. Beautiful hotel. Florida?"

"Exactly. At the Grand Victoria in Palm Beach."

"Whatever happened with that? As I recall, there were two theories at the time: either foul play or she got cold feet and took off."

Laurie was realizing she was at a disadvantage for not having followed the story while it was hot. "Over five years without a word sounds like more than cold feet."

"Nothing? No body ever found?"

Laurie was a journalist, the daughter of a cop, and the widow of an emergency room physician, but she still was not accustomed to Alex's matter-of-fact approach to speaking about crime. "According to Amanda's mother, there have been absolutely no new developments in all these years. I got the impression that police were divided—either she left voluntarily or was killed. But either way, they have stopped looking. It's a cold case."

"Meaning, right up your alley. And what's in Brooklyn?"

"The would-be groom, Jeff Hunter." Laurie quickly laid out the basic biography: Colby College, Fordham Law, a job with the Brooklyn Public Defender's office since graduation. "This is when it gets interesting." She told him about Amanda's will, leaving her trust fund to her fiancé. "Amanda's mother considers him our number one suspect."

"Are you worried that because he's a criminal defense attorney he'll take the fifth, so to speak, and not do the show?"

"Exactly. Plus his wife's a lawyer, too. Her name's Meghan White. She practices immigration law, not criminal defense, but still—"

"Even if he's willing, you're concerned that she'll try to stop him."

"Or have her own reasons to clam up. Because here's the thing: Meghan was Amanda's best friend. She was also there at the Grand Victoria, so she's a potential suspect, too. Marrying your best friend's fiancé fifteen months after she disappeared? Seems a little quick to me. I thought since you speak their language, maybe you could help convince them to do the show."

"I'm told I can be very persuasive. But do we even know if they're home?"

"I left a message on both their phones. Obviously they talked to each other and then Jeff called me back. It took a lot of persuading, but he gave the okay for us to come."

Alex leaned toward her until their shoulders touched.

"Palm Beach sounds like a good place to shoot, don't you think, Counselor?" she asked him.

"I couldn't agree more."

20

The converted brownstone looked just as it had appeared when Laurie entered the address into Google Maps' street-view function. It was a four-story walk-up. No doorman.

She pressed the buzzer for apartment B, marked "Hunter/White." Though Amanda's mother had referred to Meghan as "Mrs. Jeffrey Hunter," Laurie knew Meghan had retained her maiden name. She had already rehearsed her introduction. She looked at Alex nervously as seconds passed in silence. He pressed the buzzer a second time.

"The intercom's broken, Ms. Moran." The voice came from the second floor above them. She recognized Jeff Hunter, his head out the window, from the LinkedIn profile picture Jerry had shown her. "Are you Alex Buckley?"

Laurie could see that Jeff was astonished.

"I just used your closing argument in the J. D. Martin case in a seminar for our new lawyers. Masterful stuff. Just masterful."

Alex gave him a friendly wave. "That's very flattering. Thank you."

"Come on up." He tossed out a key ring, which Alex caught in one hand. "Nice catch."

As Alex unlocked the front door, Laurie said, "Did you see the way he looked at you? It's like he's a little kid and Derek Jeter just gave him an autograph."

"That's me: the Derek Jeter of law geeks."

"See? I knew you'd come in handy."

Jeff was waiting for them on the second floor, apartment door open. He was just about six feet tall with dark brown hair and intense hazel eyes.

"Come in please. I'm Jeff Hunter, by the way, but I guess you know that." He shook Alex's hand and then greeted Laurie.

To Laurie's relief, Jeff seemed friendly enough as he invited them to sit in the living room. The apartment was small, but comfortable, with a mix of mission-style and contemporary furniture. From a quick scan of the framed photographs arrayed on the console table, she got a sense of Meghan's appearance. Tall and thin, with long, curly black hair and sharp, angular facial features, she was the opposite of Amanda.

"Meghan isn't home from work yet," Jeff explained, "and it's very possible she won't be home for at least another hour."

Laurie had been hoping to meet both of them, but on the other hand, she knew this might be her only shot to speak to Jeff alone.

"On the phone you mentioned that you're familiar with the show," she began. "Then you know our show isn't about singling out any one person as a suspect. It's about the ways that an unsolved crime can plague the lives of everyone around it. The uncertainty. The lack of closure."

"The whispers I hear when someone recognizes my name," Hunter said bitterly.

She nodded. "So you know what I'm talking about."

"How could I not? I was in an absolute daze after Amanda disappeared. One day, I managed to walk out for a press conference wearing two different shoes. I didn't even notice that our wedding rings were missing when I was packing up to leave. My God, I felt like I was leaving Amanda behind— "

Alex interrupted. "The wedding rings were missing? Did Amanda have them? I've never heard anyone mention any kind of theft in connection with her disappearance."

"I have no idea what happened to them. I put them in my room safe when I got down there on Wednesday, but I admit I was very careless about locking it. A hotel employee must have taken them, but who knows? God, this is taking me back. Five years ago the hardest thing I ever did was to get on that plane. My friends Nick and Austin came with me to my room to help me pack, if you could even call it packing. I was a basket case. We threw my clothes, shoes, everything into the suitcase. It's possible I even tossed the rings out inadvertently. I was completely out of it. I didn't even realize I might be under suspicion, as you call it, until Nick and Austin pulled me aside and told me the cops were eyeing me as the chief suspect."

Jeff was shaking his head, remembering the moment. "They convinced me I had to look out for myself. The whole story became about money: specifically, how Amanda's family had it, and mine didn't. Reporters were calling Amanda the Ladyform Heiress. In comparison, I seemed like a gold digger from the wrong side of the tracks."

"Is that when you hired a defense attorney?" Laurie asked.

"Yes. My friends were looking out for me, but I've never had anything to hide. You know, when I first saw your show, I even thought about calling you. It seemed like a way to get people talking about Amanda's case again. But I didn't think Amanda's father would go for it."

"Why not?"

"Not his thing. Walter's super-quiet and private. Old school. Something like this would strike him as . . . flashy."

"It was actually Sandra's idea," Laurie explained, "but he's going along with it."

"Also not like him. He's the boss of that family in every way."

Laurie sensed resentment beneath the statement, but would explore it further when the time came. *If* the time came.

"They're no longer together, actually."

Jeff looked down at his feet. "I didn't know. That's very sad. We didn't . . . Well, let's say we fell out of touch. It's so strange not to know them anymore. When Amanda was sick, I was basically part of their family. By the time we were supposed to get married, I called Sandra and Walter Mom and Pops. Henry said I was like the brother he never had; we were that close. Even Charlotte—Amanda's sister—had warmed to me, and once you meet her, you'll know that's some feat. But then once I told them I was dating Meghan . . . I assume you know about that?"

Laurie nodded.

"I didn't want to hide it from them. I told Sandra I was certain that my feelings for Meghan were real. It obviously changed the way they saw me. I was no longer their 'Saint Jeffrey.' That's what they used to call me. It was kind of a joke that started when Amanda was sick."

"Amanda was ill?"

"Not by the time of the wedding, but she'd had Hodgkin's lymphoma. Diagnosed at twenty-six. We'd been dating for about a year, but on and off, the way things go when you're young."

"Only a year?" Alex asked.

"As a couple, yeah. The news kept saying we were college sweethearts, but we were just acquaintances at Colby. It was actually Meghan who reintroduced us after we all moved to New York. Meghan and I were young lawyers, and Amanda had moved here to open a New York City office for her father's company. We liked each other a lot immediately, but at first the relationship wasn't a priority. We were both working all the time. Anyway, when Amanda got the diagnosis, I realized I didn't want to spend one more second away from this amazing woman. I proposed before we even knew whether she'd make it. The chemo made her so sick, it was hard to watch, but she beat it. That's where I got the 'Saint Jeffrey' nickname. Every time she went to the doctor, every time she was sick, I was right there at her side."

Alex gave Laurie a concerned look. She knew he was thinking that this was a very different version of Jeff than the one she'd heard from Sandra. "Do you think that's why people were so willing to believe that she just got cold feet? Maybe she felt too guilty to call things off after you stayed by her side through her treatment."

"Amanda wasn't like that, at least not anymore. By the time she finished the cancer treatment, she'd lost twenty pounds, but was tougher than anyone I knew. And if anything, once the police got done questioning me, they had turned the whole thing around. Supposedly it was Saint Jeffrey who didn't want to go through with the marriage. Apparently I'd rather kill a woman than face the shame of breaking up with her. Plus, I assume you know about the will."

"Sandra mentioned it. It took Amanda's family by surprise."

"If I cared about money, would I be a public defender? If it had been up to me," Jeff said wistfully, "we would have had a tiny wedding in New York City. Amanda and her family were the ones who believed in big, lavish ceremonies. I never wanted their money, and I still don't. Even though I'll never believe that Amanda just walked away from a wonderful life, I still try to hold out some small hope that, somehow, she's still alive."

"When did you realize she was missing?" Laurie asked.

"She didn't show up for brunch on Friday morning. At first, we thought she was sleeping in. I tried calling the room to see if she wanted me to send up some breakfast. When she didn't answer, I went to check on her. Meghan came with me. Amanda didn't answer. We looked all over—the gym, the beach, the pool—and finally asked the hotel for a key. When I saw her wedding gown laid out across the bed, I was so relieved. I could imagine her trying it on one last time and leaving it out. But then Meghan told me Amanda tried the dress on before the dinner the night before. That's when she told me they never actually saw Amanda go back to her room. It was obvious that something was seriously wrong. Housekeeping had not made up her room that morning. The bed had not been slept in on Thursday night."

Jeff's description of his moment of panic when he realized that Amanda had not slept in her hotel room seemed too authentic to be fabricated. Then Laurie reminded herself that he'd had over five years to rehearse his story.

"Mr. Hunter," she said, "it's obvious that many people suspect you in Amanda's disappearance and that you want the opportunity to clear your name. We want to take on this case. Since I'm sure you'll want to see it eventually, I took the liberty of bringing the standard release we ask people to sign before production." She reached into her briefcase and slipped him the agreement.

"If I do the show, I assume that all of this would be fair game? The will. My relationship with Amanda. Were we actually happy? Was I cheating? Did she leave me at the altar? Why did I marry her best friend?"

Laurie was not going to lie to the man. "Yes, those are the kinds of things we'd get into."

He was nodding slowly as he flipped through the pages, taking it all in. "Okay."

"I can send you our previous specials if you want to re-watch them and get back to us with any questions."

"No, I mean, okay, I'll do it." He walked to his kitchen, grabbed a pen from the counter, and began signing.

"Well, that's great." Laurie couldn't remember a time when anyone had agreed this easily. Alex gave her a quick wink when Jeff wasn't looking.

"You sound surprised," Jeff said, handing her the signed agreement.

"No, just pleased."

"I'm no Alex Buckley, Ms. Moran, but I'm a good lawyer, and I can read a witness's expression. You were surprised because part of you thinks I may have killed Amanda, in which case the last thing I'd want is to sit down on camera and talk to you about her disappearance. So, Alex, I look forward to being on the receiving end of one of your trademark cross-examinations, because I didn't do anything to hurt Amanda, and never could have."

"This is your chance to tell the world that," Laurie said.

"What anyone thinks about me is less important. I just want to know what happened to Amanda. Because I know she didn't leave that resort on her own."

21

Meghan White was greeted by the smell of something delicious roasting in the oven when she got home. Jeff was in the kitchen wearing the apron she'd bought for him last year, the one that said, "Real Men Bake Cookies."

"That smells glorious." How lucky she was to have married a man who could cook. Everything about Jeff made her feel lucky. He was sweet and funny and her closest confidant. He was her best friend. She was waiting for the right moment to tell him the news. "What are we having, Jeff?" she asked.

"Rosemary and garlic lamb chops. You claim they're your favorite."

He greeted her with a hug that was longer than usual.

When he finally let go of her, he was looking at her as though something was wrong.

"Is everything okay?" Meghan asked.

"Sit down."

"You're scaring me, Jeff."

"Just sit. Please." Once she did, he poured her a glass of prosecco and waited for her to take a sip, but she did not.

"I don't need wine to have a conversation," Meghan said. "How did that meeting go? I absolutely couldn't get out of the office."

"I should have waited until we talked. I signed on to do the show."

• • •

Fifteen minutes later, Meghan sat on the edge of the bed, staring at her wineglass, still full, on the nightstand. She had changed into casual slacks and a pullover. She needed some time to think. The decision was already made. She had heard the certainty in his voice. Jeff's mind was made up. He hadn't been asking for her permission; he'd been breaking the news: He was doing this show. And Meghan knew that, in reality, he was making the decision for both of them. How could she say no? How would it look that first she took the man Amanda was supposed to marry and now was trying to block a reinvestigation of her case?

She wiped away a tear with the back of her hand. When Amanda's case had churned through the 24/7 cable channels, Meghan had managed to stay out of the story. Amanda's parents had been the ones front and center, with Jeff at their side. It was months before the reporters stopped calling Jeff for comments.

When they got married, she had been terrified that the media frenzy would start again. That's why they had gone quietly to the courthouse. It's why she didn't take Jeff's name. She didn't want the scrutiny.

But this show would put them before millions of judging eyes. Viewers would want to know what kind of woman would steal her missing friend's fiancé. They'd want to know what kind of man could marry another woman so soon after his beloved Amanda went missing. Everyone would hate them.

She started to lift her glass, and then put it back down, reminding herself that she shouldn't.

She pictured herself explaining everything about her marriage to a bunch of strangers on camera. *When Jeff and I started to develop feelings for each other, we were just as surprised as anyone else.* They'd fallen out of touch after college, but their paths crossed after law school when Meghan helped Jeff navigate a thorny immigration issue for one of his clients. He offered to take her out to dinner as a thank-you. After two dates fizzled, they remained strictly professional colleagues and friends. And then Jeff bumped into Meghan at a coffee shop near the courthouse when she was about to meet Amanda. She immediately sensed a spark between them. Maybe if Amanda had arrived a few minutes later, their paths would never have crossed again.

So how was it that they had ended up together? That's the question the television show would want to ask. It really was because of Amanda. In the aftermath of her disappearance, they had consoled each other over the loss of a woman they both loved. They had friendship first and then a deep bond that came later. And because of that bond, Meghan now knew what she had to do.

She walked back to the kitchen, stopping first in the hallway bathroom to pour her wine in the sink. Jeff was at the counter, slicing a tomato. She wrapped her arms around him tightly. "Okay, we'll do this. Together. For Amanda. And for us."

He turned around and gave her a kiss on the cheek. "I knew I could count on you. How were things at work today? When you got home, it seemed like you wanted to tell me something."

He always could tell what she was thinking. "Nothing big. I did manage to get an extension on Mrs. Tran's visa."

"That's good. I knew you were worried about that."

She would wait a few days before telling him the actual news. She did not want all this talk about Amanda to overshadow the fact that she hoped and believed she was pregnant. The home test kit had been positive. She had made an appointment with her doctor for an additional test to confirm. If the news was good, she'd need to make sure that those past problems she'd had with prescriptions wouldn't affect the baby. *Wow, a baby.* She felt a lump in her throat at the thought.

Jeff wrapped his arms around her again. She felt safe, like everything would be okay. "Don't worry about this show," he said. "We'll just explain that we never had feelings for each other until . . . after. It'll be fine. People will understand."

It wouldn't be the first time she'd had to explain the timing of their relationship. Her parents. Their friends. The familiar story they told was that their feelings developed after Amanda disappeared. It wasn't the truth in my case, she thought. I was desperately in love with Jeff. But there was no reason anyone ever needed to know that.

Meghan could lie just as well as her old friend Amanda.

22

When they left Jeff's apartment, they went directly to the Gotham Bar and Grill. The host greeted Alex with an enthusiastic handshake. "Good evening, Mr. Buckley."

Alex introduced the man to Laurie as Joseph. She had been to the restaurant several times, but was not on a first-name basis with the staff and surely would not have been able to get a reservation on ten minutes' notice with a phone call from the car.

Once they were seated, a sommelier arrived with three Cabernet selections for Alex to consider. He certainly was a regular. But she already knew that.

As Alex's chosen wine was being poured, Laurie checked her cell phone. There was a text message from her father, responding to the one she had sent from the car. *Timmy's thrilled with the pizza we ordered. Stop worrying, and have a good time at dinner.*

She knew that her father was more than happy to spend time with his grandson, but she still felt a pang of guilt. There was no way she'd be home in time to say good night to Timmy.

"Is everything okay at home?" Alex asked. Of course he would know that's where her thoughts had drifted.

"All good. It's amazing what a pepperoni pizza can do for a nine-year-old boy's happiness." Determined not to spend the entire night talking about Timmy, Laurie asked Alex what he thought about Jeff. "Did you notice that he was the one who brought up Amanda's will?"

"He struck me as a smart guy, so he knows why people are suspicious."

"Tell the truth, you just think he's smart because Alex Buckley is his idol."

"You love to get a rise out of me," Alex commented with a smirk. "So did you believe him when he said he never wanted Amanda's money?"

"I think so, actually. You saw that apartment. It was modest but comfortable. If he wanted more, presumably he could earn it by leaving his public defender job. Or he could have Amanda declared legally dead so he could inherit." Since speaking with Sandra, Laurie had learned that New York law gave Jeff the option of filing in court to have her declared dead without waiting a full seven years. A judge could evaluate all of the circumstances of the disappearance and conclude that the person is almost certainly dead.

"He may not know that, Laurie. Criminal defense lawyers don't know all the ins and outs of wills."

Whether Jeff was aware of his ability to seek to inherit Amanda's trust fund with no body having been found was the kind of detail they'd need to explore before production. Their usual approach was to use a soft touch with the show's participants at first, as they had in the apartment. Once they finished their research, Alex asked the tough questions on camera.

"Alex, thank you again for going to Brooklyn with me."

"You didn't even need my help. If anything, Jeff seemed eager to sign on. He sounded confident that he'd be able to persuade his wife, too."

"He certainly was right when he said I was surprised. I nearly fell out of my chair."

"Was it only because he's a lawyer that you were expecting him to be so uncooperative? Not all of us are so difficult." He smiled wryly.

"Amanda's mother, Sandra, made him sound like a money-grubbing ladies' man. Apparently his two best friends are flashy bachelors. Jeff, in contrast, seemed quite sweet and earnest."

"I hate to tell you how many guilty clients I've had who can put on an act when necessary. I should start handing out Oscars in my office."

"I'm sure you're right. But I have to wonder if Sandra may have jumped to conclusions. This is why I'm very careful about taking cases submitted by the families. It's too easy to get steered into one person's opinion."

"I know you, Laurie. You always keep an open mind."

A waiter appeared and began describing the new additions to the menu. Laurie nodded along, even though she already knew what she wanted. She hoped that Alex was right about her ability to remain neutral. What she hadn't told him was that something about Jeff reminded her of Greg. She realized the similarity when Jeff mentioned that he'd walked into a press conference wearing two different shoes. Greg had once come home from the hospital sporting mismatched loafers after too many hours on call. But it wasn't just that one anecdote. From the second he'd tossed his keys out the window, Jeff had struck her as easygoing and warm.

Could that really be so easily faked? Laurie doubted it.

But how was he going to react when Alex started pinning him down?

23

Twenty-four blocks north, a waiter carried three pounds of rare porterhouse to a table at Keen's Steakhouse. Nick Young gazed at the perfect char on the outside of the meat and signaled his approval. Once their martini glasses were refilled and the waiter had left, he held up his for yet another toast.

"Oh, why not?" Austin Pratt agreed.

"Here's to 'yucks' and yachts!" They both laughed.

Last year they had both signed with an upscale international boat charter service. From now on in many locations where they might be staying near water, they could request a boat to be delivered for their use to the local dock. Both men really liked small yachts with sleeper cabins, crafts they were licensed to pilot on their own. They had been doing it since the past summer, sometimes together and sometimes separately. They had already taken three boating vacations in the Caribbean.

Nick had a custom-made sign he put over the railing of whatever boat he chartered. It read LADIES FIRST, and he meant it. More ladies than clients set sail with Nick.

Austin had found that the boat was a great way to entertain potential clients, inviting them out for a lunch or dinner cruise. When he took clients out, he hired a captain to run the boat and a waitress who passed drinks and prepared the meal. Following Nick's lead, he created a sign for his boats, too. The name he chose was LONESOME DOVE.

Austin watched as his old friend downed his martini in one long gulp and signaled for another. Nick's movie-star looks had obviously attracted the attention of two young ladies seated at the next table. But he worried that Nick was drinking too much.

There was a time when he never would have questioned Nick's drinking. But he was no longer the small, shy, nerdy kid who moved in across the street when the two of them were seven years old in Baltimore. Even though they were the same age, Nick had become like a big brother, looking after him in grade school when Austin was smaller and less secure than the other children.

It was no surprise to anyone when after Nick applied to and chose to attend Colby College, I had done the same, Austin thought. Nick, naturally popular wherever he was, made sure to include me in his activities. The friends Nick made became my friends.

He did not realize that Nick was eyeing him with some envy.

He looks like a bookkeeper, Nick thought, with those frameless glasses and thinning hair. Where they'd call a woman a "plain Jane," he's a "plain Joe."

While he used to aspire to be like me, in some ways he's gone further than I have. I've done pretty well financially, but he's outpaced me. Austin is the one already managing one of the hedge fund industry's largest biotech-focused portfolios. He has homes in Manhattan, East Hampton, and Colorado. He even flies by private jet. Then Nick comforted himself by thinking, But I'm a lot better looking than he is. I'll catch up to him. Better yet, I'll surpass him.

Maybe when the check came, he'd let Austin pick it up.

They were halfway through the steak before they began to discuss the phone call they had each received from Jeff.

"I got the impression that Jeff's mind was made up," Nick said, his tone grim.

"Me, too."

"I love him like a brother, but I don't get that guy. Working like a dog for no money at all. Living in that tiny place in Brooklyn. Knowing a lot of people think he murdered Amanda, why would he stick his neck out like this?"

"He wanted my assurances that I'd sign on to the show if the producer contacted me," Austin said.

"Should we try to talk him out of it?"

Austin shrugged. "You know Jeff better than I do. You said yourself, his decision sounded final."

Nick certainly did know Jeff well. We became close friends when we were assigned as roommates our freshman year at Colby, he thought. We were both smart and confident; the girls loved us. But it ended there. Where Jeff was laid back and studious, Nick thought, I never missed a beer bash in four years. After graduation, we went in different directions. While Jeff became a public defender, I went for the money on Wall Street. After law school Jeff started dating the incredibly beautiful Amanda, the girl every guy on campus had been after. Amanda and I had a few dates in college, but it didn't go anywhere. Nick tried to suppress a smile when he recalled Austin telling him during senior year that he planned to ask Amanda for a date. "Don't bother, my friend, it's a lost cause."

To this day, Nick thought, I am still constantly playing the game of conquests; once I have her, right away I begin to lose interest.

But somehow, different as Jeff and I were and are, our friendship has always worked.

He looked over at Austin. "So are you going to do the show?"

"Sure, if you are. I mean, do we really have a choice? If there was one lesson to be learned from Jeff's experience, it's that people will suspect anyone who appears to be looking out for himself."

"You're the one who told Jeff to lawyer up," Nick reminded his friend.

"I was trying to help him. He was so out of his mind worried about Amanda that he didn't even notice the insinuations coming from the media. Amanda was from an extremely wealthy family, and he was the working-class fiancé. It was only natural that the police were going to suspect him," Austin said heatedly.

"Hey, don't get defensive. I know you were looking out for him."

Austin's intentions were good, Nick thought, but in many ways he was so hard to read. He has always been that way. Still waters run deep.

Although many had speculated that Jeff had something to do with Amanda's disappearance, no one had ever suggested the involvement of either of his college friends.

"You know," Austin said, "the show's going to ask us some questions that Jeff might not want us to answer."

"You mean what he said that night after a little too much wine."

"We never told the police."

"They never asked us the right question," Nick said coyly. "It's not up to us to do their job for them."

When it became clear that Jeff might be a suspect, he had followed Austin's advice and hired a lawyer. As his friends, both Nick and Austin decided that they would not lie on Jeff's behalf, but they also weren't going to volunteer anything that wasn't specifically asked of them.

A national television show would probably do a better job than the police had five years earlier. As they knew from when they were questioned, the police investigation could have been much more thorough.

"So if the producers ask the right question," Austin was saying, "are we going to tell them the truth?"

"It's up to you what you say. I can't make that decision for you."

"Well, we can't contradict each other."

"Are you saying you'll lie for Jeff if I ask you to?" Nick said.

"We've got a lot at stake, Nick. Investors don't want to be associated with someone caught lying in an investigation of a missing woman."

Nick ate in silence, weighing their options. "It's really not a big deal. Lots of people have cold feet a few days before they get married. It's normal. Jeff had every intention of going through with the wedding."

The night before Amanda disappeared, Jeff had told Nick and Austin that he wasn't sure Amanda was the perfect fit for him. It was only one comment, and when Nick told him that it wasn't too late to back out, Jeff quickly reassured him that he was "just nervous."

"So it's agreed," Austin said. "We'll tell the producers about that comment."

Nick nodded. "And I'll make sure Jeff knows that we plan to tell the truth. If he's going to drag us into this, we need to protect our own reputations, too."

"Weird," Austin said. "We'll all be together again, just like old times."

"It'll be just like college. We'll be chatting up two babes at the bar and they'll both be after me!"

"Okay, that does it," Austin announced. "You're paying for dinner."

"Oh, did you know that the Grand Victoria added a dock this past year? I'm going to reserve a boat. I have two clients in Boca I want to meet up with."

"Good idea. I'll reserve one as well. I'm sure we'll have some downtime when we're there."

As Nick signaled for the check, he did not see the smile that came over Austin's face.

24

By the following afternoon, Laurie, Jerry, and Grace had done enough legwork to start planning production. Jeff had called that morning to confirm that both he and his wife Meghan were willing to do the show. He also promised that his two groomsmen, Nick and Austin, would cooperate and gave Laurie their contact information. And Brett had called her in. As usual, he wanted the show done yesterday. "How soon can you get to Florida?" he asked.

It was on the tip of Laurie's tongue to tell him, *Yesterday*.

"We'll go down in one week," she said. "The camera crew can go a few days earlier. We want to film them against the background of different locations at the hotel. The wedding party had been enjoying the pool and the beach and having drinks on the veranda. We'll use those as backdrops."

Summer in Florida wasn't ideal, but at least Timmy wouldn't be in school yet.

Alex had told her that because time was so short, he could do the preliminary interviews, the ones she called his "warm and fuzzy" questions, on the telephone.

Now she and Jerry and Grace were in her office preparing to watch the security camera footage that had been taken in the three days before Amanda disappeared.

"Let's start by going over the chronology," Laurie said. "According to Sandra, the bridal party arrived late Wednesday morning and immediately went to the beach and had lunch in the ocean-side dining room. She and Walter had planned to arrive on Friday, in time for the rehearsal dinner. But Thursday was the last night anyone saw Amanda."

Laurie had immediately followed up by contacting Jeff's college friends, Nick Young and Austin Pratt. According to both, Amanda's brother, Henry, left the restaurant right after the bachelor's dinner on Thursday. Jeff and the other groomsmen had an after-dinner drink at the restaurant and then had gone to Jeff's room for a nightcap and were there for about forty minutes. They estimated that they left Jeff's room shortly before eleven P.M.

Both Nick and Austin said they were happy to help with the show if that's what Jeff wanted. They both corroborated Jeff's account of his whereabouts the night before Amanda was reported missing. More interestingly, though, both Nick and Austin agreed that when they were in Jeff's room that night, after a little too much to drink, Jeff had said he wasn't certain that Amanda was the right woman for him. On the other hand, they both construed the comment as harmless, typical of a groom just two nights before the big day.

If nothing else, Laurie thought, Brett would certainly be happy about the prospect of having two successful, eligible bachelors on the show. Her boss believed that some viewers would only watch shows about wealthy people and their problems.

"So is that everyone?" Grace asked, peering over Jerry's shoulder. Other men might be uncomfortable with Grace's ample and barely covered bosom next to their right ear, but Jerry and Grace were like siblings.

Jerry had added Nick and Austin to the list he'd been compiling on his notepad. He read the names aloud to make sure they were all on the same page. "Sandra, of course. And I've spoken to her ex-husband, Walter. He's on board, too, but I can tell he thinks we're tilting at windmills."

"Did he say why?" Laurie asked.

"I got the impression he just wants to keep believing that his daughter might be okay." Laurie nodded. As much as she had come to depend on Jerry, she was not quite ready to rely entirely on his "impression," even though this time she thought he was probably right.

She could not believe how seamlessly this installment was falling into place. Despite having met Sandra for the first time only a few days ago, they had the cooperation of everyone they needed. And so far, everyone had been able to adjust their schedules to go to Palm Beach.

"Is the video ready?" she asked Jerry.

The Grand Victoria had sent a zip file containing all of the hotel's surveillance from the wedding party's stay at the resort. Shortly after Jerry clicked on play, Laurie saw a beautiful young woman in a sleeveless floral sundress walking quickly through a tiled alcove lined with orange blossoms.

"We can go back to this one later," Laurie said. "Let's look at the footage from the lobby on Thursday night."

Jerry moved the video forward until he came across three women who stood clustered outside the elevators of the hotel. By now, Laurie was able to identify them as Amanda, Charlotte, and Meghan. She reached for the mouse and clicked on pause. The date stamp read 10:55 P.M.

"Where's Kate?" she asked.

Not surprisingly, Jerry knew the answer. "She told police that she turned in earlier than the other girls. Everyone else was still single and used to staying up late. But by then, Kate was married with a toddler who wasn't a good sleeper and couldn't keep up with the rest of the crowd."

Laurie jotted down a note on her pad and clicked on play again. The next few moments were the footage that had been played constantly on the news in the days following Amanda's disappearance.

All three women stepped into the elevator, but then Amanda walked out just before the doors closed. She was no longer in the sundress. She had changed into a blue dress and high-heeled wedge sandals. Laurie clicked on pause again. "This is where she said she lost something?" she asked.

"Yes," Jerry said. "Questioned separately, Charlotte and Meghan were entirely consistent about that. It was very sudden, like the thought just came to her. 'I forgot something' was the exact quote they both provided. At the time, they thought it might just be that she had left something in the lounge where they were having the after-dinner drink, but she had left so quickly they hadn't had time to ask her."

"But no one from the lounge remembers her going back to it?"

Jerry shook his head. "She just disappeared. But one theory is that she made up 'forgetting something' as a reason to go find Jeff. Some people think that the two of them had been fighting that weekend."

"Who are the *some people* who believe this theory?" Laurie asked.

Grace reached for a manila folder on the table and handed it to her. She opened it to find printouts from the *Palm Beach Post*. The byline on all of the articles was "by Janice Carpenter." As she flipped through the pages, Grace explained.

"Janice Carpenter was the Southern Florida reporter who did the most digging into Amanda's disappearance. According to her, she received an anonymous tip that Jeff and Amanda had been bickering all weekend at the hotel."

"*One* anonymous tip? Even with legitimate sources, reporters should have two before going to print."

"I don't think she's en route to any Pulitzers," Grace said. "She's more of a tabloid writer."

The three of them sat at Laurie's conference table for the next four hours, watching much more video than Laurie had anticipated. Jerry had managed to set up the screen to play four views at once. The hotel certainly had been diligent about saving everything that might be relevant, Laurie thought.

She started fiddling with her phone, answering texts and emails. They were playing footage from earlier in the evening, before dinner. The hotel was still busy. Amanda was still safe. Laurie found herself putting her phone down as something registered in her peripheral vision.

"Wait," she cried out. "Rewind."

Jerry reached over and did as instructed.

"That's Amanda again," she exclaimed. She recognized the sundress. Amanda was in the courtyard where most of the hotel's shops were located. She paused at a window for a few seconds, appearing to admire an outfit, and then continued to walk.

"That's definitely her," Grace said.

"This is hours before she was last seen exiting the elevator," Jerry said.

"I know, but play it again." Jerry went back a few minutes and then clicked play.

This time, Laurie took the mouse from him, waited, and then clicked pause. "See, right there." She pointed to a grainy image that appeared to be a man and then replayed the last few seconds one more time.

The man approached from the right side of the screen toward the left. He passed Amanda, who had paused at the shop window, her back toward the camera. Just as she disappeared into the right edge of the screen, the man pivoted ninety degrees and walked away from the shop windows. A moment before he was out of view of the camera, barely perceptible, he turned again. He passed the shop window and kept walking.

"Did you see it?" Laurie asked. "He was heading in Amanda's direction."

"He's following her," Grace said.

They replayed the few seconds one more time. "Or maybe he went back to his room for some reason," Jerry said.

"He's carrying something." Laurie slid the video back again and then paused on the grainy image. "Can you zoom in on it?"

Jerry tried, but the resolution turned to mush. "It's a purse or something," Grace said. The man had a strap across his chest, attached to a small case resting on his hip.

"Looks like a camera," Jerry said.

Laurie squinted, as if that might help. Jerry could be right. It looked like a camera case. "That looks like a professional camera," she said. "Five years ago, most people were already using their phones for taking pictures. Do we know who their wedding photographer was yet?" She thought about her own wedding to Greg. The photographer had been there for the rehearsal dinner. She could imagine Amanda's family asking for a few candid shots of the bridal party during their pre-wedding festivities.

Jerry effortlessly reached for a binder on the table and then flipped it open to a tabbed section. His organizational abilities were one of the many reasons he was such a key contributor to the success of the show. "The photographer's name is Ray Walker. He was questioned by the police—everyone who had anything to do with the wedding was." Jerry's eyes skimmed the report, but Laurie could tell that he already knew the contents. "He was indeed at the property Thursday afternoon to take candid pictures of the wedding party enjoying themselves, but says he left at five o'clock because he had a separate booking for another wedding that night."

His gaze returned to the image of the man who appeared to be following Amanda on the computer screen. "This video was taken at five-thirty-two P.M., so according to Walker, he would have been gone by then."

Laurie looked at the frozen image on the screen. His height was hard to estimate, but he seemed neither tall nor short. He was a bit chubby, not overweight so much as soft.

"Do we have a picture of Walker?"

"No, but according to this report, he was fifty years old five years ago."

Something about the man on the screen seemed younger, but the image was too blurred to be certain. Laurie glanced at the clock and realized she needed to leave for her meeting with Amanda's sister, Charlotte.

"I've got to go. Let's make a note to follow up with Walker," she said to Jerry, "just in case. It's probably just a tourist who's into photography.

"On the other hand," she paused, "Amanda was a strikingly beautiful woman. It's very possible that she might have attracted the attention of someone who began following her."

"You mean a stalker?" Grace asked.

"That's exactly what I mean."

25

The Ladyform waiting room was fit for a couture company, complete with wine-colored velvet furniture and black-and-white fashion photos lining the wall. Sandra wasn't exaggerating when she said the family business had shifted its "branding" in recent years. When Laurie was a child, her grandmother had bought Ladyform "foundation wear." Laurie was too young to understand all the snaps and buckles, or why her grandmother would spend so much time squeezing herself into those heavy-duty contraptions, but she remembered being scared by the entire process. Now Ladyform was synonymous with women feeling happy and comfortable inside healthy, natural bodies.

A woman about her age opened one of the double doors leading to the lobby and greeted her with a smile. She was tall, probably close to five-ten, and slightly heavyset. She had shoulder-length light brown hair and appeared to wear no makeup. Laurie recognized her from their research as Charlotte Pierce, current executive vice president of design at Ladyform and, more important for Laurie's current purposes, the older sister of Amanda Pierce.

"What can I do for you, Ms. Moran?" Charlotte asked once they were settled into her office. "Have you decided to take my sister's case?"

Laurie had scheduled an appointment through Charlotte's assistant, but hadn't yet spoken to Charlotte directly. "I should make clear that we don't *take* a case, like a lawyer or private investigator would, since your family wouldn't actually be our client. But we are looking closely at featuring your sister's disappearance in our next special."

"That's great. As I told my mother, I'm happy to participate if you need me."

"Terrific. She told me that, but we always double-check. I have the paperwork for your review." She retrieved the production contract from her briefcase and slid it across the desk. She could have emailed it to Charlotte, but she had another reason for being here. As Charlotte reviewed the agreement, Laurie pretended to make small talk. "So I'm told you were a bridesmaid."

"Hmm?" she said, her attention focused on reading. "Oh sure, that's right. I suppose the bride kind of has to ask the big sister."

"But you and Amanda were close, weren't you? Not only sisters, but co-workers."

"She probably would have said *too close* at times. It's not always easy to work professionally with family members."

Laurie nodded. It was Austin Pratt and Nick Young who'd mentioned a sense of sibling rivalry between the Pierce sisters, more on Charlotte's part than Amanda's. According to them, Charlotte showed no real interest in her sister's wedding. She had been supposed to offer the toast at the Friday brunch but had asked Nick to do it. Amanda never appeared for brunch, so the moment of the toast never arrived. Thinking about that, Laurie wondered if somehow Charlotte already knew that Amanda wouldn't be there.

"Your mother tells me that Amanda was the one to suggest this New York office. Things seem to be going very well for the company."

Charlotte's grimace was unmistakable. "Yes, it was Amanda's idea. I've managed to steer it in the right direction in her absence, but who knows where we might be if she were still here." She barely tried to hide the sarcasm.

"Sorry, I didn't mean to suggest that you didn't deserve the credit," Laurie said, even though that wasn't quite true.

"It's fine." She handed back the signed document. "So is that all?"

"What do you think happened to your sister?" Laurie asked bluntly.

Charlotte looked Laurie directly in the eye. "I have no idea. My mother is convinced she was kidnapped and probably murdered. My father seems to think she ran away to start a new life. I have dreams—nightmares—involving both scenarios and everything in between."

She spoke in a tone that was almost businesslike.

"Why would she want a different life? From everything I've heard, she had it all: a great job, a fiancé who loved her, a close-knit family."

Charlotte swallowed, and for just a moment, she looked genuinely sad. "Amanda did have it all, everything that most of us hope and pray for. But you know how some people have everything but are still yearning for something different? Almost like those people who feel like they're living in someone else's body."

Laurie knew the scenario Charlotte was describing, but didn't understand the comparison to Amanda. "Whose life did Amanda want instead of hers?"

She shrugged. "Her cancer—do you know about that?"

Laurie nodded.

"Some survivors become more grateful. Not Amanda. I think she started to doubt every choice she'd ever made, like maybe she'd taken the easy route. Job in Daddy's company. Sweet, devoted fiancé. She was only twenty-seven years old, and her entire future was already mapped out for her."

"Did she say anything to you about wanting to back out of the wedding?"

"No, but I got the sense she was looking for reasons."

"Any examples?" Laurie asked.

"Like she said she was worried Jeff only proposed because she was sick. And then she said Jeff was more excited to have children right away than she was. I got the impression she didn't want to be the one to call it off, but was sort of hoping Jeff might."

"Would she really let you all worry about her for all these years?" Laurie couldn't imagine anything more selfish.

"Not the old Amanda. But the cancer treatment changed her. She was colder. Less patient, more demanding."

"Tougher?" Laurie asked. That's what Jeff had said.

"Exactly. But still, as much as I'd like to think she's out there somewhere, doing her thing, I can't fathom her putting our parents through this much pain. Our mother still wears those yellow-ribbon buttons everywhere."

"I spent a long time talking to your mom. She seems to think that Jeff killed your sister so he could inherit her trust fund."

"Then why hasn't he tried to inherit?"

"Maybe he intended for the body to be found."

"I don't know. Jeff's a sweet guy. I actually feel pretty bad for him."

"So if someone hurt your sister, who else would it be?"

She didn't even pause. "Meghan White."

"Because she wanted Jeff for herself?" Laurie asked.

Charlotte shook her head. "I think that happened after the fact, or maybe it was an added benefit. If Meghan did it, it was because of Ladyform."

Laurie was confused. "I thought Meghan was already a lawyer by then. She was working for your family's company?"

"No, but the two of them had a major blowup right before we all flew down for the wedding. We were still in the transition then, trying to convince Dad that we could be more than the tried-and-true granny-panty company. Amanda launched a breakthrough workout line called X-Dream: high-end exercise clothing with room for cell phones, iPods, all the gadgets we want with us but don't want to hold while we're exercising. Until then, the best you could get was a loose pocket, where your phone bounced around as you ran."

"I remember that!" Laurie exclaimed. Greg had bought a sports top for her right before he died. It was her favorite running shirt because she couldn't even feel her iPod zipped into the fabric. "What does it have to do with Meghan?"

"When she saw the clothing in stores, she showed up here, screaming at Amanda for stealing her idea. It was so loud that people could hear it all the way down the hall."

"That seems bizarre," Laurie said. "Meghan's an immigration lawyer. What was she going to do with an idea about workout clothes?"

"Nothing, of course, but that didn't keep her from wanting a piece of the pie. The X-Dream line was huge for us. I could go back and show you the spike in our sales and you'll see: we literally made millions. Amanda was nervous enough that she asked our corporate counsel to prepare for a potential lawsuit."

"So was it in fact Meghan's idea?"

"Only if you call two college girls saying they wished their phones didn't bounce off the treadmills at the gym an *idea*. The real work is the execution. We actually hired an engineer with NASA experience to find the exact right way to keep everything snug and safe but still accessible. If Meghan played any role at all, it was simply identifying the need for the product—something thousands of people had probably done by then."

"So was Meghan still angry at Amanda by the time you were down in Florida?"

"She certainly wasn't *acting* like it, but anyone can compose themselves for a few days. All I know is that Amanda only quieted Meghan down by telling her no one would ever believe her. She even went so far as to warn her that as a young lawyer, she could ruin her career by filing frivolous litigation."

"Wow," Laurie said. "I didn't know your sister, but that sounds pretty cutthroat, especially toward her best friend. And just before the wedding."

"As I said, by the time she disappeared, Amanda was no pushover. Sometimes I wonder how well I really knew her."

26

Laurie found herself whispering as though she were in a library. "Your office is never this quiet," she said to Alex, who was seated next to her.

Alex shared office space with five other attorneys each of whom had his own administrative assistant and shared with them a pool of eight paralegals and six investigators. "And I would never leave someone waiting this long."

Laurie looked over to the gum-chewing receptionist to make sure she hadn't heard the comment. "Don't forget that we're here, hat in hand, begging for help he's not obligated to provide. We don't want to offend the man."

The man in question was Mitchell Lands, Esq. Laurie was enjoying the absolute silence of the sole practitioner's office, and she was savoring the excuse to read the trashy celebrity magazine she'd found on the coffee table.

Alex was not so patient. "If I were a paying client, I would have walked out ten minutes ago."

"Be careful, Alex. Stress is bad for you. I might tell Ramon that you need some more yoga in your life."

Ramon was Alex's butler. Alex had made numerous attempts to find an alternative title: assistant, house manager, scheduler. But Ramon had finally won the battle. He was a butler. In addition to running errands and preparing meals, Alex's live-in helper also had come to care for Alex like a son. When he learned recently that Alex's blood pressure was on the borderline of high, he had reduced the sodium and red meat in Alex's diet. But when Ramon had tried to enroll Alex for weekly "stress-reduction" yoga sessions, Alex had put his foot down.

"Just in the knick of time," Alex muttered, as they saw a door open.

"My girl said that you're here about Amanda Pierce's will." Mitchell Lands was a short man with unruly gray hair and glasses that were much too large for his face. Laurie felt herself blinking in shock that anyone still referred to his assistant as "my girl."

Alex jumped in before she could say anything to start an argument. She, after all, had been the one to warn him that they were here asking for a favor. "We already have considerable information from Amanda's family," Alex said, "but we can still use your help."

They had a copy of both the will and the prenuptial agreement between Amanda and Jeff. According to Alex, the prenuptial agreement was one of the least generous among standard terms for such documents. According to Sandra, Walter Pierce insisted on it to ensure that Jeff could not possibly assert any claims to the family company.

But the will was another question. Amanda had left her modest personal belongings and checking and savings accounts to her one niece at the time—Henry's daughter, Sandra—but bequeathed the entirety of her trust fund to Jeff.

"Did it strike you as unusual," Laurie asked, "that she'd leave so much money to her fiancé before they were actually married?"

Lands smiled. "I want to help you. Amanda was a lovely woman. But I've got attorney-client privilege to worry about."

"Of course," Laurie said, realizing she probably should have left the questioning of another lawyer to Alex. "Not as to Amanda specifically, but is it unusual for an unmarried person to name a fiancé in the will?"

"Good job presenting the question," Lands said. "No, at least not where the individual's other family members have significant assets, and where the couple is about to be married and have no children yet. I think I can safely add that it's especially common for fiancés to revise their wills as a way to make up for a prenuptial agreement that their family is insisting upon. Parents tend to care about prenups, but never imagine that their children will ever predecease them. If you know all the terms of Amanda's will and prenup, I'm not sure how much more I can add."

"What we really want to know," Laurie said, "is whether Jeff knew about the terms of Amanda's will prior to her disappearance."

Obviously Jeff knew about the prenuptial agreement, Laurie thought, as he was a party to it and had signed off on it. But it was possible that he had no idea until after he returned from the Grand Victoria that Amanda had also written a will, naming him as the primary beneficiary. The inheritance wasn't a motive for murder if he didn't know about it.

Alex had been the one to notice that Amanda's will was signed on the same date as the couple had signed the prenuptial agreement. Now Alex pointed out that fact to Lands.

"My guess is that they came here together to sign," Alex said. "If you went over the terms of Amanda's will in front of Mr. Hunter, then attorney-client privilege wouldn't apply. Amanda was the client, not Jeff."

"Very clever," Lands said. "And, yes, that's precisely what happened. Amanda was quite comfortable speaking about these matters in front of Jeff. Not that I'm an expert in such things, but they seemed very much in love. You don't really think he killed her, do you?"

"We haven't committed ourselves to any one theory," Laurie said.

"But working with families on their legal matters, you must understand why we'd at least want to consider Jeff as a possible suspect, and why the terms of Amanda's will might be relevant."

Lands smiled knowingly. "Oh, I certainly do understand, but I also knew my client. I think you're overlooking another possibility."

He kept looking at them, waiting for them to follow his train of thought. He seemed amused at their befuddlement. "When Amanda first disappeared, many of the news outlets called her the Runaway Bride. Cold feet, etcetera. My guess is that your show will assume that five years with no word makes a voluntary disappearance less likely."

Laurie nodded. "That's a good assumption."

The knowing smile returned. "Unless it's not." He added another hint. "Maybe the will is relevant in a way you haven't considered."

As she often did when it came to legal issues, Laurie found herself looking to Alex for guidance. But on this one, she had more knowledge than he did of the personalities involved. It wasn't a legal puzzle. It was a puzzle about human motivations.

"Both Jeff and Sandra say that Amanda would have never just walked away without a trace. But if she wanted to start over again, and felt like she owed something to Jeff—"

Alex finished her thought. "Naming Jeff in her will and then disappearing was a way to eventually give some of her family's wealth to him, despite her father's insistence that he sign a prenup."

Lands was nodding in agreement, pleased that he was being given the opportunity to share his thoughts. "I've said as much as I probably can about my own dealings with Amanda, but I can say that in general, sometimes when people have been very sick and could have died, they become keenly aware of their mortality. They want to make the most of every day. Maybe breaking your family's hearts is worth it if you can spend the rest of your days living on the other side of the world, doing exactly what you want."

27

That night at seven-thirty, Alex was thrilled to hear the sound of keys in the front door. His brother, Andrew, had made it to New York with time to spare before dinner.

He was about to pull the door open when he felt it being pushed.

"Glad to have the better-looking Buckley on the premises," Alex said with a laugh.

"Younger *and* better-looking!" Andrew said as he embraced his brother.

Ramon was hustling away his suitcase.

As much as Alex enjoyed his life, so busy with work, he felt most at home when Andrew was here. One of the reasons Alex had bought this large apartment on Beekman Place—six rooms, plus housekeeper's quarters—was so his younger brother could always have his own room and there would be plenty of space when he brought his family up for a weekend. Andrew was a corporate lawyer in D.C. who came up to New York frequently on business.

There was a reason it felt natural for Alex to have his brother under the same roof with him. For a long time, it had been only the two of them. Their parents had died within two years of each other. At only twenty-one years of age, Alex became Andrew's legal guardian. He sold their parents' home in Oyster Bay, and the two of them moved to an apartment on the Upper East Side, where they lived together until Andrew graduated from Columbia Law School. At commencement, Alex thought he probably cheered louder than any of the graduates' parents.

Alex walked over to the bar to make cocktails while Ramon continued to prepare dinner in the kitchen. Measuring shots of gin into a martini shaker, Alex asked Andrew about Marcy and the kids. He and Marcy now had a six-year-old son and three-year-old twin daughters.

"I love coming back to the city," Andrew said, "but, man, it's getting harder and harder to leave them, even for a few days. Marcy tells me I'm lucky to have a break, but I miss them like crazy when I'm here."

Alex smiled, wondering what that was like. He handed Andrew a martini, and the two of them clinked glasses.

"So what's your story, Alex? I thought I might finally meet Laurie tonight. She couldn't join us?"

Alex regretted mentioning the possibility when Andrew had phoned yesterday. "I invited her, but she's lining up a new case. When she jumps in, it's not just with both feet. She gets in all the way up to her ears. She didn't want to ruin dinner by being distracted."

Andrew was nodding. "Sure, I understand."

It was obvious to Alex that his brother, in fact, did not understand. When Laurie said she didn't want to meet Andrew until she could give him her full attention, Alex accepted the explanation at face value. Now he was seeing it as yet another wall standing between them. "Hopefully, next time."

Alex found himself relieved when Ramon appeared with a small plate of hors d'oeuvres. He had not realized until that moment how much he wanted Andrew to meet Laurie. Andrew was the only real family member he had. Would there ever be a time when Laurie would become part of this family, too?

28

"Are you sure you don't want my help, Dad?" Laurie called out to the kitchen.

"Tonight's my night with my sous chef," Leo said, popping his head around the corner. Laurie smiled at the sight of her father in the chef's hat that Timmy had given him last year for Father's Day.

Timmy's grinning face, smeared with tomato sauce, appeared for an instant and then disappeared into the kitchen again.

Her father was preparing what he called his "Leo lasagna" for dinner. She knew from eating it that it contained Italian sausage, mozzarella, and fresh ricotta, but that didn't explain why it tasted better than every other sausage lasagna she had ever sampled. Her father was so protective of the recipe that he joked about putting it in his will.

"I'll get it out of Timmy," she said. "What's that new video game you're asking for?"

"Nice try, Mom," Timmy said. "Grandpa, your secrets are safe with me."

"Laurie, I'm actually surprised you're home. Alex told me that Andrew was coming into town. I assumed you would want to join them for dinner tonight."

After Alex accepted her invitation to host *Under Suspicion*, Leo had struck up a friendship with him outside of the show. They had grown even closer since Laurie and Alex had started seeing each other. She was delighted that her father approved and had someone to talk sports with, but sometimes there were downsides to their independent communications.

"I was too wired," she said. "I needed to get some more work done before I could relax."

"Well then, go ahead and do it," her father said. "Chardonnay or pinot noir?"

With her father and son hard at work on dinner and a glass of wine in hand, it was a good time to follow up on some of the issues that had come up today on Amanda's case. First on her mind was Charlotte's claim that Meghan accused Amanda of stealing a multimillion-dollar idea. There was no reason Charlotte would make that up, but it seemed far-fetched to think that Meghan would kill her best friend over a business dispute. Besides, Ladyform continued to own the idea, whether Amanda was there to control it or not.

But Laurie's conversation with Charlotte echoed for a second reason: her description of her sister's personality. Sandra made Amanda sound almost impossibly happy about every aspect of her life. She hadn't even mentioned Amanda's cancer. But Charlotte spoke about Amanda in a darker way, as if both women were trapped beneath their parents' expectations. Laurie had gotten the same impression from Mitchell Lands. If the lawyer was right, maybe Amanda had changed her will to leave some money behind for Jeff once she disappeared for good.

She scrolled through her emails until she found the one from Jerry with all the contact information for the show's participants. She dialed a number on her cell phone. Amanda's brother, Henry, answered after two rings.

A moment later she was having a hard time hearing Henry over the sound of a crying child in the background. "I hate to say this, but I probably know less about Ladyform than you do. Maybe no one told you, but I'm sort of the black sheep in the family. I love my dad, but I had no interest in spending the rest of my life making underwear, let alone fighting with my sisters about the right to do it. I moved out west with a college buddy and started an organic wine company in Washington. Aside from both of us preferring to run our own businesses, I'm about as different from Walter Pierce as a son could be. If Meghan accused Amanda of stealing some idea, I know nothing about it. And I can't say anything about Jeff's whereabouts that night, because I crashed early. It was a party weekend for everyone else, but Holly and I had just had our first baby, Sandy. All I wanted to do that week was sleep."

"But you were at the Grand Victoria with the rest of the wedding party. You must have spent time with Meghan and your sister."

"Oh yeah, sure. I didn't hear a cross word between them. And I think if they'd been talking about the company, I would've tuned them out because, frankly, it's boring. I understand that Charlotte would blow some tiff about a Ladyform idea out of proportion, but if I had to guess, I'd say there was no bad blood between Meghan and Amanda. If Meghan came across as not being worried, that's just how she is. Maybe it's because she's a lawyer or something like that."

"What do you mean by not worried?" Laurie asked. They had received her signed agreement to participate, but even though they had exchanged messages, she had still not actually spoken to Meghan directly.

"You know, she's kind of a cool cucumber. Never gets ruffled. I can be the same way. Like at first, when Jeff was running around the resort looking for Amanda, I assumed she went for a swim or something. But once we realized she hadn't slept in her room, even I was panicked. But not Meghan. She was acting like everything was okay."

"Do you think she knew more than she let on?"

"Wow, you really are suspicious, aren't you? No, like I said, it's just her way. Different strokes for different folks. So has everyone agreed to do the show?"

"Yes, everyone we asked."

"Kate Fulton?"

"Her, too. Is there something I should be asking her? As you said, I'm suspicious of everyone."

"Touché. No, I was just wondering. I don't stay in touch with any of Amanda's friends anymore. Look, I have no idea what happened to my sister, and I still miss her like crazy, but I've got to be honest: I don't think you're going to learn anything new with this show."

"And why is that?"

"Because, as much as it pains me to say it, my best guess is that she went out late for a swim or a walk and crossed paths with the wrong kind of person—the kind of person who doesn't get caught. I for one am not looking forward to being back down there."

29

Laurie was trying to picture Amanda's best friend remaining calm while everyone else panicked. Maybe Henry was right. Not everyone responds to worries in the same way. Or maybe, as Amanda's best friend, Meghan had been in denial, refusing to believe that anything could have possibly gone wrong.

She looked at her watch. It was just past seven-thirty, not too late to call someone in Atlanta. She picked up her phone again and called Kate Fulton.

Laurie introduced herself and asked if Kate had time to review some basic information. Kate confirmed that she was a homemaker in Atlanta, a mother to four children, and wife to her high school sweetheart, Bill. Laurie found comfort that Kate's bio lined up with the information they'd gathered so far in their research. Preparations had been moving so quickly, she was worried they would overlook something important. Not to mention that several of the participants were spread out across the country, so she was forced to question some people by phone.

"How did you feel when you realized that Amanda was missing?" Laurie asked.

"Terrified. I don't even know how to describe it. It was like time stopped, and everything went blank. I just knew in the pit of my stomach that something had gone horribly wrong. I couldn't stop crying.

In retrospect, I'm sure I only made things worse for Amanda's poor family."

"What about Meghan? Did she react the same way?"

"Oh, God no. Meghan? She's the exact opposite. Her way of dealing with bad news is to try to fix it. In college, we called her TCB—always Taking Care of Business. She's a planner and thinker, but Amanda's disappearance was something that even Meghan couldn't fix. She was at a loss for what to do, but no, she's not a crier."

"Did you find it strange when she began a relationship with Jeff?"

Kate paused for a moment. "Of course we were all surprised. I didn't even know they were dating. Meghan called me after the wedding—or what she referred to as their *non-wedding*. Just vows exchanged at the courthouse."

"Is it possible they might have been seeing each other before Amanda disappeared?"

This time she didn't need to reflect before answering. "No way. Jeff was head over heels for Amanda. Meghan had tried getting his attention before, and they just didn't click. I think it was actually their mutual love for Amanda that helped to bring them together later."

Laurie heard her father tell Timmy to be careful of the heat from the oven, and resisted the temptation to walk to the kitchen to supervise. "What do you mean, she had tried getting his attention?"

"They'd gone on a couple of dates. Meghan was always interested in Jeff, even in college. If you've seen him, you know he's very attractive, and they were both drawn to public interest work. They're a good match, but for whatever reason, they didn't hit it off at first. I think Meghan was sort of disappointed."

"So Meghan played matchmaker for Amanda? That was thoughtful."

"Not really. Jeff bumped into Meghan in the neighborhood, and Amanda happened to be there."

That was interesting. Laurie had gotten the impression that Meghan had intentionally set up Amanda with Jeff. She was about to ask for more details when Kate shifted the conversation back to Amanda's disappearance. "More so than anyone except maybe Mr. Pierce, Meghan really wanted to believe that Amanda left on her own. I always thought it was her way of coping."

Laurie shook her head in frustration. She still had no sense of Meghan as a person. After she and Alex met with Jeff, she had called Meghan twice to try to schedule a meeting, but got voice mail both times. Meghan had replied only by email, saying that she was busy at work but "looked forward" to talking "soon."

"That's what we keep struggling with on our end," Laurie said. "To us, it seems far more likely that something bad happened to Amanda. Why would anyone possibly disappear for all these years?"

"They wouldn't, or at least Amanda wouldn't. But at the time, it hadn't been a matter of years. And we were all trying to convince ourselves there was some explanation. It was the day before the wedding, and Amanda was having doubts."

"She was?" Charlotte said she sensed her sister was having second thoughts, but this was the first time anyone had claimed to have heard Amanda express them.

"Doubts might be too strong of a word. But when we were alone, she was asking me if I was happy. If I wished I had met Bill later in life. Whether I'd had enough adventure before settling down. But if I thought she was really going to back out of the wedding, I wouldn't have been so terrified when she was missing. I can't bring myself to say this to Sandra, but I'm convinced my friend is dead. I know for a fact she wouldn't put her family through this."

"How can you be so sure?"

"Back when we were at Colby, a girl named Carly Romano disappeared. It was nearly two weeks before they found her body in Messalonskee Lake. Actually, this will give you some idea of how

Meghan and Amanda were so different. We didn't really know Carly, but the entire college was affected. Amanda was the one who organized the prayer sessions and candlelight vigils; Meghan was the one who helped organize the on-campus search teams and handed out flashlights and safety whistles. Amanda was a caretaker. Meghan was a pragmatist. Anyway, one night, while everyone was still searching, Amanda told me that she nearly broke down when she met Carly's parents. She said she almost hoped they'd find a body, because she couldn't imagine anything worse for a parent than not knowing."

Laurie thought she was living in hell those five years when Greg's murder was unsolved. She couldn't imagine how she would have felt if he had simply failed to come home one night. How do people go on?

30

Leo hadn't allowed Laurie into the kitchen while he was cooking, but he seemed more than happy to let her help with the cleanup. Timmy was off the hook because of his work as sous chef and was in his room practicing the trumpet Leo had bought him last month. He was an enthusiastic student, but as far as Laurie was concerned, his weekly lessons couldn't kick in soon enough.

While she transferred the leftover lasagna into a Tupperware dish, she made a point of using the spatula to prod between the layers. "Provolone cheese?" she asked.

"Nope."

"Gouda?"

Her father shook his head. "I'm not going to tell you."

"Can you at least tell me if it's a dairy product?"

"It is not." That was the biggest hint her father had ever given her.

"Spinach?"

"Laurie, I know you're not the world's most knowledgeable cook, but please tell me that even you would notice if there were chunks of spinach in your dinner. And you certainly know I could never sneak that past my grandson."

Generally, Timmy was not a finicky eater, but he had decided in kindergarten that "Popeye food" was not for him. He said it made his teeth feel "yucky."

"Dad, I've been so busy with work we haven't had a chance to talk about the Amanda Pierce case. I can't stop thinking about her."

"When you first mentioned it, the case seemed perfect for your show," Leo replied as he started the dishwasher.

"At first, I was drawn to it because I knew it would attract viewers. But the more I learn about Amanda, the more interesting she becomes. She wasn't just another pretty face from an impressive family with a storybook wedding. She was complicated—and still getting to know herself. She was so young, but had already survived a serious illness. Some of the things I've heard about her remind me of myself and what I would have done, like organizing prayer vigils for a missing girl in college. But she wasn't perfect by any means either."

Laurie continued to talk about the case as she wiped down the countertops. When she'd brought him up to speed, she glanced around the kitchen. "I guess we're almost finished here."

She turned to face Leo. "Bullying Meghan into retracting her claims that Amanda stole an idea from her seems especially cold, but do you think it could possibly have anything to do with her disappearance?"

Before Leo could answer, Laurie's cell phone began buzzing on the counter.

"No rest for the weary," Leo commented.

The number on the screen was unfamiliar, but Laurie did recognize the 561 Palm Beach area code.

When she answered, a man's voice said he hoped he wasn't calling too late. "I spoke this afternoon to your assistant, Jerry. He told me I should call you if I remembered anything more about Amanda."

"And this is—?"

"Oh, I'm sorry. This is Ray Walker. I was supposed to photograph the wedding for Amanda Pierce and Jeff Hunter."

"Yes, of course, Mr. Walker. Jerry briefed me on your conversation earlier today."

The photographer had confirmed that he was not the man in the hotel surveillance video, the one carrying a camera as he appeared to turn to follow Amanda. According to Walker, he had left the property by then to work with another client. More important, Jerry had learned that Walker was six-foot-four and thin, and had been five years earlier as well. The man in the video was slightly overweight and of average height.

"After I hung up, I kept thinking about that weekend. It's hard to retrace your steps so many years later, but of course the events stand out because of what happened. I've had weddings canceled at the last minute before, but never because the bride disappeared. It was very upsetting."

"We very much appreciate any help you can give us, Mr. Walker. I believe Jerry explained we were trying to identify a man from the hotel surveillance system."

"He did, and that's what got me thinking. I was at another wedding the evening Amanda disappeared, so I assumed I had nothing that might help the police. But when Jerry called, he said the video you were interested in was earlier, at five-thirty."

"That's correct."

"Well, it dawned on me that I had an intern back then. His name was Jeremy Carroll. He was self-trained, but quite good. He had a real eye for candids, which is why I took him on. In photography, sometimes assistants can be more trouble than they're worth. Anyway, he was with me at the Grand Victoria earlier in the day. We spent about two hours there on some informal shots with the wedding party. He would've been carrying a camera and was about the same height and weight as the man Jerry described from the video."

The intern's name didn't sound familiar from the reports Laurie had read. She began drying the salad bowl her father had just rinsed. "Do you know if the police ever spoke to Jeremy about that night?"

"I doubt it. Like I said, I assumed he left when I did at five o'clock. But now I realize I can't say that for certain. Here's the thing: a couple months after that, I wound up letting Jeremy go. He made some of the clients uncomfortable."

Laurie's radar went up. "How so?"

"Socially. They mentioned that he didn't seem to respect proper boundaries. When you're photographing intimate events like weddings, it can be tempting to think that you become part of the inner circle. You don't. Anyway, I never thought too much more about him until your show called today. Now I'm thinking, maybe he took it upon himself to keep hanging around. It's a long shot, but I thought I'd mention it."

Laurie found a notepad and jotted down the name Jeremy Carroll. Walker didn't have contact information for him, but he said Carroll was around twenty-five years old when he worked for him. Laurie thanked Walker profusely before saying good-bye.

"I take it your caller had something interesting to say," Leo observed.

She summarized her conversation with Walker. "If Jeremy's the man from the video, I need to talk to him. It really did look like he turned around to follow Amanda. But all I have is a fairly common name and an approximate age."

"No, you have more than that. You have a father who still knows a thing or two about basic police work." Leo snatched the piece of notepaper from the counter, and Laurie knew that First Deputy Police Commissioner Farley was on the case.

31

The next morning Laurie had no sooner reached her desk than her phone rang. She suspected it would be Brett. I swear whenever he calls, even the ring sounds angry, she thought.

Keeping her fingers crossed, she picked up the phone. It was Brett. Typical of him, there was no exchange of greetings.

"Laurie, I'm very upset," he bellowed.

It was obviously the beginning of a wonderful day.

"Can you please tell me why some local-yokel reporter in Palm Beach, Florida, is calling me for a comment on our plan to shoot the Runaway Bride segment at the Grand Victoria? That was supposed to be kept under wraps."

"Brett, we tried to keep it quiet. We had to be in touch with the hotel manager, the director of security, and other personnel. Obviously, somebody spoke to the reporter."

"Who cares who blabbed? The point is that your supposedly cold case is hot again. Laurie, don't worry about expenses."

That's a first coming from him, Laurie thought.

"Get your team down there yesterday. I don't want *60 Minutes* to do a piece on the Runaway Bride and beat us to the punch."

The click of the receiver hitting the cradle signaled that the conversation was over.

32

Yesterday turned out to be six days later.

Six days. In the past, Laurie had spent weeks reinvestigating an entire case, from beginning to end, before starting to film. But now they were at the Grand Victoria, just hours away from turning on the cameras. Even worse, those six days had been spent almost entirely on coordinating the logistics. Laurie felt as though she needed another month to dig into the facts, but the accelerated schedule gave her no choice other than to plow forward.

She felt the stress of the situation wash away as she walked through the breezeway at the hotel entrance. For a brief moment, it felt as though she had stepped back in time. She remembered Greg reaching for her hand. *Happy Anniversary, Laurie.* She assumed at the time they'd have at least fifty more.

"Mom!" Timmy was already heading toward the pool. "This place is awesome!"

The one upside of the ridiculously rushed timeline was that Timmy was still on summer break, so he and Leo were treating the trip as a vacation. It was ninety degrees and humid, but if Timmy had palm trees and a pool to splash around in with a few other kids, he'd be happy to stay year-round.

The resort was even more beautiful than she remembered—modern but inspired by classic villas of the Italian Renaissance. A man in his fifties wearing a tan poplin suit was heading directly for her. "Are you Ms. Laurie Moran, perchance? Irwin Robbins, general manager."

She returned his friendly handshake and thanked him for all the help he'd already provided. Robbins hadn't been kidding when he said that the resort wanted to help in any way possible. They had donated rooms for Amanda's parents and the entire wedding party and provided a generous discount for the production team.

"And who's this young man here?" Irwin asked, gesturing toward Timmy. "Your number one investigator?"

"Don't tell anyone," Timmy piped up, "but I'm undercover. I'll be needing a pool for my work."

Two hours later, Grace turned in a circle, gawking at the enormity of Alex's suite. "This room's the size of all of ours put together."

For once, Grace wasn't exaggerating. Alex's suite was more like a large apartment, with an enormous living room. He generously suggested that his living room serve as a conference area for the team.

It was four o'clock, and they were meeting for one last team discussion before the first production session this evening—a reunion cocktail gathering for the wedding party and Amanda's parents in the ballroom where Amanda and Jeff were supposed to have had their wedding reception

"Alex, the front desk clerk probably upgraded you when she saw those beautiful eyes," Grace said.

Alex laughed. He was used to Grace flirting with him, and Laurie knew he got a kick out of it.

"Have you met Jeff's college friends yet, Laurie?" he asked.

"Not in person, but I spoke to them on the phone. According to Sandra, they're both rich bachelors."

"The tall one, Nick, is a hunk," Grace interjected. "But that other one? Austin? He's lucky he's rich. Now, Jeff, on the other hand?" She pretended to fan herself. "He looks so sweet and innocent, and has no idea how gorgeous he is. Of the three of them, he's the catch."

"Do I need to remind you he might be a murderer?" Jerry asked.

Timmy bounded into the room from the terrace, where he had been checking out the view of the ocean below. "Alex, did you bring a bathing suit? There's a water park here with a slide that's four stories tall!"

Laurie gave her son a hug. "Alex and I have to work. I told you: Grandpa's going to be the one to take you. And believe it or not, Jerry was very excited about the possibility of joining you. If I can spare a few hours without him, he just might race you down the slide."

"You don't *race* on a super slide, Mom." Timmy corrected her as if she had suggested that the Yankees were a football team. "It's only wide enough for one person. And you didn't even let Alex answer. Anyway, if Jerry can miss part of a day, why can't Alex?"

"Because he's busy," Leo said, taking charge. "Come on, buddy. Let's go down to the pool. We've got time for a short swim before dinner."

Laurie shifted into work mode once Leo and Timmy were gone. She kept waiting for something to go terribly wrong, given how they'd rushed into production. "Jerry, have you confirmed that everyone is here?"

"To a person," Jerry reported cheerfully. "I also did a walk-through in the ballroom with the camera crew. The hotel has staged it to resemble a smaller version of the reception Amanda and Jeff had planned. The room is absolutely stunning. White flowers and candlelight everywhere. I imagine that everyone seeing it—and all being together once again—should have quite the impact."

Once they did a quick run-through of the participants and the points they wanted to cover in each individual interview, Laurie stood up and tucked her notebook in her bag as a signal that their meeting was ending.

"And what exactly is my role this evening?" Alex asked, smiling. Tonight's gathering was not for interviews, Alex's forte on the program.

"Just be your usual charming self." The show always worked best when the participants were comfortable enough with Alex to let their guard down on camera. Without preliminary in-person interviews, he'd have to find alternative ways to build a rapport.

"And don't forget the tuxedo," Grace reminded him with a wink, as she followed Jerry out of the room.

"I apologize on behalf of my boy-crazy assistant," Laurie said once they were alone. "I may have to call the human resources department to give her a refresher course on sexual harassment."

Alex stepped toward her and took her into his arms. "Are we in any position to complain about romance occurring within your production team?"

She looked up at him as he leaned down to kiss her. "No, Counselor, I suppose we are not."

Laurie found her father and son at the "active" pool, the most family-friendly of the resort's four oceanfront pools. Timmy was hanging off one side of a float being steered by a slightly smaller child. It was just like her son to make a new friend within minutes of arrival. His father had been similarly outgoing. He was so much like Greg.

Her father was on a nearby lounge chair, one eye on his grandson, the other immersed in the latest Harlan Coben thriller. Years ago, he had given his business card to the author at a book signing, with an offer to answer any police-related questions he might have down the road. Laurie had never heard her father yelp so excitedly as when he spotted his own name in the acknowledgments of his favorite author's next book.

Laurie made herself comfortable on the chair next to him. "I can take over from here so you can keep both eyes on your book for a while."

"Timmy's easy to watch these days. The kid would be more likely to save me from drowning than vice versa. Hey, by the way, I made another call to the local police about that photography intern, Jeremy Carroll."

"Any luck?" she asked.

"Maybe. There's a Jeremy Carroll, thirty-one years old, longtime local resident, whose height and weight listed on his Florida driver's license would seem to fit the general description. He's got a clean record except for a contempt conviction for violating some kind of court order. I called the court clerk and asked for a copy of the records. I'll let you know what comes of it."

"Thanks, Dad. I should talk to Brett about adding you to the payroll."

"No amount of money would be worth having to take orders from Brett Young. By the way, don't you need to get dolled up for the big reunion party?"

"You know me. Dolled up means brushing my hair and putting on some lip gloss." Laurie knew that she was an attractive woman, but she never felt comfortable beneath layers of makeup and hairspray. She kept her honey-colored hair in a simple shoulder-length bob and rarely applied more than a single coat of mascara to highlight her hazel eyes. "And I do have a new cocktail dress that cost too much money, but I know I look good in it."

"You're beautiful just the way you are," Leo said. "I know you've been stressed out about the ridiculous pace Brett's expecting, but let yourself have some fun. You and Alex will both be dressed to the nines tonight. I'm happy to stay up with Timmy if the two of you want to make a night of it after the reception. Who knows? Maybe all this talk about the wedding that never came to pass will prove to be motivational."

Laurie was stunned by her father's suggestion. "Dad, we are *so far* from anything like that. Please don't plant those seeds in Timmy's head. Or Alex's either, for that matter."

"Okay, okay, I was only kidding. Lighten up."

"Good. You scared me for a second."

Her father was looking at her, his book now closed on the table next to him. "Laurie, I was only kidding about a proposal being around the corner, but I do want to say one thing. I've seen the way you keep Alex at a distance. Most of the time you're very formal around him. You steer the conversation back around to work. And when Timmy asked about Alex going with him to the water park, you said no before Alex could even answer."

"Dad, what are you trying to tell me?"

"I'll be blunt. It's as if you're afraid of letting him see the real Laurie."

"Alex sees plenty of the real me, Dad, but we're not spring chickens who are going to drop our entire lives and run off together. We're taking things at our own pace."

"That's fine, and I know you're a grown woman and don't need your father telling you how to live your life. But let me say this once, just in case it needs to be said. I know how much you loved Greg. We all did." Leo's voice cracked briefly. "The two of you had a great five years, but that doesn't mean the rest of your life has to be lonely. Greg, of all people, would not want that for you."

"I'm not lonely, Dad. I have you and Timmy, and Grace and Jerry, and, yes, I have Alex. You may want me to leap in faster, but we are in a good place, trust me."

He opened his mouth to speak again, but she interrupted.

"Dad, do I ask why I haven't seen you keeping any ladies' company since Mom passed? There are several lovely widows I can introduce you to at church. They're never shy about asking how you are."

He gave her a sad smile. "All right, you've got me there."

"Don't worry about me, Dad. I know Alex cares for me. If it's meant to be, it will happen naturally. We shouldn't have to overthink it."

Laurie's own words echoed in her mind as she walked back to her room.

With Greg, there had been no time to overthink. She had met him because she got hit by a cab on Park Avenue. They used to joke that they were the only couple who legitimately had different versions of how they met. When Greg first met Laurie, she was unconscious. When Laurie first met Greg, he was shining a penlight in her eyes to see if she would finally blink. They were engaged three months later.

If it's meant to be, it will happen naturally. When Laurie spoke those words to her father, she had been thinking about Greg, not Alex.

33

Jerry had told Laurie that the ballroom was decorated beautifully, but words didn't do justice to the setting. It felt like a scene from a fairy tale. White roses and lilies were everywhere, and tiny white lights shimmered from the ceiling like stars on a country night. Grace and Jerry were dressed for the event. Grace wore a surprisingly unrevealing cobalt-blue gown, and Jerry looked dapper in his slim-fit tuxedo.

"The two of you clean up nice," Laurie remarked. "Well done. We should get some great footage to set the tone for the show's opening sequence."

She glanced over at the camera crew. The lead cameraman gave her a thumbs-up to signal that he was ready. They would not be recording their voices, but they wanted to capture the moments when the participants first saw each other in the room. Then Alex in a voice-over would narrate the scene and identify the people.

Sandra and her children, Henry and Charlotte, were the first of the participants to arrive for the reception. Even with her elegant silk pantsuit, Sandra had found a place for a button of Amanda's photograph, complete with the image of a yellow ribbon, on her lapel. Laurie greeted Sandra and Charlotte with hugs, and then introduced herself to Amanda's brother, Henry.

"Oh, Amanda would have loved this." Sandra wiped away a tear. "Everything is precisely the way she wanted it."

Charlotte placed an arm around her mother and gave her shoulder a little squeeze. "As I recall, this is just the way *you* wanted it, Mom."

"I know it is. I love to plan a party, it's true. And the joy of planning this one—I wanted everything to be so perfect."

"It would have been, Mom," Henry tried to assure her. He then began fiddling with his bow tie. He was a handsome man, but with shaggy dark hair and more than a few days of stubble, he did not seem comfortable in formal wear.

Charlotte nudged her mother. "Jeff just walked in."

Sandra stole a glance and then quickly turned away. "With Meghan, of course." Her tone was reproachful. "I know I pushed for this, Laurie, but now that we're here, I have no idea how to act. I truly believe one or both of them is responsible for Amanda's disappearance. I wanted them to be here, but I didn't think it would be this hard to be in the same room with them."

Laurie placed her hand gently on Sandra's arm. "Just do what comes naturally, Sandra. You don't even have to speak with them if you don't want to." The beauty of reality television was letting the cameras capture human behavior, completely unrehearsed and unscripted.

"Wow," Charlotte exclaimed. "Kate looks terrific. She hasn't aged a day."

Laurie turned to see a third person with Jeff and Meghan, hugging them both. She was slightly shorter than Laurie, around five-foot-four, with chin-length, bright blonde hair and round, rosy cheeks. In the old college photographs Laurie had seen, Kate had been the plain one compared to her two friends. But obviously she had put her best foot forward for an occasion like this.

"Did she bring the family?" Henry asked.

"Her mother is minding the children," Sandra replied. "I guess a true-crime TV show isn't the best family vacation."

Except in my household, Laurie thought, amused. She excused herself to make her way over to the Colby crowd of participants, pausing nearby to eavesdrop. She heard Jeff tell Kate and Meghan that it was "surreal" to see his planned wedding reception with Amanda re-created.

"It's certainly a far cry from our reception," Meghan said. "Margaritas and take-out barbecue in our apartment was more our speed."

Laurie couldn't tell if she sensed resentment in Meghan's tone. If Kate was at all suspicious of Jeff and Meghan, or disapproving of their marriage, she didn't show it. They sounded like three old friends catching up.

"I'm sorry to interrupt," Laurie said, "but I wanted to introduce myself." Meghan never had found the time to talk to Laurie directly, and she had only spoken to Kate on the phone. Meghan seemed to withdraw as both Kate and Jeff said they were excited about the possibility of discovering new clues about Amanda's disappearance once the show aired.

Kate suddenly turned toward the entrance. "Take a look, guys. Nick hasn't changed a bit, but get a load of our little Austin, all grown up!"

Kate leaned in toward Laurie to fill her in on the backstory. "Nick was always a ladies' man, even in college. Austin was Nick's sidekick, but very much in his shadow. A complete disaster with women, he was always coming on too strong."

"Well, I don't know about his success in the dating market," Laurie said, "but I doubt he's in Nick's shadow in all respects these days. The two of them flew down here on Austin's private jet."

The men were making a beeline for their old college friends.

"La dee da," Kate exclaimed, when Austin reached them. "A private jet, I hear. Who'd have thought that the Austin we knew in college would be doing that?"

"Careful, Kate," Austin protested good-naturedly. "I can probably dig up some old pictures from when you stayed way too long at happy hour."

Clearly these friends were used to good-natured banter.

Laurie noticed Nick nudge his friend Austin. "Heads up," he said. "We may have some competition for female attention at the bar tonight."

Laurie turned to see Alex walking into the ballroom. She felt a catch in her breath. His face was slightly tanned already, and his tuxedo fit him perfectly. Laurie immediately looked down at her own dress and was glad she had splurged on it. But she wished she had put on more makeup.

"You look beautiful, as usual," Alex said as she walked toward him.

"And of course you're the essence of the man about town." As she spoke, she was aware of the instant warmth from the closeness of their bodies.

The last person to arrive was Walter Pierce, the family's patriarch. Unlike his ex-wife Sandra, he marched directly up to Jeff and greeted him with a strong handshake. He even congratulated him and Meghan on their nuptials and wished them a lifetime of happiness.

As Laurie scanned her cast of characters, she couldn't help but notice how the dynamic changed once Walter entered. Having said his hellos to Amanda's former fiancé and their friends, he moved directly to his family, where he remained for the rest of the night. The exchanges she had heard between Sandra and her children flowed less naturally. Every member of the Pierce family now seemed to focus on Walter. Was his flight okay? Did he like his room? Did he need another drink? Even with everything that had happened, he was still the head of the family.

Were there ever children who didn't care what their father thought of them? Laurie wondered. Then she answered her own question. No.

After ten minutes she went over to the lead cameraman.

"I just asked the wedding party and Sandra's parents to stand together for a group shot," she said. "We'll close with that."

As they lined up and faced the camera, it was clear that this was not a typical wedding photograph. The earlier polite veneer was gone. Jeff had his arm protectively around Meghan. Tears were spilling from Sandra's eyes. No one was even attempting to smile.

Is it possible that someone in the wedding party could have hated Amanda enough to take her life? Laurie wondered. Unless the man in that grainy surveillance video or some other random stranger was the killer, it was highly likely that one of the people staring at the camera had killed Amanda.

But which one?

34

It was ten o'clock the next morning, and the cameras were ready to go in room 217 of the Grand Victoria. Jerry had chosen this room as the location to interview Sandra and Walter Pierce. He had learned that this had been their suite when they came to Palm Beach for their daughter's wedding but ended up searching for her instead.

According to the plan Laurie had sketched out with Alex, Sandra would speak on camera first. Over the last five years, she had become the public face of the search for her daughter. She was the one who appeared on television regularly, pleading for the public's assistance.

Noticeably nervous, her hands clenched, Sandra settled in on the love seat across from Alex's chair. She was wearing a turquoise linen blouse and white slacks. It was the same outfit she'd been wearing when she found out her daughter had disappeared. She told Laurie she could never bring herself to get rid of it.

She took a deep breath and nodded toward Laurie, indicating she was ready.

Alex began by asking Sandra to describe the moment when she first realized Amanda was missing.

"I think I felt it in my bones the second I walked into the lobby. I saw Jeff, Meghan, and Kate gathered at the front desk, and I could tell something was wrong. And then Jeff said Amanda was gone, and

I felt the ground disappear beneath me. Everyone else was worried, too, but also certain there would be some good explanation in the long run. But not me. I just knew something was dreadfully wrong."

"Was there a moment when those fears felt most confirmed?" Alex asked.

She shook her head. "That might be the worst part of not knowing what happened. I was numb, stunned, bewildered. But the moment when Amanda's disappearance really kicked in was when the police asked for her laundry to give to their canine team. The idea of dogs tracking my baby's scent . . ." Her voice trailed off.

"In the early days of the search," Alex said, "many in the media referred to your daughter as the Runaway Bride—"

Sandra began shaking her head scornfully before Alex finished the sentence. "It was terrible. There were stand-up comedians guessing how long it would be before she showed up drunk on a dance floor in Miami. My daughter is not some flighty, whimsical girl in a wedding veil. She is tough and smart."

"I notice you're speaking of her in the present tense," Alex said.

"I try to, yes. It's my way of saying I won't stop fighting for her, ever. She's out there—somewhere, Amanda Pierce is out there, whether alive or not—and she wants to be found. I'm as certain of that as anything I've known in my entire life."

Alex looked to Laurie to see if she had any notes to give him before they moved on. She did not.

"Sandra," Alex said, "if it's okay with you, we have asked Amanda's father to join you in the discussion."

Less than a minute later Walter entered the room, clearly uncomfortable, and sat next to Sandra on the love seat. Laurie noticed that even though there was plenty of room for them both to sit comfortably, Walter chose a spot close to his ex-wife. She warmly gave his knee a gentle pat.

Alex began, "Walter, many of our viewers will recognize Sandra.

Initially, you were in front of the cameras, too. But after about three months, from what I can tell, Sandra seemed to take the lead in the continuing search efforts. Are you as convinced as she is that something terrible happened to your daughter the night she disappeared?"

Walter looked down at his lap, then to Sandra. "I've never been convinced of anything other than my love for Amanda and the rest of my family. I trust Sandra when she says she has a mother's connection to Amanda. That she knows in her blood and her bones that Amanda crossed paths with evil that night. I don't purport to have that kind of a sixth sense, but they were always connected that way. Back before the days of crib monitors, Sandra would even wake up in the middle of the night only to realize that Amanda had done the same. Remember that?"

Sandra nodded and said softly, "I do."

Alex continued, "My understanding is that Amanda, by all accounts, was already a tremendous asset to Ladyform, your family business."

"She was indeed," Walter confirmed proudly.

"Some have speculated that the expectation to carry on your legacy may have been a burden on the next generation of Pierces. She was only twenty-seven years old, and her career was already mapped out. Now she was about to get married. Is it possible the pressure was too much? Do you think Amanda simply escaped and started a new life?"

"When it comes to what happened to Amanda, I'm guessing just as much as anyone watching your show. But I want to say this, just in case there's any chance my daughter is watching. Please come home, sweetie. Even just a phone call to your mother, so she knows you're okay. And if someone out there has our daughter, please, we will do anything, pay anything, to get her back."

Walter was on the verge of tears, and Laurie could tell that Alex wished he didn't have to move on to the next question. Laurie had to hope that all of this would lead to something good.

"I'm sorry to bring this up," Alex said, "but since our show is about crime and the toll it takes on loved ones, it's worth mentioning that, after thirty-two years of marriage, the two of you divorced a little more than two years ago. Did Amanda's disappearance contribute to the end of your marriage?"

Walter turned to Sandra. "Do you want to take that one?" he asked with a nervous smile.

"Walter and I never thought we'd be one of those divorced couples. We didn't believe in it. People used to ask us the secret to a long marriage and Walter would say, 'Neither one of us leaves!' But, yes, Amanda's disappearance changed us, individually and as a partnership. We were on separate paths. Walter wanted—no, *needed*—to get back to our normal life. He had his company to run and we had two other children, plus our grandchildren, whose lives needed to continue. I try to move on, for the sake of Henry and Charlotte, but I realize I've stayed frozen. I'll be in limbo until I find Amanda. That put an enormous strain on our marriage."

"Walter," Alex said quietly, "is there anything you want to add to that?"

"If you're lucky enough to live to our age, inevitably you'll have some regrets. My biggest one is making Sandra feel the way she just described. But the truth is my life never went back to normal, and it never moved on. In my own way, I'm still in limbo, too, Sandra, but alone." He looked at his ex-wife. "Because here's the thing you never realized: I wasn't the tough one. You were. I couldn't walk with you on your journey to find Amanda because I wasn't strong enough. I didn't want to find out she was dead, and I couldn't take the thought of her resenting me so much that she'd leave the whole family behind. So I hid myself away in my work and pretended that we had to move on. But I'm not hiding anymore. I'm here with you and Henry and Charlotte. And I'm ready for the truth, no matter where it leads us."

Laurie gave a hand signal to the cameraman to stop shooting and let the room become quiet. She turned away as she saw Walter wipe a tear from his face. The Pierces deserved some semblance of privacy. It was a moment of silence for Amanda.

35

When Laurie got back to her room, her father was sitting on the couch watching cable news. He hit the mute button on the remote control, and she kicked off her shoes and settled on the couch next to him.

"That was pretty heavy," she sighed.

She and Leo had adjoining rooms, each with two beds. The door was open, and she could see Timmy at his Wii in Grandpa's room.

Having watched Sandra and Walter's raw emotions about their missing daughter, she could only think again how blessed she was that her father was always there for them.

Leo put his arm around her. "I'm sure it was tough, but I think I have some good news for you. Your new lead, the man in the surveillance footage, may have paid off, and it's pretty interesting."

As Laurie waited, Leo got up and walked over to the desk in the corner of the room.

"Remember I mentioned that the photographer's intern only had one conviction?" he asked.

"Sure. Something about violating a court order? What did he do? Fail to show up for a traffic ticket?"

"That wouldn't be nearly as intriguing as this." Leo's expression was serious as he handed her a manila file folder. "Start with the first document. That's the court order in question."

The header on the first page read *Order of Protection*. It was filed by Patricia Ann Munson and Lucas Munson, Petitioners, against Jeremy Carroll, Respondent. In the first paragraph, the court concluded that Carroll had caused the petitioners to suffer "substantial emotional damage or distress" by harassing them repeatedly with "no legitimate purpose." The court order prohibited Carroll from being within 840 feet of the Munsons or intentionally contacting or communicating with them by any method whatsoever.

"This is a stalking order," Laurie said, continuing to flip through the pages. "Why eight hundred and forty feet? That seems like a strange number."

"The Munsons were his next-door neighbors. My guess is that was the number of feet from his front door to their property. The court can't force him to move from his home."

The next document was an affidavit from Lucas Munson, swearing to the allegations that formed the basis of the stalking order.

"Whoa," Laurie said, "he sounds like a complete nut. No wonder some of the photography clients complained he couldn't respect boundaries."

She read quickly through the court papers. According to the Munsons, who were in their sixties, they initially appreciated Carroll's attempts to be neighborly. He would help them carry in the groceries and eventually began bringing them fresh vegetables from the farmers' market on weekends. But then they noticed his curtains moving when they were mowing the lawn or sitting on their back deck enjoying a cocktail at sunset. Twice, Lucas was certain that he had seen a camera lens between the parted drapes.

When Lucas asked Jeremy whether he had been photographing them, he went inside and returned to the front porch with an album full of pictures. Patricia pruning her rosebushes. Lucas firing up the barbecue in the backyard. The two of them watching television on the sofa, visible through the living room window. Lucas was so stunned, he didn't know what to say and just left. Jeremy apparently took the lack of a negative response as approval and began leaving photographs of them on their front porch for them every Saturday, a small collection of what they thought were private moments. The final straw that led the Munsons to seek the protective order was when Jeremy started calling the Munsons "Ma" and "Pa." When Lucas mustered up the courage to ask why, Jeremy's only explanation was "I'm estranged from my biological parents."

When she was finished reading, Leo handed Laurie a printout of a very different kind of photograph, a mug shot. The man was holding a sign that read "Jeremy Carroll," followed by his date of birth and the date of his arrest, five months ago. Laurie could tell from the height chart on the wall behind the suspect that Jeremy was five-foot-ten. He had thinning brown hair and pale, chubby cheeks. His shoulders slumped.

"This could definitely be the man I saw turn and follow Amanda on the surveillance tape," she said excitedly. "I see he was convicted of violating the order."

"It was a relatively minor violation. He left a framed photograph of a roseate spoonbill in their mailbox, along with a note apologizing for what he called a 'misunderstanding.' "

"A *roseate spoonbill*? What the heck is *that*?"

"A bird. Sort of looks like a pelican. They're cute."

"I won't ask how you knew that."

"Timmy Googled it."

"You don't even want to know the things I was imagining. A picture of a live bird? That doesn't sound so creepy."

"Not in isolation. That's the whole point of stalking laws. Context matters. It really scared the Munsons. The judge wasn't cutting Jeremy any slack. He found him in contempt and sentenced him to two years of probation with an extension of the stalking order. He warned him that one more violation and he'd be in jail."

"Dad, if this Jeremy guy thought he'd found surrogate parents in his next-door neighbors, what kind of relationship did he imagine with a stunning beauty like Amanda?"

36

Laurie had been so engrossed in the conversation with Leo that she was almost late for the next filming session. They were interviewing Amanda's brother, Henry, at the edge of the resort property, next to the ocean. By the time she walked all the way there, the cameras were already situated, and a makeup technician was adding a final dash of powder to Henry's sunburned cheeks.

Last night, Laurie had sensed Henry's discomfort in formal wear. Her intuitions were apparently correct. Today, he wore khaki pants and a short-sleeved camp shirt, and he seemed like an entirely different person than the man she'd met the previous night.

"Sorry I'm late," she whispered to Jerry, who was attaching a wireless mic to Henry's shirt collar.

"I knew you'd get here in time. You always do."

Henry fidgeted in his chair, as though trying to find a comfortable spot. "Do you really think this show might help us find out what happened to Amanda?"

"No guarantees," Laurie said, "but our two previous specials certainly paid off."

Alex had also opted for a more casual look. Laurie made a mental note that his green polo shirt brought out the color in his blue-green eyes.

"Is everything okay?" he asked.

Normally Laurie was the first person to show up on the set. "All good. I hate to throw a curveball at you, but can you be sure to ask Henry about the wedding photographer and his intern, Jeremy Carroll? I'll explain it all later."

"Henry," Alex said once filming began, "can you start by telling us about the last time you saw your sister."

"It was right around five o'clock on Thursday. The eight of us—Amanda, Jeff, and the wedding party—had met with the photographer for a few informal shots around the property. When we were finished, we all went back to our rooms for some downtime and to get dressed for dinner."

"You joined Jeff and his college friends, Nick and Austin, at eight o'clock, correct?"

"That's right. I thought it was sort of silly to split into separate bachelor and bachelorette parties, but I went along for the ride. With Nick and Austin involved, I was dreading some horrible antics involving scantily clad dancers, but Jeff insisted they keep the evening civilized."

"Yet you still turned in early for the night."

Henry nodded. "We had a newborn at home, so my wife didn't come. The highlight of my trip was sleeping uninterrupted all night. Besides, I was a bit of a hanger-on with the rest of the boys. The three of them were buddies, but I only knew Jeff. Basically, I was just there as Amanda's brother."

"You mentioned the photographer," Alex said. "Is that Ray Walker?"

Henry shrugged. "I don't remember his name, but he was supertall. Like, even taller than you, I think."

"Do you remember an intern who was with him? His name was Jeremy Carroll."

Laurie smiled. Alex had a way of making every question seem like it had suddenly come to him off the top of his head.

Henry squinted, and then a flash of recognition registered on his face. "Oh yeah, that guy. I do remember him. He was the one who came up with the idea of all of us standing at the edge of the pool, pretending we were about to jump. The tall photographer gave the pictures to my parents afterward as a gift, and that one was my favorite."

"How long was the group with the photographers?"

"About forty minutes."

"Did you happen to see them at the hotel after that?"

"No, but I wasn't really around. I was in my room until I met the other guys in the lobby a little before eight, and we took the jitney to the Steak and Fin restaurant next to the golf course. I left when they were ordering after-dinner drinks. I went back to my room and called it a night."

"You took the jitney?" Alex asked. "Did any of you have rental cars?"

Laurie was constantly impressed at how nimble Alex was in these interviews. Whether other members of the wedding party had access to cars was another detail that Laurie should have thought of before production began, but Alex had caught it immediately with one mention of a bus.

"I didn't," Henry said, "and neither did Charlotte. But I know Amanda and Jeff rented a car. She wanted to be able to go shopping on Worth Avenue without bothering with cabs."

"Were you ever in the rental car?" Alex asked.

Henry nodded and then laughed. "Believe it or not, the guys had to take a shopping trip, too. We all managed to forget something—a belt, socks, shaving cream. The four of us drove downtown Wednesday afternoon."

"Just to be clear, was this the same car that was missing when Amanda disappeared?"

"Yes, it was."

"Did anyone else in the wedding party have a rental car?"

"I don't think so."

"Okay, returning to the subject of the photography intern, did you notice anything unusual about him?"

"Like what?"

They always tried not to lead their witnesses, but in a cold case, it was often necessary to refresh a person's memory.

"Did he maintain a professional demeanor during your interactions?"

"Yeah, I'd say so. But, now that you mention it, I remember Kate saying that he was being a little too chummy."

"How so?" Alex asked.

"Nothing striking. More like, he was around our age, especially compared to the head photographer, and seemed interested in hanging out with us, like he was part of the gang or something. I didn't notice it, but I'm not exactly an expert on social etiquette."

"You seem like an upbeat person," Alex said.

"I like to think I am."

"Is that part of the reason you wanted to go your own way and not work in the family business? I imagine that with siblings trying to run a company together, it could get a bit tense."

"I went my own way because I like making wine more than ladies' 'foundational garments.'" Henry made air quotes with his hands. "I can actually partake in the merchandise."

"But you'd agree, wouldn't you, that there could be some rivalry between your sisters?"

Laurie could tell that Henry didn't approve of the question, but in Laurie's short phone call to him last week, he had alluded twice to the work drama between his sisters. He couldn't deny it now.

"All siblings compete for their parents' affections, and the way to my father's heart was always his business. And, sure, everyone wants to be respected at work, and my sisters were no different."

"But the rivalry didn't always cut both ways, did it?" Alex asked.

"Amanda was always more confident than Charlotte."

"Is it fair to say that Charlotte could be jealous of Amanda at times?" Alex had slipped into cross-examination mode. He was in complete control.

"I suppose."

"Even angry?"

"At times."

"In fact, didn't Charlotte resent the fact that your father allowed your sister to open a New York office and expand the company's operations, even though she expressed doubts about the idea?" Laurie had gleaned that tidbit from Amanda's former assistant.

"Yes, she was very upset. But if you're suggesting that Charlotte hurt our sister, you're crazy. See? That's why I didn't even want to do this stupid show."

"We're not accusing anyone, Henry. We just want to get a better understanding—"

Henry was pulling off his microphone. "You said I'm an upbeat person? That's because I call things how I see them, and this is what I see: you're pointing the finger at everyone Amanda knew and loved, when what you should be doing is tracking down the local creeps. I'm out of here."

Alex shrugged once they realized Henry wasn't coming back. "Sometimes that's going to happen."

Given the nature of her show, Laurie was used to being accused of aiming her suspicions in the wrong direction, but this time, Henry's words stung. Everyone they had brought here was someone Amanda loved enough to include in her wedding. Most murder victims were killed by someone close to them, but Amanda could have been hurt by someone she never knew before she came to this beautiful place, Laurie thought.

Maybe that someone was Jeremy Carroll.

37

Sitting in the resort's cocktail lounge, Laurie perused the adventurous options on the list of "signature drinks." According to the menu, they were all handcrafted by the resort's in-house mixologist. With the art deco surroundings, she felt like she had stepped into a speakeasy.

She felt a gentle hand on her shoulder and looked up to see Alex. He gave her a quick kiss. "I hope you haven't been waiting long."

"I just sat down myself. So who won?" Alex and Leo had sneaked off to a nearby sports bar to watch the Yankee game on a big screen. Leo had vowed to stick to the heart-healthy diet he'd been following since having two stents inserted in his right ventricle last year, but Laurie would bet her life that he'd been unable to resist a few chicken wings.

"The Red Sox," Alex groaned. "Nine to one, a complete blowout. How was your mother-son dinner?"

"Excellent. Timmy ate an entire plate of spaghetti and meatballs, as well as half of my lasagna. My little boy has a very big appetite. And he's still pestering me about getting you to go on that water slide with him."

"I'm happy to take him," Alex said. "We could go early in the morning before we're shooting for the day."

"And ruin that perfect hair?"

"First Grace, and now you." He grinned. "As long as you think it's perfect."

A waitress arrived with two glasses of water and a tray of olives. Laurie asked for a vodka martini, and Alex ordered a ginger ale. "Your father and I already knocked back a few. And you don't want my eyes puffy on camera tomorrow, do you?" He reached across the table and held Laurie's hand. His hand was warm; it felt good.

"I, on the other hand, was a teetotaler at dinner. When your date is a nine-year-old, you're the designated driver. Switching topics," Laurie said, "is anything Henry said today about the rental car helpful to us?"

Alex sighed. "Not really. I bumped into Austin a little while ago in the lobby. He confirmed Henry's story about the four of them using the car to drive downtown. I assume Kate, Charlotte, or Meghan will verify that the women in the bridal party used the car for a shopping trip, too."

"I'll recheck the police report about the search of the rental car," Laurie said. "Jerry said there was no relevant evidence found there, but I'll make sure."

"I reread it after the interview with Henry." He took a sip of his drink and chuckled.

"An older gentleman found the car three days after Amanda's disappearance and reported it to the police. When the police pressed him on what he was doing behind the abandoned gas station, he admitted he had to relieve himself and was concerned that he wouldn't make it home."

Laurie smiled. "What made him call the police?"

"He wasn't going to, but then he spotted a set of keys on the ground near the driver's-side door. He assumed the car was stolen and abandoned and called 911 when he got home."

"Any DNA or fingerprint evidence?" Laurie asked.

"The police checked for both. They were able to lift prints belonging to Amanda and Jeff from the steering wheel. They cross-checked Amanda's prints against some personal items from her room. Jeff volunteered his. Both had driven the car, so the results weren't surprising. The DNA trail also didn't lead anywhere. All six members of the wedding party had been in the car so finding their DNA wouldn't tell us anything. And remember, this was a rental car. Even though it would get a quick wipe and vacuuming between uses, it would be loaded with the DNA of previous occupants. The police checked the DNA samples they found against their database of sex offenders but didn't find any matches."

"So the car tells us nothing," Laurie said.

"That's not exactly true," Alex replied. "If they had found blood or clumps of hair, that would have suggested a struggle took place. But they didn't. And one more thing: The night before the car was found it had rained really hard. Footprints that might have been made by Amanda or anybody who was with her or potential tire tracks from another car would have been washed away."

"A dead end," Laurie sighed.

"Oh, don't look now, but we have company, at the bar," Alex said in a low voice.

Laurie stole a glance to the front bar. Austin and Nick were drinking what looked like scotch. Their heads turned in sync as a group of young women in cocktail dresses walked by.

"Looks like they're on the prowl," Laurie said.

"It sure does."

"Think they'll mind if I interrupt? I want to ask them if they remember Jeremy Carroll."

"I was thinking about him this afternoon," Alex said. "I bet the police have never connected him to Amanda."

"I'm sure they haven't. The photographer, Ray Walker, didn't think of it himself until Jerry called him. It was only after Amanda disappeared that any clients complained about Jeremy. And the neighbors didn't seek a protective order until last year. There would be no way for the police to realize that Jeremy had been working on Amanda's wedding photographs."

"Have you considered approaching him for the show?"

"We certainly can't ignore him. If only there were some way to know if he was the man who turned to follow Amanda in the surveillance photo. Let me see what Nick and Austin remember."

"Want me to go with you?" Alex asked, beginning to stand.

"No, I think you intimidate them. Too much competition for best-looking man at the Grand Victoria."

He was smiling as he watched her walk away.

"Ms. Moran," Nick exclaimed. "Let us get you a drink." Laurie noticed that Austin did not look happy at the suggestion that she join them. Hers was probably not the kind of female company he was hoping for tonight. "Please call me Laurie, and thank you, but I already have one." She gestured to Alex, who gave a small hand salute. "I don't want to interrupt for long, but something's come up in our investigation. Do you happen to remember a younger man who was working for Jeff and Amanda's wedding photographer? His name was Jeremy Carroll."

"The intern," Austin said immediately. "Kind of a nosy, nondescript fellow. He took good pictures as I recall."

"So you do remember him!"

"Austin remembers everyone," Nick said. "He's the Rainman of people-watching. Me on the other hand? I don't even remember there being a wedding photographer."

Austin launched into a detailed description of the photo shoot by the swimming pool the afternoon of the bachelor party, but Nick's face was still blank.

"Did you notice anything unusual about him?" Laurie asked.

"Are you thinking he might be a suspect?" Austin asked, his voice tense. "We've been telling people all these years that there's no way Jeff would hurt Amanda. Henry said from the beginning she probably went for a walk and ran into a dangerous creep. Is it possible this intern's the one?"

"At this point, we're just trying to make sure we have a complete list of people Amanda would have encountered down here."

"Come to think of it, the guy did seem very interested in everyone," Austin said. "I thought he was just too eager, the way interns can be."

"Did he seem especially interested in Amanda?"

"Yes, I think so." His voice was deeply concerned now. "That seemed normal at the time. After all, she was the bride. Maybe someone should have mentioned it to the police."

"It's a big leap from being overly interested in your job to hurting someone." She saw no reason to mention Jeremy's more recent problems with the law.

Nick downed the rest of his scotch and signaled for the bill. "Is that all we can help you with for now, Laurie?" They were clearly eager to move on to more fun conversations with more available women.

"Just one more question while I have you here: We were trying to clarify who had access to rental cars that week. Jeff and Amanda rented a car; did either of you have one?"

"No, only Jeff had one. On this trip we're yacht people," Nick said with a smirk at his own joke. Austin began to tell Laurie in agonizing detail about their newfound love for boats and putting their *Ladies First* and *Lonesome Dove* nameplates on their charters.

"So is that it?" Nick asked. Laurie had the impression that he either needed to leave right now or would be ordering another drink.

"Yes, and, please, let me get this," she said, reaching for the tab. "It's the least I can do."

Nick placed a gentle hand on her forearm. He certainly was a flirt. "I hate to break this to you, Laurie, but you've been picking up more tabs than that one. We've put everything on our rooms."

Brett Young will be so thrilled, Laurie thought.

38

"How'd that go?" Alex asked when she returned to the table.

She related the new information to him.

As usual, he processed it quickly. "So that's one more person saying Jeremy Carroll is a little off."

Jeff, Austin, and Nick had all given the same timeline to police. According to the three friends, after dinner, they went to Jeff's room for a nightcap. Around eleven o'clock they said good night and Nick and Austin went to their own rooms and to bed.

"Alex, think about this. All four men supposedly were in their hotel rooms alone by eleven o'clock. Henry claims that he went to bed earlier, close to ten o'clock. That means that nobody can confirm the whereabouts of those four after eleven the night Amanda disappeared."

"Yes, it does," Alex agreed.

"And it was about eleven o'clock when Amanda stepped back from getting on the elevator."

"Do you think she was meeting one of the four?"

"I don't know. And the question is, was Jeremy hanging around the hotel at that time? If so, he could have seen Amanda and followed her again."

"I know your father found Jeremy's address and it's not far from here."

"That's where my mind was going. After the shoot tomorrow, I want to pay a visit to Mr. Carroll."

"Laurie, please don't tell me you're planning to go alone."

"Don't worry. Armed Commissioner Leo will be going with me."

"That makes me feel better. Switching to another subject, can you and I have dinner tomorrow night? There's a new gourmet restaurant in town that I hear is wonderful."

"Really? Just the two of us?"

"Over a romantic dinner you can tell me all about your meeting with Jeremy Carroll."

Laurie laughed and said, "What could possibly be more romantic? You're on."

Half an hour later they were walking to the elevator. Laurie found herself thinking about Jeremy Carroll. Her gaze drifted to the now dark atrium outside the bar. She could picture Carroll lurking there, his camera strapped across one shoulder. She imagined Amanda walking past him that night, never noticing that the young photographer was watching her. And following her.

39

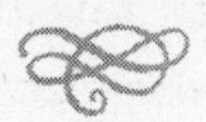

Jeremy Carroll's neighborhood, a mix of ranch-style and bungalow homes, was modest but well maintained. The one exception was his address. The split-level ranch was in dire need of both a paint job and a lawn mowing. According to his neighbors' application for a restraining order, Jeremy had inherited the home three years earlier from his great-aunt.

Laurie paused on the sidewalk. "Now that we're here, I'm worried that we should have called the local police instead."

"I was on the job three decades, Laurie. I know police work. If we took our suspicions to the police department here, they'd spend the entire day mulling things over. They'd probably even call in an Assistant District Attorney for advice. Jeremy would lawyer up the second they started asking questions about Amanda. But we're just a couple of civilians from a New York City television show. We can use that to get him talking."

"Is it safe to just walk up there and knock on the door?"

"While I'm around, we're fine."

Laurie saw Leo's hand reach inside his jacket to where he kept his gun. After all those years with the department, he felt unnatural without it.

Laurie felt her heart start to race as her father rang the doorbell. Were they about to look into the face of Amanda's killer?

As the door slowly opened she immediately recognized Jeremy from his booking photo. He even had the same trapped, fearful expression.

"What are you doing here?"

On instinct, Laurie looked at his hands and clothing to see if he might be armed. His hands were empty, and he was wearing a T-shirt and sweatpants, not ideal for concealing a weapon. She felt her pulse begin to return to normal.

But then her gaze moved past Jeremy, into his home. A worn brown sofa and an old television were the only furniture in the living room. Past that, she saw a small table and two chairs in what was meant to be a dining room. Despite the paucity of furniture, the house was cluttered beyond belief. Old computers, video equipment, and printers were scattered in random places. Stacks of magazines and newspapers stood five feet high. And everywhere Laurie looked, there were photographs—on the floor, strewn across the table, pinned to the walls, lining the stairwell.

Her eyes widened as she looked at Leo.

He took the lead. "We're with Fisher Blake Studios and wanted to talk to you about your photography work."

It was a smart move. The name of their show would put Jeremy on high alert. Fisher Blake Studios sounded like a photography company. Even so, Jeremy looked wary.

"I've sent my work to every major photographer in Southern Florida. I've never heard of you, Mr. Blake."

"Oh, I'm not Mr. Blake. My name's Leo." He offered a handshake. "This is Laurie. And we're not local. We're from New York."

Jeremy's eyes lit up at the mention of the Big Apple, then immediately lowered as Leo handed him a still photograph from the Grand Victoria surveillance video. Laurie could tell that he recognized himself. There was no doubt in her mind: Jeremy was the man she had spotted walking behind Amanda at five-thirty the night she disappeared.

"This is from the Grand Victoria Hotel," Leo stated. "See the date stamp at the bottom of the picture? Do you remember that night?"

Jeremy nodded slowly. He wasn't denying being the man in the security video.

"Ray Walker, the photographer who hired you, told us that the two of you had finished taking pictures at five o'clock. But you were still there a half hour later, with your camera. And when you saw Amanda, you changed your direction to follow her. We have the whole thing on film."

"I don't understand. Who are you?"

Laurie decided that it might be best to let Jeremy experience a bit more fear and told him they were from *Under Suspicion*, investigating Amanda Pierce's disappearance. "Can we come in?" She stepped inside without waiting for a response, and Leo followed her. She was no longer afraid. This man was a coward, finding power in the shadows, behind a camera. He was not going to lash out with her father around.

"Why didn't you tell the police that you saw Amanda after you and Walker finished taking pictures?" Leo demanded.

"Because nobody asked me if I'd seen her. And I knew if I told them, they'd suspect me. Everybody always suspects me."

"You like taking pictures when people aren't looking." Laurie gestured to all the photographs strewn around his house. Even at a superficial glance, she could tell that most were taken with long-distance lenses, their subjects unaware of the stranger watching them.

"It's my art. I don't photograph flowers or landscapes. I photograph people, and not when they are posed and artificial. I capture their reality. Isn't that what everyone really wants? Look at all the selfies posted all over the Internet. People love having their picture taken."

"Even your neighbors?" Leo said. "They didn't seem happy with your art."

"That was all a misunderstanding. I tried to explain. Once I realized they were offended, I got rid of all my images of them. It wasn't right to keep them."

"What about Amanda?" Laurie asked. "Do you have pictures of her? Ones she didn't know about?" Laurie walked to the dining room and began rifling through the photographs spread across the table.

"Stop it!" Jeremy's voice was booming. Leo lunged in Laurie's direction, placing himself between her and Jeremy. "Please," Jeremy said, lowering his voice, "you need to go now. You have no right to be here. You're trespassing. Get out."

Laurie looked to her father for guidance.

"I'll call the police if you don't leave," Jeremy threatened.

Leo took Laurie's hand and led her to the front door. They had no choice.

"Dad," she said once they were safe in the car, "he has photographs of Amanda. I could feel it. He's going to destroy them now."

"No he won't," Leo said grimly as he started the engine. "They mean too much to him. They're his mementos."

40

Alex embraced Laurie when she walked into his suite.

"I didn't want you to know how worried I was, but thank God you're both back in one piece. How did it go? What was he like?"

Laurie sat on the sofa and pressed her hands to her face. "Scary."

"Major creep," Leo said. "Seriously off."

"He's living like a hoarder," Laurie explained. "Floor-to-ceiling photographs everywhere. It was like something out of a horror movie. When I pressed him about whether he had pictures of Amanda, he threw us out of the house. Dad, should we call the police now?"

"And tell them what?" Leo said. "We don't have any evidence. But I'm telling you: he's the guy, the one the police missed all those years ago. Tying him to the case is a big breakthrough."

"I don't understand," Alex said. "You just said you don't have any evidence. How can you be so sure he's guilty?"

Leo shook his head. "Sometimes I forget you're a defense attorney. Trust me, we were the ones who were there. Jeremy Carroll knows something."

"Leo, with all due respect, that doesn't mean he's guilty. I see clients all the time who get railroaded by police simply because they were nervous, or were trying to protect some harmless secret."

"No one's railroading anyone—"

"Okay, please, don't argue," Laurie pleaded. "Alex, Dad's right. You weren't in that house. There's no question that Jeremy's—" She paused, searching for the word. "A weirdo. And he didn't even deny being the man in that video. He turned around to follow Amanda, and he's been convicted of stalking people."

"But you're suggesting he did something far worse," Alex pointed out.

Laurie turned to her father. "Dad, Alex is right that until we have solid evidence, we shouldn't leap to conclusions."

"So what do you want to do?" Alex asked. "It's up to you."

"Dad," Laurie began slowly. "Based on your experience, you don't think Jeremy will make a run for it or destroy evidence if we don't move against him right now?"

Leo shrugged. "You never know, but if the guy can't throw out old newspapers, I don't think he'll dump pictures he's been holding on to for more than five years. And that house is probably his only asset. He's not the type who can hop on a jet and live a fugitive lifestyle on the other side of the world."

"And keep in mind," Alex said, "just because he might know something about Amanda's disappearance doesn't mean he was involved."

Laurie nodded. "What do you think about this? Jerry can call him and try to smooth things over. He can say that we're reaching out to everyone who was at the Grand Victoria that weekend and didn't mean to invade his privacy. That might calm his nerves."

"Good idea," Alex said.

"And Alex, none of us want to rush to judgment. We'll keep an open mind for now, but that makes it all the more important that we hold everyone else's feet to the fire. Don't go easy on anyone."

"I have no intention of going easy on anyone." There was a glint in Alex's eyes.

"Next up is Meghan. I can't wait to hear how she wound up marrying her best friend's fiancé," Laurie said as she stood up and headed for the door.

41

"Are you almost ready, Ms. White? We have the cameras set up with the current light, and the shadows can change quickly outside."

Meghan White held up one finger. She would have finished by now if she could have gotten a better phone signal. When she told Jeff that she would be part of this awful show, she assumed they'd have plenty of notice to make arrangements with work. Instead, they'd been hauled down here on the spur of the moment, as if Meghan could put her entire caseload on hold with the push of a button.

She was doing her best to telecommute, but hotel Wi-Fi connections were infamously insecure, so she had created her own using her cell phone's hotspot. She watched the progress bar move slowly on the download of this appellate brief. The production assistant—was his name Jerry?—was obviously getting antsy. She wanted to tell him that if time was of the essence, they should have filmed inside. "Just another second, I promise."

When the download was finally complete, Meghan closed her laptop and followed Jerry to the set of rattan furniture Laurie Moran had arranged on the promenade behind the main building. She resisted the temptation to wipe all the makeup off her face. The woman who caked it on had promised her that she would look natural on camera, but to Meghan, it felt as though she were wearing a layer of mud. She had stopped arguing when the makeup artist said, "You don't want to look washed out on the screen. It makes people look scared."

Meghan was scared, but she didn't want to look that way. She asked for a little more blush.

Laurie Moran, the woman who had been hounding her on the telephone for the previous week, seemed amiable enough, but Meghan thought she had noticed a hint of sarcasm in the producer's voice when she said she was happy to *finally* meet in person. Meghan was more nervous about going toe-to-toe with Alex Buckley. His cross-examination skills were well known.

Her laptop tucked away, she no longer had an excuse for delay. Okay, she said to herself, let's do this and then Jeff and I can go home and move on with the rest of our lives.

The minute they were past introductions, Alex Buckley began by asking Meghan to explain the timing of her courtship with Jeff.

He clearly isn't pulling any punches, Meghan thought. He's going for the jugular.

"You had to have known that some people would disapprove of your starting a relationship with him when Amanda—his fiancée and your best friend—was still missing."

Meghan had practiced her answer hundreds of times, but now that she was here, all she could think about was those hot lights and cameras pointing at her. She had worked so hard to avoid all this attention.

She managed to make it through her memorized response. "We were both as surprised as anyone, Alex."

"You've told people over the years that you were the one to reintroduce Amanda and Jeff."

"That's right. At a coffee shop in Brooklyn. Amanda loved their bagels," she said sadly.

"But you didn't intentionally get them together, did you?" he asked in a sympathetic tone. "Isn't it true that Jeff just happened to bump into you?"

"Yes, I guess that's right."

"In fact, weren't you romantically interested in Jeff all the way back in college?"

She shrugged. "College crushes come and go."

"So you did have a crush. And then you were excited when you both ended up in New York after law school and he invited you out."

"Yes, I suppose I was."

"And were you the one to tell him you didn't want to see each other anymore, or was that his decision?"

"It wasn't like that. We didn't even have that discussion. We just never went out on a third date."

"And is that because Jeff didn't invite you?"

"Sure, I guess."

Meghan could feel the implication in the pause that followed. The show had scored a point at her expense. All these years, she had allowed people to think that she played cupid between Amanda and Jeff. Would everyone see the truth now? Would they know that she had loved Jeff all along? That she had sobbed for hours after Amanda called her the day after the coffee-shop run-in to say that Jeff had invited her to dinner? Meghan had known instantly that she had lost her shot. She never could compete with Amanda.

Now in desperation, she tried to turn the tables on her interrogator. "Have you ever heard of tunnel vision?" she blurted. "Let me explain it. It's when an investigator gets suspicious of one person and views all the evidence through that lens. I could point to any person in the wedding party and start raising questions. It doesn't mean any one of us is involved. Take Kate, for example. On the night Amanda disappeared, she said she had too much to drink and needed to go to her room. But when I went to check on her, there was no answer, even though I banged on the door. In the morning, she claimed not to have heard the knocking, even though Kate is the lightest sleeper I've ever met. In college, she would wake up if someone played a CD two rooms away. Do I know where Kate was that night? Not really. But did Kate have anything to do with Amanda's disappearance? I'd bet my life she didn't. Are you going to play gotcha with all of us? Are you trying to make us all look guilty?"

Meghan felt like she had made a valid point, but realized the producers could always edit anything they didn't like. By the time they were done with their creative splicing, she might come across like a defensive lunatic.

Alex shifted gears. "Did you threaten to sue Amanda for stealing a product idea from you?"

Meghan's worst fears were coming true. Well, not her *very* worst fears, but she knew this interview was not going well. She felt even more nauseous than she'd become accustomed to in the past week. How in the world did they even know about the fight at the Ladyform offices? She thought Amanda's disappearance had long ago overshadowed their argument. It must have been Charlotte. That woman never forgot a grudge.

"I didn't *threaten* her, but I did let her know my feelings were hurt. Back in college, the two of us came up with a trick to hold our keys and our iPods while we were working out. We sewed neoprene pockets onto our exercise clothes. It kept the contents dry and tucked snugly into place. Plus, we thought it was pretty cute. When I saw Ladyform's X-Dream collection in stores, I was so upset that I went to Amanda's office. We argued over whose idea it was. I thought it was mine, or at least a joint idea. She insisted the real work and the ownership was hers and the company's. In my opinion, if she didn't think she was doing anything wrong, she would have told me in advance."

"You were screaming loudly enough that people could hear you all the way down the hall. Did the fact that Amanda was going to marry a man you were still interested in add to your anger?"

Meghan was beginning to regret not trying to dissuade Jeff from coming here. Now she was trapped. She had no choice but to keep talking. "I admit, the argument in her office was heated. But she called me the next day. We met for lunch. She explained all the design work and experimentation that had gone into turning our simple little trick into a breakthrough product. She apologized for not telling me in advance, and I told her she could make it up to me by paying for the very nice bottle of champagne we were drinking and sending me a box full of free workout clothes." She smiled at the memory. "In the end, it was a minor snit between friends. And it was over the same lunch that we had the conversation I always go back to. It's the reason I truly believe that Amanda left this hotel on her own."

Alex leaned forward. Meghan prayed that he would believe her. She had never told anyone this before, except Jeff. "Amanda's illness fundamentally changed her. She told me that she would no longer do things only out of loyalty or obligation. She was going to live for herself. It was her reason for not giving me credit for X-Dream. In her heart, she didn't believe I deserved it, so sharing credit with me would diminish her own accomplishment."

"And how does that relate to her disappearance?" Alex asked.

"She was so different than the Amanda I knew before she was sick. In retrospect, I think she was trying to tell me she was no longer going to be the good girl. The good daughter. The good friend. The good wife. She wanted freedom, and she wanted power, and she didn't want to feel guilty for being the strong, independent woman she'd grown to be. But, she couldn't do all those things in the shadow of her family and friends and her impending wedding."

"Friends have said that you were less frantic than everyone else when she disappeared. Why didn't you tell anyone this before?"

"In time, I did tell Jeff. But it didn't feel right saying it to anyone else. I felt like I was criticizing her, as if I was saying cancer made her selfish. Doesn't that sound terrible? But that's not how I saw it. I was happy for her. I thought she had found a way to start over again. That's why I didn't feel guilty when Jeff and I became closer. Do you know that the wedding bands were missing?"

She had been hoping to surprise Alex, but he was ready for the question.

"Yes, Jeff explained that he did not realize the rings were missing until he got back to New York. He admitted he was careless about always locking the hotel safe. He thinks an employee could have stolen them."

For the first time since she took her seat, Meghan felt like she had the upper hand. Did they really believe that the rings *happened* to disappear along with the bride? "What a coincidence that would be," she said. "And I bet if you check, theft is extremely rare here. These are excellent jobs. I can't imagine the employees would take the risk."

"So what is your theory?" Alex asked.

"I always thought Amanda took them as a memento. She may have wanted a new life, but she did love Jeff. I just loved him more, and that's not a crime." She looked directly into the camera. "Amanda, I'm happy and I hope you are, too."

That was the best Meghan could do. When Jerry removed her microphone, it felt as though he had lifted a thirty-pound weight from her chest. She wanted to go home. Please, Jeff, she thought to herself, let's just go home. I have something to tell you.

42

"If you believe that woman, I've got a bridge I'd like to sell you, and it's made of gold." Grace pointed a French-manicured index finger for emphasis.

The team was meeting in the living room of Alex's suite, rehashing the interview with Meghan. It was the first time they had ever gone directly on camera without first having a more wide-ranging conversation off-camera.

Jerry and Grace had wildly different impressions of Meghan. "You're so cynical," Jerry told Grace. "She struck me as very straightforward. I believe that's what both of Amanda's siblings told us to expect. She's unemotional. Matter-of-fact. Everything she said seems credible to me."

Grace looked as though she wanted to jump out of her skin as she waited for Jerry to finish. "You could tell she memorized every last word. Even her pauses seemed rehearsed."

"That doesn't mean she's lying," Jerry retorted.

"No, but it does mean she thought she had something to hide. The only question is whether Alex got her to come clean, or if there's more to learn. At the very least, that woman's been lying over the years about her feelings for Jeff. She didn't reintroduce him to Amanda, at least not intentionally. My guess is she wishes they'd never bumped into each other at that coffee shop. I bet she was pining for Jeff since college. Maybe that's even why she went to New York after law school and just happened to live near him in Brooklyn."

Laurie was following the conversation but was distracted by her own thoughts about Meghan.

Alex adjusted his black-rimmed glasses after tipping them up to review his notes. "I agree with you, Grace, that she was probably more interested in Jeff prior to Amanda's disappearance than she ever let on. But I believed her when she said she and Amanda smoothed things over after the blowup at the Ladyform offices."

"Really?" Grace asked. "That's a whole lot of money to put behind you with one champagne lunch and a box of gym clothes."

"If they were feuding, would Meghan still be her maid of honor?" Alex paused. "What did you think, Laurie? A few people have mentioned Amanda's illness, but this is the first time anyone tried to explain how it really did change her."

That was the part of the conversation that Laurie had been replaying in her head for the last half hour. The way Meghan described the transformation in her friend sounded completely authentic. And as her friend, she may have been in a better position to recognize the change than either Amanda's family or even her fiancé. For the first time, Laurie believed it really was possible that Amanda had wanted to break free. Maybe she ran away, as Meghan believed. But maybe she told Jeff she didn't want to go through with the wedding. And if that happened, they were right back where they started: with a finger pointed at Jeff.

"The missing rings," Laurie said suddenly. "I didn't think much of it when Jeff first mentioned them. But Meghan made a good point that it's quite a coincidence that they went missing during their stay at the resort. Jeff said he assumed an employee slipped them from the safe during the chaos, but that would be quite a bold move. To be caught with wedding bands belonging to a missing woman would make that person a prime suspect in her disappearance."

"And wedding bands aren't worth much compared to what many of the guests probably lock in their safes," Jerry added. "Meghan's right: they were more likely to be taken as a keepsake than loot. It really got to me when Meghan looked into the camera and said she loved Amanda. Wouldn't that be amazing if Amanda saw our show and contacted her family?"

"Oh boy," Grace said. "You really bought her bull—hook, line, and sinker!"

Two days into filming, Laurie thought, and I don't feel any closer to the truth.

43

"Grandpa, come in with us!" Timmy and four other kids were immersed in an epic round of Marco Polo. "Jake's dad says he'll play if we get another grown-up."

Leo scanned the pool area. A man in his mid-forties caught his eye and subtly shook his head, a pleading expression in his eyes. Jake's father, as Leo expected, had been looking for a way to avoid getting chased by a pack of children in the water.

"I think you guys have taken over enough of the pool on your own."

As the rhythmic chants of "Marco . . . Polo" continued, Leo smiled to himself and took another sip of his piña colada. Laurie wouldn't approve of the calories, but he felt entitled to a little celebration. When he and Timmy had left Alex's suite, Laurie, Alex, Jerry, and Grace were all bouncing around the various theories of what happened to Amanda.

But Leo was ready to close the case. The more he thought about it, Jeremy Carroll had to be their man. Leo had felt the old, familiar kick in the gut when you're certain you've discovered the missing link in the investigation. Usually, you find it within twenty-four hours: the spouse gets caught in a lie, or one of the victim's colleagues fails to show up for work the next morning. But when the key to the case is a minor player in the victim's life—the landscaper or the grocery store bag boy or an intern working for the wedding photographer—it can take years to make the connection.

Jerry said that the phone call to Jeremy had gone well; he accepted the apology and seemed to go along with Jerry's explanation that this morning's visit to his house was a routine research visit clumsily conducted by two overeager staffers. With Jeremy feeling safe, Laurie and Alex could finish interviewing the rest of the show's participants, but then Leo would convince his daughter to go to the local police with what they knew. Leo already had an idea about using Jeremy's probation officer to search his house. If they found pictures of Amanda—and Leo knew they would—a good detective could use them to get a confession.

Leo felt the old police muscles working again. He could envision every piece of a renewed investigation falling into place. He had no regrets about retiring to help Laurie raise Timmy, but he would never stop missing the job.

Now that Timmy was getting older, he thought, I might think about doing some private detective work on the side. I'd be good at it. He closed his eyes and felt the sun warm his face. As his thoughts wandered, he remembered Laurie mentioning that Amanda had organized prayer vigils for a girl who was killed at her college. He wondered if the case was ever solved. Maybe that could be Laurie's next cold case.

He reached into Timmy's beach bag, pulled out his iPad, and connected to the hotel's Wi-Fi. He couldn't remember the woman's name, so he searched for "missing student Colby College."

Her name was Carly Romano, a twenty-year-old sophomore, putting her one year behind Amanda and her friends at the time of her disappearance. She was from Michigan and was last seen at an off-campus party. No one saw her leave, but the assumption was that she tried walking back to campus alone. She was missing for two weeks before they found her body, strangled, in Messalonskee Lake.

Leo looked up to make sure that Timmy was still okay in the pool. He was convinced these kids were going to keep playing until they passed out from exhaustion.

He continued to click through the news results. As far as he could tell, no one had been arrested and no suspect had ever been named by police.

He looked up the phone number for the police department in Waterville, Maine, where Colby College was located, and emailed it to himself along with the name, Carly Romano. I may not be ready to open my own private detective business, he thought, but that doesn't mean I can't do a little independent research now.

44

"Are we really going to let them drink scotch during their interview?" Jerry was staging the bar table just so in the cocktail lounge. From the right angle, the cameras would be able to catch both the dark wood of the hotel bar and the sunshine and palm trees waiting just outside.

"Trust me," Laurie said. "This is the place where Nick and Austin will feel most at home. That's what matters most, which means giving them their beverage of choice."

Laurie had decided to question the two friends together. They seemed to open up around each other, and that was what she wanted.

As for wardrobe, Laurie couldn't have hoped for more if she'd selected their clothing herself. They both showed up wearing tan summer suits with open-collared bright blue shirts. The only difference was the pattern of their pocket squares. Though their clothes were nearly identical, they looked nothing alike. Nick was strikingly handsome and fit, one of those men who wore a suit well. Austin was at best average-looking with the early signs of a paunch over his belt. His suit was impeccably tailored, but it did little to boost his overall appearance. She remembered what the mother of one of her friends had observed about her daughter's date: "He does not yet look comfortable in his Paul Stuart suit."

"Let's get straight to the point," Alex said once they were filming.

"By all accounts, you two are successful, eligible bachelors. Even our assistant on the show says you can't help but flirt with every woman you encounter. As the saying goes, birds of a feather flock together. Was your friend, Jeff, ready to settle down with Amanda?"

Laurie wasn't surprised when Nick took the lead. He was definitely the alpha male of the pair. "Absolutely," he said with confidence. "Look, Jeff and I were tight from the second we were paired up as college roommates, but he was never a wingman."

"And can you explain for our viewers what that means?" Alex asked.

"Oh, yeah, sure." Nick and Austin exchanged an amused glance. "A buddy when you're out talking to women. A partner in the hunt, so to speak."

Laurie wanted to edit both of them out of the show entirely. No wonder she had always avoided the dating scene.

"Jeff wasn't like that?" Alex asked.

"Definitely not," Austin said, trying to get a word in. "In college, he was focused on his studies. He'd hang out mostly in groups."

"What about later, once he was a lawyer in New York?"

Austin clearly didn't know the answer. Nick was the one who was closer to Jeff. "He'd go out on the occasional date," Nick said, "but nothing serious. I was actually the one who got into a serious relationship for a while—"

"Melissa," Austin said. "That didn't last for long."

"True. I had one misstep at a buddy's bachelor party. Melissa found out about it and was gone. I haven't tried again, but hey, unlike *some people* here, at least I gave it a shot. Anyway, once Jeff started seeing Amanda, she was all he talked about."

"But weren't they on and off for a while?" Alex asked.

"At first," Nick said. "One or the other would be so busy at work that they'd shift the relationship to the back burner. But, wow, once they started going out for real and then Amanda got sick, every minute he wasn't at work he was with her. When she told him she had cancer, he asked her to marry him the next day."

"What about after she was sick?" Alex asked. "Did you ever see them fight?"

"They argued like any other couple," Austin said, "but he would never hurt her."

Nick shot a disapproving glance to his friend. "Trust me: whatever happened to Amanda, Jeff had nothing to do with it. He was crushed when she went missing."

"Until he became involved with Meghan," Alex said.

A flash of anger crossed Nick's face. "That's not fair. Was the guy supposed to become a monk for the rest of his life? Is it that surprising that he'd fall for someone Amanda also loved and respected?"

"You'll have to forgive Nick," Austin observed. "He's fiercely protective when it comes to Jeff."

Laurie thought she detected a note of jealousy in Austin's voice.

"Now, you've both said that you last saw Amanda around five o'clock, after you finished group photographs."

Both confirmed the same timeline they'd provided to police. After the photo shoot, they'd gone to the bar for an hour and then to their rooms. A little before eight, they met in the lobby and went to dinner at the Steak and Fin, finishing around ten. Henry left while they stayed for an after-dinner drink there. Then they had a nightcap in Jeff's room and went to their rooms around eleven.

"It's our understanding that you were down here around the time Amanda and her girlfriends were coming back to the hotel. Did you cross paths with them?"

Nick shook his head. "No, I didn't see Amanda again after they took pictures."

Austin gave the same answer.

Laurie listened intently as Alex hammered questions at them.

"So you two fun-loving bachelors left Jeff's room and went to bed around eleven o'clock. Isn't that a little on the early side for both of you?"

"We'd been out late the night before. We'd been in the sun all day. We had plenty to drink before dinner, at dinner, and then in Jeff's room." Nick turned to Austin. "I don't know about you, but I was beat."

As usual, Austin quickly agreed. "I'd had enough. I went straight to my room and to bed."

"Okay, let's go back to when you two were alone with Jeff in his room. You have both told me previously that Jeff expressed reservations about marrying Amanda. What did he actually say?"

"I jokingly asked him if he was getting cold feet," Nick said. "We were both astonished when he said, 'Yes.' "

"And what was said after that?"

This time it was Austin who answered. "Jeff said that Amanda wanted him to change jobs. That he was too good of a lawyer to waste his time working for peanuts at the Public Defender's office. Jeff told her that he liked being a public defender and helping people, and he was really good at it."

"What was your response to that?" Alex asked.

"We laughed it off," Nick said. "I told him getting married always means she's going to start managing your life. Get used to it."

"And what was Jeff's response?"

"He laughed with us," Nick said. "But we got the impression he was sorry he had started this conversation. It was right after that that we said good night and headed to our rooms."

"So you went to your respective rooms at eleven o'clock and you contend that you stayed in your rooms all night. Is that right?"

"Yes," they both answered.

"And as far as you know, Jeff was not planning to leave his room after eleven?"

"That's right."

"And is it fair to say no one can confirm that you were in your rooms for the night beginning at eleven o'clock, which is approximately the last time anyone ever saw Amanda?"

A flash of anger came over Austin's face. "I guess not." Nick nodded in agreement.

"Were you aware at the time that in her will Amanda had left Jeff her two-million-dollar trust fund?"

"We found out about that after she disappeared," Nick said.

"Do you think Amanda would have told Jeff about his potential inheritance?"

They looked at each other. "It's entirely possible," Austin said quietly.

Laurie could tell that they both desperately wanted to vouch for their friend, but they couldn't. There was no getting around one basic fact: Jeff had the most to gain by Amanda's disappearance.

45

"Mom, those ladies over there are drinking blue martinis." Timmy was pointing to a group of four women. Their drinks were the color of dishwashing liquid. "You wouldn't want one of those. You like martinis dry."

Alex's eyes sparkled with amusement behind his glasses. "Timmy certainly does know his mother."

Laurie and Alex had postponed their plans for a dinner alone at a Michelin three-star restaurant after Timmy pleaded to go to the hotel's sushi restaurant. Leo could not stand the thought of eating raw fish. He called it *sea slime*.

Timmy, on the other hand, was even more adventurous with a sushi menu than Laurie. But she suspected that her son's excitement about this particular restaurant was less about food than about the two L-shaped aquarium bar counters where live fish swam beneath the glass.

Alex was about to check in with the hostess when Timmy asked if they could sit at the bar. "You're always saying we should try new experiences," he argued. "We don't have this back home."

Alex broke the bad news. "You're a little young for the bar, buddy. Try again in about twelve years."

"I can't wait to be old enough to sit at the bar."

"Just what a mother wants to hear," Laurie said dryly. "I don't want him to end up like those two barflies Austin and Nick."

Once they were at the table, Alex said, "Speaking of the two Romeos, what did you make of their interview today?"

She shrugged. "They're exactly as Sandra described them. I don't get the appeal, personally, but I know Brett will be happy. At least they're entertaining for television."

"Enough about those two," Alex sighed. "So Leo's already convinced the photography intern was involved."

Without new facts, Laurie wasn't eager to revisit this topic. "I know you think he's jumping to conclusions," she said. "Maybe we should leave it on the back burner for now."

Later, as they walked through the lobby, Timmy asked if he could sleep in Grandpa's room tonight. Laurie found herself happy to have even more time to spend with Alex.

46

Laurie was shocked the next morning when Charlotte Pierce arrived on set at the courtyard behind the hotel. She wore an impeccably tailored white suit with a black silk shell. Her hair and makeup were camera-perfect. This did not look like the same woman she'd met in the office at Ladyform.

"Don't look so surprised," Charlotte said, perching herself comfortably on the love seat they had staged for the occasion. "You didn't think I'd go on national television looking like the ugly duckling, did you?"

Alex took his place, nodded, and the cameras began to roll.

Five minutes later, Laurie checked her watch. Charlotte had already recited the same information she'd given Laurie when they met in New York. She was a businesswoman who was used to communicating efficiently.

But part of Alex's talent was to introduce questions that his subjects hadn't anticipated. "What was it like being Amanda Pierce's sister?" he asked casually.

"I have no idea what you mean by that. It's like asking me what it's like to breathe. She was the only sister I ever had."

"Yet I sense in you a woman who could in fact describe what it's like to breathe, if someone asked you the question."

She gave him a half smile. Laurie could almost hear her deciding to play along. "Fine. It was like being the weed next to the rose. In any other family, I would have been a superstar. I graduated at the top of my class from the University of North Carolina. I'm a pretty nice person. I work hard. But Amanda was special. Men wanted to marry her, women wanted to be her. She knew how to please people."

"Jeff's friends sensed that you weren't especially happy about the wedding. *Disinterested* was the word one of them used."

"Well, first of all"—Charlotte waved her hands dismissively—"Jeff's friends are idiots. Second of all, I wasn't *disinterested*. I was worried, and not about Amanda. I thought Jeff was the one making a mistake. I loved my sister, but I was probably the only person who really knew her. She looked like a princess from a fairy tale, with bluebirds brushing her hair. But she was cunning. Ambitious. And there's nothing wrong with that, but she hid it behind this perfect, gentle façade."

Laurie found herself fascinated by Charlotte's description. It felt utterly honest.

"So why were you worried about Jeff?" Alex asked.

"Because he had no clue what he was getting himself into. He started dating Amanda and then almost immediately she became very sick. Weak," she added sorrowfully. "It was the only time in her life when she was vulnerable, but if anything the experience only hardened her. I can tell you this. She was going to put him through the ringer. She was going to change him the way she changed Ladyform. Her idea of a successful husband was not a public defender."

Alex leaned toward Charlotte. "So do you suspect Jeff Hunter in your sister's disappearance?"

She paused a long time before answering. "I guess that depends."

"On what?"

"On whether he figured out that if he married Amanda, he'd be under her thumb as I always was."

47

Leo woke up feeling completely rested. This bed is great, he thought. It had been ten years since Eileen passed. Since then, it was only on trips with Laurie that he slept somewhere other than in his own bed or in Laurie's guest room. He realized it was probably time to buy a new mattress. Maybe he'd think about it when they were back in New York.

He looked at the clock. It was already ten A.M. He saw a note beneath the door that joined his room to Laurie and Timmy's. He felt his hamstrings ache as he bent down for it. At sixty-four years of age, he was in good shape but needed to stretch more. *Figured I'd let you two sleep in*, the note read.

Timmy was getting older. He could sleep until noon if undisturbed.

Leo walked over to the small desk in the corner, opened the laptop Laurie had bought him for his birthday, and clicked on the Internet browser. He could spend a few minutes working on his pet project before waking his grandson for a late breakfast. He used two fingers to type *facebook.com* into the search window. Grace was the one who was teaching him how to "cyberstalk," as she called it. When he was on the job, gathering background information had required knocking on doors and pounding the pavement. These days, people posted their entire lives, including what they ate for breakfast, on social media.

He typed "Carly Romano" into the search window of Facebook. He read recently that it was increasingly common for families and friends to maintain pages of those who had passed, as a place for loved ones to post memories. Sure enough, he found her wall, with a posting as recent as two months ago, from a Jenna Romano: *Happy Birthday, Sis. You're still in my heart. Xoxo.*

He had called the police in Waterville and confirmed that Carly's case was still unsolved. According to the detective he spoke to, the primary suspect was her high school boyfriend back in Michigan. The two had tried a long-distance relationship during their freshman year, but Carly broke things off when she returned to campus for her sophomore year. He didn't take the news well. But police had never been able to build a case against him.

It seemed like a good case for Laurie's show.

Leo clicked through the photographs on Carly's profile, searching for one of the old boyfriend. He checked the dates. He was still browsing the college years. He needed to keep scrolling back to high school.

He couldn't help but notice that Carly looked happy and lively in every photograph. She had thick, dark hair and big brown eyes. She seemed to always be smiling. He was scanning the pictures so quickly that he almost missed it: a familiar face.

He flipped back two pages. The caption on the photograph read, "DJ Night at the Bob-In!" Carly looked straight at the camera. The man next to her in the booth had his arm around her. He was younger, Leo thought to himself, but that's definitely him.

Younger, but familiar. He spotted him two more times in other photographs taken within a few days of this one.

He clicked over to his email and found the production schedule that Jerry had sent everyone prior to the trip. Alex was interviewing Charlotte at nine A.M. in the courtyard behind the hotel, with Kate to follow at 10:30. If he hurried, he could find Laurie on a break in between.

Leo waited until he saw Charlotte Pierce leave the set. Laurie smiled when she saw him, but then a moment of panic crossed her face. “Dad, where’s Timmy?”

“He’s fine. I woke him up and he’s in your room getting ready for breakfast.” They had lived for five years in the shadow of a killer’s threat that he would someday return to kill both Laurie and her son. That kind of fear doesn’t fade easily. “I think Alex may have been right when he said I was jumping to conclusions about Jeremy Carroll. You need to see this.” He opened his laptop screen.

Laurie’s mouth opened in surprise. “Is that—? Oh my God, it is.”

He clicked to the other two photographs. “His arm’s around her here. And check out the way he’s looking at her in this one. I think Jeff was dating Carly Romano. Amanda may not have been his first victim.”

48

Jerry was waving in Laurie's direction. "Is everything okay? We're ready to go over here." They had scheduled Charlotte Pierce and Kate Fulton in back-to-back interview sessions.

"Just a second." She turned to Leo and said, "Dad, let's not share this discovery yet. If word gets back to Jeff that we've connected him to Carly, he might panic. We're supposed to question him this afternoon."

Leo nodded. "I agree."

Laurie approached the set, smiling calmly at Kate, and then explained she just needed to speak to Alex briefly before they began.

Alex knew her well enough to know that something unexpected had occurred. They stepped aside, out of earshot of the others.

"Remember how I told you that a girl was killed near campus when they were all in college?" she asked.

He nodded.

"Dad found some photographs of Jeff and Carly together online. It looks like they may have dated."

"How come no one ever mentioned that?" Alex asked quickly.

Laurie shrugged, still trying to process the new information herself. "The girls probably didn't know; Kate said they weren't friends with Carly, and they weren't close to Jeff yet. But Jeff's friends presumably knew."

"Should I ask Kate? Or maybe we should just wait until we have him on camera."

"Don't ask Kate anything about this. I want to make sure we catch Jeff off guard later."

Grace was making her way toward them, her tanned legs revealed by an impossibly short minidress. "How are we doing over here? I told Jerry to calm down, but you did look a little worried." Grace's ability to read Laurie was almost eerie.

"We're all set," Alex said confidently. He reached over and squeezed Laurie's hand. Don't worry, Alex is a pro, Laurie reminded herself. He'll handle this perfectly.

"Now, Kate, you said Amanda expressed doubts about going through with the wedding. Can you tell me exactly what she said?" Alex asked pointedly.

Kate pressed her lips together, appearing to concentrate deeply. "I don't recall every word, but we were alone in the pool, and she was asking whether I ever wondered if I got married too young. She wanted to know if I had regrets, if I would have experienced more in life if I hadn't—that kind of thing. She even asked if I thought it was too late to call things off."

"That sounds like more than last-minute nerves," Alex said. "She actually mentioned the possibility of canceling the wedding?"

"She didn't say she *wanted* to cancel, but yes, I remember she said, 'How bad would it be to pull the plug at this point?' I told her it was normal to be nervous, but that she shouldn't go through with a wedding just to avoid upsetting other people."

"If this is true, Kate, you're the only person we know of to whom

Amanda expressed her reluctance. Pardon me for saying this, but wasn't Meghan closer to her than you were? She was the maid of honor, after all. Why wouldn't Amanda have disclosed these concerns to her?"

She shrugged. "Maybe because Meghan was also friends with Jeff? She might have been worried Meghan would tell him."

"Are you sure that's the only explanation?" Alex persisted. "Meghan made it sound as if she and Amanda were extremely close friends. Wouldn't Amanda trust her with such an important confidence?"

Kate cleared her throat. "It's possible that over the years, I may have let it slip that, yes, I did used to wonder if I married too young. That I would picture how things might have been different if I had ventured off on my own for a while. But I told her when she asked if I loved my husband and my children. How could I possibly regret them? Later, when I asked whether she was seriously having second thoughts about marrying Jeff, she was a bit evasive."

"How so?" Alex asked.

Laurie leaned forward, not wanting to miss a single facial expression or syllable.

"She said that something had come up—she was very vague—and that she needed to learn more about it before making a final decision."

"What exactly did she need to learn?"

"I have no idea. That's all she would say."

"Was it something about Jeff?" Alex suggested. "Was she planning to talk to him?"

"I honestly don't know," Kate said.

Alex turned and looked to Laurie to see if he should press any further. She gave him a small headshake, indicating not to push. She didn't want Kate to tip off Jeff that they were leaning in his direction.

Alex was bringing the session to a close when Laurie saw Sandra

Pierce walking quickly toward the hotel lobby, a handkerchief in her hand, her husband one step behind her. What was this all about? Seconds later, Amanda's brother, Henry, emerged from the same door and ran toward Laurie.

"Mom asked me to find you. The police said they found a body that they believe is Amanda's."

49

The detective's name was Marlene Henson. Laurie remembered Sandra mentioning her when she first came to Laurie's office. She was short—barely five feet tall—with long red hair and round, full cheeks. She stood with her feet hips' distance apart, sturdy like a tank.

"Are you sure you don't want to keep this strictly within the family, Sandra?" the detective asked. Laurie detected a hint of a southern accent in her voice.

The entire Pierce family was gathered in the living room of Walter's suite. Laurie suddenly felt all eyes on her and Alex, standing next to each other near the door. They were the interlopers.

"I want Laurie and Alex here," Sandra affirmed. "Their show is the reason we may have finally found Amanda. I know they're committed to helping us."

"But they're also reporters, Sandra. There are things we can't divulge to the public without jeopardizing the investigation."

"We're not typical reporters," Laurie said. "Anything you say in this room will remain between us for now. You have my word."

"And unlike the police," Alex said, "we have agreements with everyone in the wedding party to speak to us voluntarily. No arrests, no Miranda warnings. That could come in handy."

Detective Henson looked one more time at Sandra and appeared satisfied. Sandra's eyes were still bloodshot and puffy from crying, but she seemed ready to hear the details. Walter put his hand around her shoulder.

Her voice remarkably calm, Sandra asked, "Do you believe you have found my daughter's body?"

"Allow me to explain the events that brought us here today. A phone call came into the station house last night, a few minutes before midnight. The caller's voice was muffled. At this point we're not even certain if it was a man or a woman. The caller provided specific information about the location of your daughter's body. Of course we tried to trace the call but it came back to a phone you can buy and throw away."

Walter pursed his lips. "That was over twelve hours ago. No one thought to tell us?"

"The department wanted to investigate first. I didn't want to distress you if it was a crank call, but we acted on it immediately. The address the caller provided was for a parking lot across the street from St. Edward's Church, which is two miles from here. We checked the records. That parking lot was being resurfaced at the time your daughter disappeared. The instructions were very specific regarding where the body would be found.

"We had GPR—that's ground-penetrating radar—out there in the middle of the night. Based on what we saw on radar, we began excavation of the parking lot at sunrise and unfortunately did locate remains at that location. We'll do further testing to confirm if they belong to your daughter, but we found these on the left ring finger."

Detective Henson handed Sandra a photograph of two platinum rings: a classic Tiffany-style diamond engagement ring and a matching wedding band. The setting was caked in dirt.

"I think these are hers," Sandra said. "The engagement ring was engraved. A and J—"

Detective Henson finished the phrase with her. "*Semper amemus.*"

"It means 'Let us always love' in Latin," Sandra explained, choking back a sob. "It's definitely our daughter. It's my baby. It's Amanda."

Walter wrapped both arms around her, and she leaned her head on his shoulder.

"I'm so sorry to have to tell you this," the detective said softly. "I'll give your family some time alone. I've always hoped there might be a different ending."

50

On the way to the hotel elevator, Laurie asked Detective Henson if they could have a moment. "Detective, there's something you need to know about the wedding band that you found with Amanda's body. Jeff told us that when he got back to New York, he couldn't find the rings in his luggage. He said that with all of the distress over Amanda's disappearance, he hadn't realized they were missing."

"I was wondering why she would have been wearing the band before she was actually married."

"She wouldn't have been," Alex said. "And here's the thing: both the bride and the groom's rings were supposedly being kept in Jeff's room safe prior to the ceremony. And one of Amanda's friends just told us that Amanda seemed to be having second thoughts about the wedding. She said there was something she needed to find out before she made a final decision about whether to go through with the ceremony."

Detective Henson raised her eyebrows. "Well, that certainly is interesting. Sandra already told me about the will. Now that we've found her body, Jeff will finally get his money without having to call attention to himself by asking a court to declare her legally dead."

Laurie saw the pieces of the puzzle falling together. "If Amanda went up to Jeff's room that night after their separate parties, she might have wanted to try on her ring—maybe as a test to see how she felt about it. If she changed her mind and decided to call things off, a fight might have ensued. Jeff could have killed her and buried the body without remembering to remove the ring."

As usual, Alex was following her logic step by step. "When he realized his mistake, filing an insurance claim for the stolen rings after he got back to New York could have been a way to cover for the fact that her wedding band was missing. But he never filed a claim."

The detective smiled. "I appreciate the information, but you should leave the police work to us."

"Are you sure about that, Detective?" Alex asked swiftly. "Because we're supposed to question your number one suspect in half an hour, and for now he has no idea you found Amanda with that ring on her finger. And rest assured, I'm going to ask him about that."

51

Jeff looked handsome in a tan summer suit and plaid bow tie. They had asked him to wear something similar to what he had planned to wear for the wedding ceremony. He was showing Alex the beachside pergola where they were supposed to exchange vows in front of their family and closest friends.

"It's a truly beautiful setting," Alex observed. "I can't resist asking about your somewhat unusual choice of footwear."

One of the videographers moved forward with a handheld camera to get a shot of Jeff's sandals.

"Amanda loved the idea of being on the beach for an afternoon wedding," he said, reminiscing, "but was worried about wearing heels in the sand. She was thrilled when I suggested that we both wear flip-flops for the occasion and encourage our guests to do the same. Then she could change into her white satin Jimmy Choos for the reception."

Laurie smiled conspiratorially to the woman who handed her the bottle of water she'd requested. Detective Henson had looked like the result of a casting call for a police detective when she was delivering the bad news to the Pierce family. But clad in blue jeans and an *Under Suspicion* T-shirt, she now blended right in with the rest of the crew. Alex had been the one to convince her that it was in the police department's interest not to disrupt the production schedule.

So far, the police had been able to prevent the news about the discovery of a body beneath the concrete of a parking lot from leaking to the media.

If Jeff was the one who called in the anonymous tip, he might know they had already conducted an excavation. But he would have no way of knowing for certain that they had located either Amanda's body or the wedding ring. They still had the upper hand.

Jeff seemed comfortable in front of the cameras, telling Alex once again how much he admired his skills as a lawyer.

"We'll see if you still like me when we're finished here," Alex said wryly. "Let's start by getting something clarified upfront. You married Amanda's best friend, Meghan, just fifteen months after you were supposed to marry Amanda. You must have known that was going to raise some eyebrows."

"Of course we did, Alex. That's why we didn't have a big wedding and kept the news relatively private. But we were deeply in love. Getting married to each other was a way to remind ourselves that life needed to move on. We wanted to move on together."

"You don't think that sounds cold?"

"Maybe it does, but it didn't feel cold to either of us. We both loved Amanda. It was losing her that brought us together as a couple. We helped each other through the grief."

"So you're officially going on the record to say there was nothing going on between you and Meghan prior to Amanda's disappearance."

"I swear on my very life," he said, holding up one hand as an oath.

"Your wife told us that Amanda changed after she survived her illness. That she developed a harder edge. Was less patient. I think she even used the word *selfish*. Amanda's own sister echoed the sentiment. That must have placed some strain on your relationship."

"I doubt Meghan meant to use that particular word, but yes, it's fair to say that Amanda was a different person once she was past the treatment. Who wouldn't be affected by having a brush with death at such a young age? If anything, it made me admire her even more. She was determined to live her life to its fullest."

"We've heard from one of your friends that the two of you would sometimes argue."

"I mean, sure, like any couple. But nothing unusual. Look, it's true that our relationship wasn't perfect, and that was related to her getting past the illness. We really fell in love while she was sick. Once she was better, she was less dependent on me, and sometimes it was unclear how our lives fit together. In a crazy way, it was almost like there was a void without the illness."

"Amanda even spoke to Kate about the possibility of calling off the wedding."

Jeff appeared surprised by the assertion. "I can't imagine why. We were both so excited to be husband and wife."

"Amanda told her that something had come up and that she needed to find out more. Are you certain that you did not see Amanda the night after you separated for your bachelor and bachelorette parties?"

"Of course I'm certain."

"I want to shift gears and talk to you about your wedding bands. You were holding on to them until the ceremony?"

Jeff seemed completely unfazed by the question. "Yes, they were in the safe in my hotel room, but were stolen at some point during our stay."

"When was the last time you recall seeing them?"

"Let's see—I guess it was the same day Amanda disappeared. The photographer was taking some early pictures of the bridal party and snapped a couple of stills of the rings up in my room."

"And you returned them to the safe afterward?"

"Yes, I'm sure of it."

"And Amanda wasn't in your room at any time after that?"

"No. You're asking so many questions about those rings. They weren't particularly valuable. I couldn't have afforded expensive ones. Is there a reason you're so interested?"

A chill ran down Laurie's spine. Was Jeff testing them? As Laurie watched Alex's face, she made a mental note never to challenge him to a poker match. He was absolutely unreadable. "Meghan suggested that Amanda may have taken them as a memento."

Jeff nodded, apparently satisfied by the explanation. "She's mentioned the possibility to me, too. I think she truly wants to believe that Amanda's out there somewhere, churning butter on a farm in Montana. Wouldn't that be nice?"

"Amanda's not the only woman you've known who disappeared, is she?"

"What kind of question is that? Of course she is."

"We've been looking into the murder of a woman named Carly Romano. She was a sophomore at Colby, one year behind you. She was missing for two weeks before her body was found. The medical examiner determined she was strangled. Isn't this a photograph of you with Carly taken three months before her death?"

Jeff's face flushed with anger. "You can't possibly be suggesting—"

"All I did was ask a question, Jeff."

"This is crazy. Colby's tiny, eighteen hundred students total. Everyone basically knew everyone."

"But your arm is around Carly in this picture. You look quite enamored with her."

"You're blowing it way out of proportion. I would guess that was at Bob-In, a nearby stomping ground. I think Nick was trying to endear himself to one of her friends. I wasn't dating her or anything."

"There were other pictures of the two of you together."

"Those were probably the only times we ever hung out. Carly was one of the great beauties on campus. Everyone would flirt with her at parties, but in my case, it was nothing serious, just simple college fun. This is ridiculous. I've gone all these years with people wondering whether I hurt the woman I loved, but are you seriously suggesting I'm some kind of serial killer?"

Alex let the pause linger. By the time he spoke, Jeff was pale. "There's something I need to tell you, Jeff. The police found a woman's body this morning, buried beneath a parking lot that was under construction at the time Amanda disappeared."

Jeff's mouth opened and closed like a marionette's. "Is it Amanda?"

"There's no final identification yet, but they did find what appeared to be her engagement ring."

"*Semper amemus*?" he muttered. "That was the engraving."

"Yes," Alex said, "that's the same ring. And that wasn't the only piece of jewelry. The police also found a matching wedding band, the one you said was last seen in your hotel room."

Jeff rose from his chair, ripped off his mic, and walked quickly off the set.

52

An hour later, Laurie was pacing yet again in the living room of Alex's suite.

"Laurie," Alex said, obviously concerned, "I've never seen you so nervous. You're going to wear a hole in the hotel carpet at this rate."

The only other people in the room were her father and Detective Henson. Jerry was out with the camera crew gathering footage of local scenery to use during the narration between interviews. Laurie had asked Grace to watch Timmy so her father could be here while they met with Detective Henson.

"You're right," Laurie said. "I am a bundle of nerves. Shouldn't we tell Sandra and Walter about this latest development?"

So far, only her production team—and Jeff—knew about both the significance of the wedding band found with Amanda's body and Jeff's connection to Carly Romano.

Leo grabbed Laurie's hand abruptly as she passed his wing chair. "Stop pacing. The detective here knows what's she's doing, and for what it's worth, I'd make the same call. When you're working a case, you can't always tell the family everything in real time."

Alex had been able to extract some helpful information from Jeff. He had admitted knowing Carly, and he had locked himself into a very specific story about the wedding bands. But Detective Henson couldn't make an arrest until the Medical Examiner's Office completed the autopsy that might produce physical evidence connecting him to her death.

Detective Henson had changed back into her black pantsuit. "I've got police officers in plain clothes all over the property, and I have Jeff Hunter's name flagged with all the airlines, rental car companies, and Amtrak. If he tries to flee before his scheduled flight back to New York, we'll know."

"And what about when he's back in New York?" Alex asked.

"We'll deal with that when the time comes, but trust me, we're not going to lose sight of him."

"Good," Leo said. "If we're right, Jeff's gotten away with too much for too long."

"There's one thing I still don't understand," Laurie said, her pacing commencing once again. "Was Jeff really the one to call the police? But why would he tip us off to the location of the body? He had to have known that the wedding band would only call attention to him."

"I thought of that, too," Alex said. "But I've had clients who are extremely calculating about the costs and benefits of the choices they make. Jeff may have been confident that the ring wouldn't be enough proof for a conviction—because it's not. But now that Amanda's body has been found, he can finally inherit her trust fund without having to sue to declare her dead, which would have made him look like a real heel in the public eye."

"The account was worth two million dollars more than five years ago," Henson said.

Leo let out a whistle. "It's probably considerably more by now."

Laurie said, "Is there any way to analyze the voice on the tape to see if it's Jeff's?"

Henson shook her head. "You can buy a voice distorter in any spy shop. As I told you earlier, the caller could be a woman for all we know. We traced the call, and it came from a burner—a throwaway phone, no name attached to it. According to the cell site information, the call originated through a cell tower two blocks from here. So any of the people you are interviewing could have made the phone call. So, nothing helpful." Henson continued. "Can I trust the three of you to keep all this to yourselves? Don't make me regret this."

Laurie assured her that they would not let on that the police were closing in on Jeff, but as she shut the door behind the detective, she just couldn't picture Jeff making that phone call. They had to be missing something.

As she and her father left Alex's room, she asked if he could join her for a ride in the car after taking Timmy to the water park.

"No need to wait," Leo reported. "I just saw Jerry, who was quite proud to have finished scouting locations with the camera crew early. Much to my surprise, Jerry announced he'd been looking forward the entire trip to checking out the four-story slide Timmy keeps carrying on about."

"I'll see if Jerry is joking or if he minds staying with Timmy so you can keep me company."

"Dearly as I love my grandson, at sixty-four I'm not up to the water slides. But Laurie, give yourself a break and spend your free time with Alex. I know you're done shooting for the day."

"I am, but there's something I need to do, and I'd feel safer if you came along. But you have to promise that this time, we do it on my terms."

53

Laurie knocked on the door for the third time. "I know you're home." She peered through Jeremy Carroll's front window, but couldn't see anyone in the living room. At least it didn't look as though he had thrown out his photo collection.

She stepped toward the edge of the front porch to make sure that her father was staying put in the rental car parked across the street. She wanted him within view in case things went terribly wrong, but she thought she had a better chance of getting Jeremy to open up if she talked to him alone.

She'd seen a curtain part when she walked up the driveway. She wasn't going to leave until he answered.

"I know you didn't hurt Amanda," she cried out. "I'm sorry that we were so pushy last time, but I think you want to help. Please!"

The front door cracked open by an inch. Jeremy peered out from beneath unkempt brown bangs.

"Are you sure you're alone?" he asked fearfully.

"Yes, I promise."

He opened the door fully and stood back, allowing Laurie to step inside. She hoped she wasn't making a terrible mistake.

• • •

"I didn't like that man who was with you," he said once she was settled next to him on his living room sofa. "He seemed like a police officer or something."

"He's actually my father," she said, allowing that to serve as a response. "You were right to worry that people would be suspicious of you if they found out you were taking photographs of Amanda and her friends when they weren't looking. But I understand now. You take pictures because you care about people. You want to see them in their most honest moments, not just when they're smiling for the camera."

"Yes, that's exactly right. I don't want to see the faces that people put on for the world. I want reality."

"You said you got rid of the photographs you took of your neighbors once you realized that they were truly upset. What about the pictures of Amanda?"

He stared at her, blinking. He still didn't trust her.

"I saw you in the hotel surveillance footage. She walked past you, and you turned around to follow her. You had your camera. You're an artist. You must have taken a few snapshots."

"They're not *snapshots*, like some amateur Instagram account. They're my art."

"I'm sorry, Jeremy, I didn't mean to use the wrong words. But Amanda was a beautiful and, more important, smart and complicated woman. Did you know that she had been diagnosed with a very serious disease?"

He shook his head.

"Hodgkin's lymphoma. She was terribly ill. She lost twenty pounds and could barely get out of bed most days."

"That sounds terrible," he said sadly.

"It's a cancer of the immune system. It keeps your body from fighting infection. She was lucky to make a full recovery, and she knew it. She told her friends she wanted to live her life to the fullest."

He nodded. "I knew she was special."

"You must have some . . . ," she struggled to find the right word, "*portraits* of her. You kept them, didn't you?"

He nodded slowly. She was beginning to earn his trust.

"You kept them for a reason. You think maybe there's something in those images that might lead us to the truth about Amanda?"

"Do you promise this isn't a trick?"

"I swear, Jeremy, I only want your help." It was only a matter of time before reporters found out that Amanda's body had been located, but so far, the story hadn't broken. "There is new evidence that I'm not allowed to tell anyone. Based on that evidence, I don't think anyone's going to believe that you did anything to harm Amanda."

Next to her on the sofa, he began breathing so quickly that she thought he might be having a panic attack. When she reached over and placed a hand on his arm, he felt both warm and clammy.

"It's okay, Jeremy," she assured him. "You can trust me."

He stood quickly, as though he was trying to act before he changed his mind. He walked to the dining room and began sifting through a tower of newspapers and magazines. Holding her breath, Laurie followed him into the room. From the bottom of the stack, he pulled out an oversized mailing envelope and handed it to her. Clear, block letters on the front read "GRAND VICTORIA," with the date when Amanda was last seen.

"May I open this?" she asked.

He nodded. His face looked pained, as though he was expecting her to turn on him.

Laurie slid the pile of photographs from the envelope and began to spread them across the dining room table. There have to be at least a hundred pictures, she thought. A few looked like the posed shots that the wedding party had taken with Ray Walker, but most of them were obviously taken without the subjects' knowledge.

As she flipped through the images, Laurie saw one of the entire wedding party gathered at a large round table near the pool. She could tell from the picture that it had been taken from a distance with a long-range zoom lens. Jeremy was actually a very good photographer. The focus was perfect. She was surprised to see two people holding hands beneath the table. There was no mistaking who they were. Trying to keep her expression impassive, she pulled it from the pile.

"Do you mind if I keep this one?" she asked.

"That's okay."

Laurie hesitated, then said, "Jeremy, I want to hire you to do exactly what you did last time. Come back to the hotel now and take pictures of people on the set and also take some long-distance shots of those people when they don't know you're doing it."

"I'd like to work for you. Does that picture have anything to do with Amanda?"

"In a way it does," she said, even though she was sure that the picture bore no relation to Amanda's murder. She wanted the photograph because she knew someone who would want to keep this image private.

She realized as she continued scanning the pictures that Jeremy had filed them in the progression of the day. The sunlight grew dimmer toward the bottom of the pile. She paused on an image that appeared to be of Amanda, taken from behind. She was in the sundress she'd worn for their afternoon session with the photographer, and the hotel bar was visible in the background.

Laurie held up the photo for Jeremy. "This is when you saw her in the promenade and turned around."

He nodded.

"Jeremy, this is so important. It's just as you said. You were able to see beyond the false faces people put on for the public. Did you see

Amanda and the groom arguing? Is it possible she was going to call off the wedding?"

He shook his head, moved close to her side, and began sorting through the pictures himself. She could almost feel his breath on her neck.

"Here, let me help you," he said as he began pulling individual images from the ones she had already bypassed. "See how they look at each other? They had no idea I was looking. People don't fake these feelings."

Jeremy was right. The pictures he singled out showed undeniable affection. Jeff wrapping his arm around Amanda's waist as she stepped into the pool. Amanda looking up adoringly while Jeff took the seat next to her at the restaurant. Their fingers entwined as they strolled next to each other on the beach. Amanda and Jeff would have had no idea they were being photographed, but they appeared to be head over heels in love.

"But here's the thing," Jeremy said, pulling out a new subsample from his collection to tell a different story. "I don't think the bride and groom, and the two lovebirds holding hands beneath the table, were the only people in love that week."

Laurie now understood what he meant when he said that his photographs captured the truth about people. "Can I take these, as well?" she asked.

"Yes, you can have anything that's helpful," Jeremy said.

Laurie could tell that he finally felt at ease with her.

He volunteered one last image. "And I know you'll want this one."

The final photograph he handed to her showed two people. One of them was Amanda. She was pulling her arm out of the other person's grip. Her mouth was open. She looked angry. Hurt. The two were clearly upset. But the other person in the photograph was not Jeff.

"What time was this?"

"Not long after I saw her in the courtyard. It was around six o'clock, before they all left to get ready for dinner."

"What happened after that?"

"The other college friend came down to meet them. Her name was Kate? It looked like they forced themselves to act like everything was fine once she was there."

"Did you take any pictures after that?"

He shook his head. "No, they were wearing false faces again. There was no point."

"And did you leave the hotel after that?"

"No. I stayed. The Grand Victoria is a beautiful place to be. It was nice to just walk around and take pictures of people on vacation."

"Did you see Amanda again that night?"

"Yes, I did."

Laurie couldn't believe her ears.

"You know how when she disappeared they kept playing the video of her walking with her friends to the elevator and then turning around?" he asked.

"Of course. It's the last time anyone ever saw her."

"No it's not. I saw her."

"What happened next?" Laurie was practically screaming she was so excited.

"She was alone, heading down to the parking garage."

"Did you see her get into a car?"

"No, I followed her to the staircase and then stopped."

"Why? Why didn't you keep following her?"

"It's so quiet down there. Every noise echoes. I was afraid she'd hear my footsteps. I didn't want to scare her."

Laurie could only imagine how different it might have been that night. If the killer had been lurking in the garage, the sound of Jeremy's footsteps might have frightened him off.

54

Leo Farley kept his eyes on Jeremy Carroll's front porch as he hit refresh on his cell phone's email app for what felt like the thirtieth time in three minutes.

He had a love-hate relationship with computers. Sometimes he thought about how much easier his job would have been if he had had all this technology at his fingertips back with the NYPD. And then there were moments like this when he wished he had an actual human being on the other end of a good old-fashioned telephone call.

He had seen the worry in Laurie's face when she stepped out of the car. Laurie's show had been a phenomenal success so far. In both of the previous specials, the show had played a key role in identifying the murderer.

Laurie's work at the Grand Victoria would prove instrumental, but this might be the first time that she only managed to move the ball downfield, without going over the goal line. I was a cop for nearly thirty years, Leo thought. I've learned to know the difference between a gut feeling and proof beyond a reasonable doubt. But for Laurie, the sense of uncertainty was new. They still needed more evidence before the police could even possibly arrest Jeff. And Leo was determined to find it.

Maybe I made a mistake, he thought, not insisting on going inside with her. He had intensely lobbied Laurie to allow him to accompany her inside Jeremy's house, but she insisted on questioning him alone. She was so driven to get to the truth. But at least she didn't come here alone. She had allowed him to make the drive with her.

To keep his mind occupied, Leo had called the Office of Student Services at Colby and asked for help searching the college yearbooks for any information about Carly Romano. According to Jeff, he was only a casual acquaintance of the young woman who'd been murdered near the campus. If Leo could prove that Carly and Jeff had been an item, they'd be one step closer to building a case against him.

When Leo explained he was a retired first deputy commissioner of the NYPD looking into Carly's case in his spare time, the secretary volunteered that the yearbooks all contained an index by students' names. She would scan any page mentioning Carly and email it to him. It was the only thing he could think to do as he sat restlessly in the car.

Laurie saw her father lean his head back in the driver's seat when she reemerged from Jeremy's house. She wondered how many times he had started to leave the car to check on her.

"Laurie, that might have been the longest twenty minutes of my life," Leo said as she hopped into the passenger seat.

"Dad, wait until I tell you," she said as she dropped the package on the floor and began to put on her seat belt. Then her cell phone buzzed. It was a new text from Alex.

Local news just reported the discovery of Amanda's body. CNN is covering now. I'm taking Timmy to the pool but will follow updates online.

She was still reading the message when her phone rang. It was Brett Young.

She answered immediately. "Brett, I know. Big developments."

"Huge! Please tell me you're almost finished filming."

"We've got everyone who matters on film, yes."

She could almost picture him popping the champagne on the other end of the line. "So how long before you finish? I want to start advertising now."

"We don't have any answers yet, Brett."

"We need to strike while the iron's hot. I want to go to air as soon as possible. Wrap it up. Pronto!"

"There's a little problem. We still only have questions, not answers." She realized that the connection was already broken and Brett had not waited for her response.

Leo shifted the car into gear. "Brett must think you're Houdini."

"The news got out about the police finding Amanda's body. Did you hear it?"

"No, I had the radio off. I was making some phone calls."

"He wants me to finish as quickly as possible."

"To what end?" he protested. "At this point nobody knows who killed Amanda."

She thought about the photographs Jeremy had given her. Did she finally know who killed Amanda?

Maybe.

55

Leo dropped Laurie off at the hotel entrance and waited for the valet to take the car while she went to see Alex. She had just walked into the hotel lobby when she saw Kate Fulton make a beeline in her direction.

"Oh, Laurie, thank goodness. I've been looking all over for you. I feel terrible thinking about anything other than Amanda right now, but it's really important. I already talked to Jerry, but he said he couldn't make any promises. I know I signed that agreement, but I don't want you to use my interview after all."

This was the last thing Laurie wanted to deal with right now. She had Brett breathing down her neck, and she desperately needed to talk to Alex. She could feel the photographs in her briefcase pulling at her. She and Leo both thought she should take them to Detective Henson, but she wanted Alex's advice before making a final decision.

"Kate, I think I know why you're having second thoughts about your interview," Laurie said, "but can we please talk about it later? I'm sure we can easily edit out the segment you're worried about."

"Wait, do you know? Did Henry say something?"

Laurie reached into her bag and pulled out the first photograph she had taken from Jeremy, the one of the entire wedding party sitting around a table. Even from a distance, Jeremy had been able to capture Henry's hand entwined with Kate's. "An intern for the wedding photographer had this," Laurie said, giving her only copy to Kate. "And trust me, I'll edit out the part where you said you wondered if you got married too young, and no one ever needs to know."

Kate had been the first to turn in for the night after the bachelorette dinner. Amanda's brother, Henry, was the first of the men. They were the only married people in the gang. They were both parents to young children, eager for some downtime. After saying good night to their dinner companions, they had gotten together in one of their rooms.

"I love my husband," Kate said. "It was just one night. It was a terrible mistake, for Henry, too."

"You don't need to explain."

Kate gave her a huge hug. "I felt so guilty for thinking about myself when they've finally found Amanda. Poor Sandra and Walter. Austin offered the whole family the use of his jet if they needed to get home, but they said they wanted to stay here."

"They're actually holding up okay," Laurie said. "After all these years, I think they were ready to hear the truth. There is one more thing you can help me with."

"Anything."

"Were Meghan and Amanda arguing while you were all down here?"

"Not to my knowledge," she said. "But, as you now know, I had other things on my mind. Why?"

"Amanda told you she was having second thoughts about the wedding and needed to find something out. Is it possible she figured out that Meghan had feelings for Jeff?"

"I don't know—maybe. You don't think Meghan killed Amanda, do you?"

"Oh, of course not," Laurie said quickly. "We just try to cover all our bases."

She watched Kate head toward the elevator, knowing she was going to destroy that photograph. The pictures that mattered to Laurie were still in her briefcase. Five of them showed Meghan at various times during the week, staring longingly at Jeff as he doted on his fiancée. But it was the final photograph that was most shocking: Amanda pulling her arm from Meghan's grip during a heated argument.

56

Leo had just returned to his hotel room when he heard a knock at his door, followed by a familiar voice. "It's Laurie. Dad, are you there?"

She sounded concerned. He jumped from the chair to let her in.

"Have you seen Alex and Timmy?" she asked immediately. "I can't find them anywhere."

"Timmy left a note saying Alex was joining him and Jerry for the water park. He used five exclamation points."

The sight of her son's carefully printed words on the Grand Victoria stationery only partially calmed her. "When Alex texted me saying he was going to the pool with Timmy, I thought he meant the hotel."

Leo expected his daughter to worry once again that Timmy was getting too attached to Alex, but she changed the subject back to the case. "Dad, I can't decide whether to take these pictures to Detective Henson." She removed the photos from her briefcase and spread them out on the bed. Leo hadn't had time to study them closely in the car.

"Look," she said, pointing to a picture of Meghan glaring in the background as Jeff and Amanda posed under a poolside marble archway. "You can tell she's in love with him, and he has no idea. And then in this final picture, it's obvious Amanda and Meghan were fighting. Meghan never said anything about a confrontation after that one incident at the Ladyform offices."

"You think they were arguing about Jeff?" Leo asked.

"Somehow Amanda could have learned Meghan was in love with Jeff. Maybe she even sensed it was mutual. She told Kate she had to find something out before she could go through with the wedding. This picture may have been taken when she confronted Meghan about her real feelings. I think they cut the argument short because it was time to get ready for dinner, but agreed to meet privately later. That's probably why Amanda was heading for the parking garage. If only Jeremy had followed Amanda all the way to the car."

"I thought you told me that Meghan and Charlotte rode up together on the elevator after Amanda said she forgot something."

"They did, but once Meghan went to her room, she was alone. We'll need to check with the hotel, but there must have been a way for Meghan to double back out of the hotel from her room without being seen. The camera footage is grainy. If she changed out of her dress into jeans and a baseball cap, she could have passed for a man. Plus, I was thinking about Carly Romano. If she and Jeff were dating, and Meghan was already interested in Jeff, then Meghan might have been the one to hurt Carly, too. She wanted Jeff to herself."

At that very moment, Leo's laptop let out a high-pitched *ping* from the desk in the corner. He had a new email message. He nearly ignored it, but sneaked a quick glance. It was from the Office of Student Services at Colby.

"Speaking of Carly," he said, "I checked with the college to see if I could track down more details about her connection to Jeff. They scanned every yearbook page with Carly's name on it."

He opened the attachment to the new message. "I don't see any mention of Jeff here," he said, "but take a look at this."

Laurie scanned the tribute to Carly in her sophomore yearbook. She was the president of the debate team. *Without Carly, the club had no choice but to elect a new president. "Carly's death was a tragedy and loss to our team and the entire Colby community. I only hope to do half the job she did."*

Beneath the quote was the smiling face of the new debate team president, Colby junior Meghan White.

As Leo's laptop pinged with the incoming message, Jeff Hunter's cell phone rang. It was an unexpected call from New York City. Jeff was shocked by who the caller was and what he said about Meghan.

57

As Jeff ended his call, Austin signaled a poolside waiter and ordered a scotch. "By the time it gets here, it will be five o'clock. Who am I kidding? I started at lunch. You want anything, buddy?"

Jeff shook his head but said nothing. Once the waiter was gone, Austin said, "I'm sorry, I can't imagine what you're going through. I guess most of us suspected Amanda was—you know—but it's got to be rough to finally know for certain. What was that call? You sounded upset."

Jeff told Austin he was fine and then quickly changed the subject. "Where's Nick?" he asked, even though the person he was eager to see was his own wife. Meghan was with Kate at the hotel spa for the afternoon. After that phone call, Jeff was tempted to storm into the spa and demand an explanation. But in light of today's grilling by Alex Buckley, he knew everyone was suspicious of him. For all he knew, the police had undercover officers at the hotel, watching his every move. The last thing he needed was to lose his temper in public, but he was hurt and confused, and desperate to speak to Meghan. He took a deep breath and tried to remain calm.

Austin said, "Nick's getting his boat ready. You know him. He takes forever." Austin and Nick, always competing, Jeff thought.

Jeff looked at his watch. "I doubt you two have time for a cocktail cruise before dinner." All the college friends were planning a group dinner tonight. After Amanda's body was found, Kate moved the reservation up to six-thirty. It would be an early, somber evening, not the reunion they'd been expecting. Jeff didn't even want to go, but Meghan felt bad about leaving Kate to mourn alone.

"Not a cocktail cruise," Austin corrected. "Nick's leaving early to woo a billionaire, remember? A client meeting in Boca Raton."

Right. With everything that was going on, it had slipped Jeff's mind.

"Speak of the devil," Austin called out. Nick was headed their way in madras shorts and a Polo shirt, his captain's hat already donned and a can of beer in his hand. "You finally got that poor excuse for a boat ready to hit the water?"

"You're just jealous that I got the nicer boat." Only then did Nick seem to notice Jeff's pensive mood. "Hey, we're just trying to keep things light. We're all sorry about Amanda."

Jeff nodded.

"Where are the ladies?" Nick asked. "I'll see Meghan soon enough back home, but I wanted to say good-bye to Kate."

"They decided to get facials and massages to take their minds off all this," Jeff said. His eyes drifted to the corridor leading to the spa. No sign of them. Every minute without an explanation about that phone call felt like hours.

"Were you able to say good-bye to Amanda's family?" Austin asked.

"I just came from Sandra's. I almost walked away from her room without knocking, but I couldn't leave without expressing my sympathies."

Jeff didn't tell his friends that he had knocked on the same door earlier in the day, only to have Sandra slam it in his face.

Austin asked how the Pierces were holding up.

"Honestly?" Nick said. "Not well. I got the impression they wanted to be left alone. They'll be having a family dinner tonight to talk about their memories of Amanda."

Austin held up his scotch and said quietly, "To Amanda."

"See you boys back in New York," Nick said. "You hang in there, buddy."

Nick gave Jeff a comforting pat on the back, and Austin followed suit. Was Jeff being paranoid, or did even his best friends seem to be looking at him differently now?

He needed to talk to Meghan.

58

Laurie pushed her chair back from the desk in her room the second she heard the beep of a key card in the door. Timmy and Alex were back from the water park, both in swim trunks and Knicks T-shirts.

She gave Timmy a hug. His hair was still warm, and he smelled of chlorine and sunscreen. "So how was it?"

"It was awesome! I think it was even better than Six Flags." Coming from Timmy, that was the equivalent of Shangri-la. He surprised her by saying that he wanted to tell her all about it but was hot and wanted to take a shower. He was growing up so fast.

Once she heard the water running, she began briefing Alex on what he'd missed this afternoon. She showed him Jeremy's photographs of Meghan, as well as the yearbook information from Colby. When she was finished laying out her case, he put his hands on his hips and exhaled. "Just when we thought we were getting somewhere."

"I know. I was sure it was Jeff. Now I think Meghan was involved. And I'm wondering if I'm missing something once again."

"But what about the ring Amanda was wearing?"

"Amanda could have been the one to take the bands from the safe. Maybe she wanted to try hers on to see how she felt about it, and maybe Meghan didn't realize she was still wearing it later."

"That's a lot of maybes."

"Exactly. Which is why I have no idea what to do with this evidence. In the other specials, we found clear enough proof to be absolutely certain about the truth. We were able to produce our show *and* identify the killer, all at once. But now I have this evidence against Meghan, and I want to keep digging. But Brett's breathing down my neck to finish so we can go to air. Plus, I feel like I should tell the police what we know—"

Alex finished her thought. "But right now it's exclusive to you. And if you share it with the public—"

"There goes my scoop. And Brett will want my head on a platter."

"Is he really that ruthless? He'd want you to sit on evidence?"

"Unless it's subpoenaed, absolutely. He told me once that the Nielsen ratings were his religion." She felt a hot coal forming in the pit of her stomach. "I don't know what to do."

Alex placed his hands on her shoulders and looked her in the eye. "First of all, try not to panic. The last Meghan knew, I was giving Jeff the third degree. She has no idea you have these pictures, right? Or that Leo called Colby?"

Laurie nodded and was already starting to calm down. Alex always had that effect on her.

"Okay," he said confidently, "that gives you some time to think. Why don't I clean myself up and we can all have an early dinner. Grace and Jerry, too. We'll go over everything we know, and then you can decide whether to go to the police now or keep working."

"That sounds good," she said, moving into his embrace.

"Now, is there any chance I can take your mind off this by telling you about the trip to the water park today?"

"I would love that," Laurie said with a smile. "I can't even picture Jerry with wet hair in a swimsuit, hurling himself down a slide."

"You would have loved the sight of it. He was like a big kid, and Timmy was overjoyed to have a friend who was at least as excited as he was to play in the water."

"And what about you?" she asked. "If I ask Jerry, will he have pictures of you bouncing into the waves?"

Alex put on an intentionally haughty expression. "I'm much too dignified. But it's possible I had an identical twin on the premises. And I imagine he looked ridiculous with six feet and four inches of arms and legs sticking out everywhere."

"If Jerry has pictures," Laurie quipped, "I'm sending them to the *Law Journal*."

59

Jeremy had forgotten how sprawling the Grand Victoria was. He'd been roaming the property for nearly twenty minutes without crossing paths with any of the bridal party members he was supposed to be watching.

It had taken him longer to get here than Laurie might have expected. He needed to pack a variety of lenses for the job. Taking shots from a distance could be tricky, plus the light would change as sunset approached. He hoped he wasn't too late. He didn't want to disappoint Laurie.

He had been surprised and excited when Laurie hired him to take photographs without the subjects' knowledge. The first time she came to his house, she and her father made it sound like such a horrible thing to do. Then she did a complete about-face, offering him money to do exactly the same thing.

He suddenly stopped walking. What if this was all a trick? The last thing he needed was another restraining order.

He was thinking about calling this whole thing off when he finally recognized someone. It was Jeff, the groom from five years ago. He hadn't changed much. He was rushing into an alcove leading to another section of the hotel. Jeremy was about to follow him when he saw Jeff reemerge, this time with a dark-haired woman at his side.

Jeremy looked through his camera lens and zoomed in for a closer look. It was Meghan, Amanda's maid of honor.

Neither Jeff nor Meghan looked happy.

Jeremy immediately began taking pictures. Maybe he'd give them to Laurie, or maybe not. Either way, he couldn't help himself. He loved to watch.

60

"Shhh! Everyone on the floor can probably hear us."

Jeff Hunter didn't care if the entire state of Florida heard them fighting. He had never been this angry with Meghan before. Worse, he felt betrayed.

The phone call he received while Meghan and Kate were at the spa had been from Mitchell Lands, Amanda's estate lawyer. At first, Jeff assumed he was calling to express his condolences. The news of Amanda's body being found was all over the news.

But that wasn't the only reason the attorney called.

Jeff was so angry now he could barely recognize his own voice. "Amanda's body was found only hours ago, and Lands was already calling to explain the process for moving her estate into probate. I told him I never wanted Amanda's money," Jeff said, "and then came the bombshell. Imagine my shock when he told me *you* called him this morning to ask about my inheritance. Why in the world would you call Amanda's lawyer behind my back asking how to get the money from her trust fund? You know I've never had any interest in one penny of Amanda's money, not even when we were supposed to get married."

"Marrying Amanda is what you always really wanted, wasn't it? I knew this day would eventually come, the moment when you realized that she was the only one you ever loved. You only married me because I was her best friend, the next closest thing to your beloved Amanda."

Jeff couldn't even recognize the woman who was sobbing on the hotel bed. Did she really doubt his love for her? Is that why she called the lawyer? Was she planning to leave him and take half of the inheritance? He would give her every cent if she wanted. He just wanted her to act like the wife he thought he knew better than anyone on the planet.

"Meghan, talk to me. Why did you call that lawyer? You should have told me. Do you realize how horrible this will look now that they've found Amanda's body?"

Meghan buried her head in the pillow, leaving mascara stains on the crisp white cotton. "It was just one phone call. I wasn't thinking about the show, and I certainly had no idea they'd find Amanda's body, today of all days!"

"They found her rings. Amanda's dead. All these years, you said you thought she was out there living a happy life. You must feel something."

Now her volume outmatched his. "Of course I feel something. She was my best friend. You know how the producers asked me about that stupid fight we had over X-Dream workout clothes? I couldn't have cared less about Amanda taking that idea. I was looking for an excuse to lash out at her because she was marrying you. Don't you realize, after all these years? I've loved you since college, and I had to sit there and pretend to be happy for Amanda while you fell in love with her. I've always been your second choice."

Jeff had never seen his wife this emotional. "That's not true, Meghan. Amanda was—we were so different. And people change. I've never felt as right with someone as I feel with you. But you've got to tell me why you called that lawyer."

"I promise, it's not what you think. I can explain. You just have to wait."

There was a knock at the door. Meghan looked through the peephole, then wiped her face with her palms.

"It's Kate. I told her to swing by here before dinner. Now can you please stop yelling and have a little faith in me?"

In an instant, her outburst was over, and she was back to her cool, levelheaded self. At this point, Jeff had no idea where to place his faith.

Five years ago, when he was about to marry Amanda, he had nagging doubts about how well he really knew her. Now after the bewildering rush of today's events, he found himself questioning how well he knew his wife.

61

Sandra Pierce suppressed a wince as her son, Henry, confirmed with the hostess that their reservation was for four people. All these years, she knew that something terrible had happened to Amanda. Despite what the police and public wanted to believe, Amanda would never have vanished on her own. But some part of Sandra had always held out a glimmer of hope that they'd find Amanda alive—that they might be a table of five again.

Walter was remarking on the unusual aquarium bar when Sandra saw a familiar group already seated at the back of the dining room. She let out a gasp, and Charlotte immediately grabbed her hand.

"Mom, are you okay?"

Walter, Charlotte, and Henry followed her gaze. Jeff Hunter was there, with that traitorous Meghan, along with Kate and Austin. Sandra could not stop staring at Jeff. As Jeff lifted his water glass, Sandra pictured that same hand around her daughter's throat.

"I can't stand the sight of him," she hissed. "He killed Amanda, I just know it."

The hostess had obviously overheard her. "Shall I change your table?" she asked. "I have one at the other end of the dining room."

Sandra felt a comforting hand on her back and turned to see Walter, looking at her softly. "You know what?" he said. "Now that we're here, I'm in the mood for steak. Would you mind if we went across the street? We can have the concierge call them for us on our way out."

As they left the hotel, Henry pointed out the beginning of a beautiful sunset. The sky was purple and gold. Amanda would have loved it. That's why she wanted to get married on the beach.

Sandra felt Walter's strong arm around her. "I'll never rest until we get justice for Amanda," Walter said. "But tonight is about our family. We deserve a night in peace to remember Amanda." They walked to dinner as a family.

Jeff Hunter saw the Pierce family turn away from the hostess stand and walk out. He had seen the expression on Sandra's face. She was judge, jury, and executioner.

He wondered if he looked at Meghan in the same way. He wanted to stand up in the middle of the restaurant and scream at the top of his lungs, "I did not do this!"

His cell phone buzzed in his pocket. It was a text message from Nick: *Boca's a beautiful place, but I wish I could be there with you guys. Hope you're doing okay, man.*

Jeff would tell Nick later he was lucky to have left early. This dinner was a terrible idea. Austin was clearly bored without Nick. Next to Austin, Kate kept inching her chair farther away from him, probably remembering all of Austin's awkward passes in college. Meghan was sipping water and barely talking. And Jeff wanted to leave this dinner table right now and demand that Meghan explain why she called Amanda's lawyer about the will.

Was this her plan all along? To marry Jeff once Amanda was out of the way, then spend his inheritance? He couldn't believe he was even entertaining the possibility.

As they continued to eat in silence, he thought he saw a man in the distance staring at them from the courtyard. Of course, he thought. The police are definitely watching me.

The man in the distance was not police, but Jeremy. He had followed Jeff and Meghan until they entered the elevator, then watched the numbers click in order until a stop on their floor. When Jeremy followed, he could hear raised voices. But then he saw a man lingering in the hallway. He didn't want to call attention to himself by wandering around without a room to enter, so he rode back down to the lobby. He waited until he spotted Meghan and Jeff again, this time with Kate in tow. He could sense the coolness between them. Even without words, body language told the story.

He could also read the Pierce family. Their mood was heavy when they walked into the seafood restaurant. Of course it was, after the news about Amanda. But within minutes, they walked out, and this time, they all looked even more upset. When they left the hotel, Jeremy had a choice to make. Watch the family or watch the bridal party. The answer seemed clear.

Now he was wondering if he'd made the right decision. There was still tension between Meghan and Jeff, but the preppy male friend looked bored, and the other woman was sad. Nothing much to see.

Then Jeremy saw another familiar face. It was Laurie's father, walking through the lobby, the man who had scared him so much at his home. Jeremy stepped behind a palm tree, and watched the older man go down the path toward the Italian restaurant. Once he was out of sight, Jeremy followed and, through the window, saw him join Laurie and several other people at a large round table in the back.

Laurie had asked him to take photographs of people participating in her show. She didn't tell him *not* to photograph her and her friends, too. Besides, whether this was part of the job or not, there was nothing illegal about standing here and taking pictures.

He changed to a longer-distance lens. Once he started shooting, he couldn't stop. The young woman with the long black hair was gorgeous. And the man sitting next to Laurie was remarkably photogenic. Plus the boy was adorable. These would be wonderful photographs for his collection.

Jeremy was so engrossed that he didn't notice when Jeff, Meghan, and their friends left the seafood restaurant and disappeared into the elevator.

62

Laurie tasted salt on her lips as the night wind from the Atlantic Ocean blew into her face. Her linen pants were rolled up high on her calves. She carried her sandals in one hand while Alex held the other. They must have walked a mile by now.

As Alex had suggested, they'd talked through everything they knew about Amanda's case over dinner. There was evidence against Jeff, but against Meghan, too. It could be either of them, or both working together. At this point, they may as well flip a coin. Then there was the question of whether to keep investigating or to rush to air. If it were up to Brett, the show would be on television tonight.

By the time dessert arrived, Laurie knew in her gut what she had to do. She just wanted one final talk with Alex alone before committing to a final decision.

"I really thought we'd solve another one before calling it a wrap," she said wistfully.

"That's not always going to happen, Laurie. And look at how much you've accomplished. You've brought closure to a family who were forgotten by the system. Sandra told me today how grateful she was to finally have an answer about Amanda."

"But it's a bad answer. She's dead, and we still don't know who killed her."

"But at least they're able to say good-bye," Alex said. "It sounds like you've reached a decision."

"I have. We'll have one more film session tomorrow when you can lay out everything we know. You might want to repeat some of what you just said to me about saying good-bye," she said with a sad smile. "It would be the perfect way to end a story that doesn't really have an ending."

Alex stopped walking and turned to face her. "Speaking of my wrap-up for the program, there's something I need to tell you."

"That sounds ominous." Maybe my father was right, she thought. I told him Alex and I were fine, but maybe we aren't.

"No, not at all. But I won't always be able to keep working on the show."

"Is it because of us—"

"No, not at all. It's my practice. As much as I love an excuse to leave New York for days at a time, and with you no less, it's too hard to juggle my schedule. So far, it has worked out, but that won't always be the case."

It was hard to imagine ever doing the show without Alex. And Laurie immediately wondered how it would affect their relationship. She didn't want him to see how disappointed she was. "You mean judges won't halt the wheels of justice so you can be a TV star?"

"Apparently not," he said.

His smile made her heart swell. Laurie grasped his hand more tightly and continued walking along the beach. "Brett won't be happy until I find another narrator as handsome as you."

"Well, that's impossible, of course," he said dryly. "But I already have someone in mind. Besides, it's about time Brett realizes you're the show's real special ingredient."

• • •

They were on their way back to the hotel when Laurie felt her cell phone vibrate in her pocket. If that's Brett again, she thought, I'm throwing this thing into the ocean. She checked the screen to find a New York phone number, but not Brett's.

"This is Laurie," she answered.

"Ah, good, I caught you. I'm sorry to call at night. It's Mitchell Lands."

It took Laurie a moment to place the name of the lawyer who had written Amanda's prenuptial agreement and will. "Oh hi, Mitchell. You're working awfully late." She whispered an apology to Alex. She shouldn't have even answered.

"The life of a lawyer, I'm afraid."

"I imagine you're calling because you heard the terrible news about Amanda. I'm so sorry."

"I hate to say it, but in my business, you get accustomed to hearing about death. I feel terrible for poor Sandra and Walter. They must be heartbroken."

"They are. Is there something I can help you with?" she asked.

"No, but something's been eating at me all night, and I finally thought I better call you. It's about Jeff Hunter. He told me he's down there as part of your show."

"You spoke to Jeff?" She stopped walking. Alex's expression grew concerned.

"Yes, I called him as soon as I heard about the discovery of Amanda's remains. I thought he should know the next steps before Amanda's estate enters probate."

"Not to question your tactics, Mitchell, but isn't that awfully soon? The identity hasn't even been officially confirmed yet."

"I know, it's not my usual process, either. But since there seemed to be an urgency to have the funds dispersed, I figured there was no harm in getting the ball rolling. But then he told me he was being questioned for your show. Is Jeff considered a suspect? If so, Amanda's parents could intervene to try to freeze the assets until the investigation is complete. I hate to call them about a legal matter at a time like this, but, as I said, it's been eating at me all night. Maybe I shouldn't have phoned Jeff after all."

"What do you mean an urgency? I thought Jeff had never sought to collect on the will before?"

"He hadn't. And I guess he still hasn't. So I was a little surprised this morning when I got a phone call asking me about the inheritance."

"Jeff called this morning about the will?"

Alex's eyes widened.

"No, not Jeff," Lands said. "His wife, Meghan."

Laurie's suspicions had been right. "Meghan was the one asking about the inheritance? What time was this?"

"First thing when I showed up at nine A.M."

Not even Amanda's parents had known yet about the discovery of her body. Laurie remembered Detective Henson saying that the person who called in the anonymous tip could even have been a woman, given the easy availability of voice-distortion equipment.

"And she knew Amanda's remains had been found?" Laurie asked.

"No, I'm sorry. I don't think I'm being very clear. Jeff's wife called prior to the news reports. She was asking about the process for Jeff to inherit—how to go about having Amanda declared legally dead and the timing. I told her they'd have to hire their own lawyer since I represent the estate. But then once I heard the news, I called Jeff as the beneficiary to let him know that he wouldn't need to pursue a declaration once the death certificate was signed."

"How did Jeff handle the news?"

"That's the thing. He seemed very upset, and quite surprised when I told him that Meghan had called this morning. I don't think he had the foggiest clue she was asking. She must have done it on her own. So that had me thinking he wasn't a suspect, but I decided to check with you to be sure."

"When did you talk to Jeff?"

"A few hours ago. Just before five."

Laurie said good-bye and turned to Alex. "We thought there was no rush telling the police about Meghan, but she called Mitchell Lands this morning, asking about the inheritance. And then Lands called Jeff."

As usual, Alex immediately understood her point. "Which means Jeff has probably already confronted Meghan about it. She'll know it makes her look guilty. We have to tell Detective Henson."

"I'll ask Dad to do it. She trusts him more than either of us. But I need to call him right now."

63

Just as Meghan expected, Jeff laid into her as soon as they were alone again in their hotel room.

"Why do you keep telling me I need to wait?" he demanded. "Are you trying to buy yourself time to come up with a lie?"

"I would *never* lie to you. I just can't talk about it right now. Not like this."

"Why in the world did you call that lawyer this morning?" Jeff insisted. "After all these years, and just hours before we all learned about Amanda's body. I can't get my head around it."

"I promise, there's a reason—"

"Then tell me!"

"Stop screaming at me!"

"I'm asking you one simple question, Meghan. I deserve an answer."

Jeff could not believe his eyes when she stood up, grabbed her purse, and walked out of the room, slamming the door behind her and leaving him in silence.

Meghan used the short amount of time in the hotel elevator to wipe the tears from her face and catch her breath. She and Jeff rarely argued, and neither of them had ever walked out on the other when they did, but leaving the room felt like the only way to keep her blood pressure from rising. The doctor had warned her to avoid unnecessary stress.

Good luck with that, she thought, as she placed a hand on her belly. She had no way of knowing whether the baby could feel it, but resting her palm near her unborn child was calming to Meghan, if to no one else. Don't worry, she thought, everything's going to be just fine. Once your father calms down, I'll go back to the room. He'll believe my side of the story, I'm sure of it.

Meghan had been planning to give Jeff the news once they were back in New York. She wanted a clean break between this place and their baby. She wanted it to be a perfect moment.

But she never should have called that lawyer this morning. Of course it looked terrible, especially in light of the police finding Amanda only hours later. No wonder Jeff was demanding an explanation. She turned back toward the elevator, ready to tell him the truth, even though it wouldn't be anything like the moment she had imagined.

Her cell phone buzzed with an incoming email message. There's no way to escape work, she thought. How can I be on twenty-four-hour call once I'm a parent? But the message wasn't about a client. The subject line said "from Kate."

She clicked on it. *Hey there. I didn't want to say anything in front of everyone at dinner, but I have something important to tell you about Jeff. I think that TV show is trying to railroad him. Meet me by the pier behind the hotel so we don't run into anyone from the show?*

Perfect, Meghan typed. Jeff could use a few more minutes to cool down before we talk, she thought. *Headed there now.*

64

Detective Marlene Henson sprawled on the area rug in her den and allowed her two standard poodles to jump on top of her. They were three-year-old sisters named Cagney and Lacey. Even on days when her daughter Taylor stayed with her father, these two sturdy girls gave Marlene someone to come home to.

Their exuberance about Mommy coming home temporarily quelled, the two dogs ran into the living room to continue an epic round of wrestling. She had learned the hard way when she adopted them as puppies not to leave anything breakable within a few feet of the floor. The upside was she no longer had so many knickknacks cluttering the house.

She felt her eyes begin to close involuntarily. Marlene loved her job, but today had been a rough one.

She had inherited the Amanda Pierce case—already cold—three years earlier when homicide detective Martin Cooper died of an aneurysm in his sleep. She reached out to Sandra and Walter the following week. She had told them that no new leads had come in of late, but Marlene had a standing alert with the department that she be called—day or night—if that ever changed. Then last night came the tip about the body. Since then she'd been working more than twenty hours straight.

She was starting to doze off right in the middle of the floor when her cell phone buzzed on the coffee table. It was a New York City area code.

"Henson," she said, stifling a yawn.

"Detective, it's Leo Farley."

The ex-cop, she thought. He'd been invaluable in dealing with his daughter and her team. She was usually distrustful of the media, but she trusted Leo, and he seemed to trust the people who worked for that show.

"Hi, Leo. What can I do for you?"

"We know you've got officers watching Jeff, but they need to keep their eyes on his wife, Meghan White, too. Laurie got some photographs from that intern we told you about—"

Marlene sat up immediately. "She did what?" So much for trusting them.

"She thought she had a better shot getting him to open up if she went in alone. I waited outside, worried every moment. But she was right. It worked. Jeremy gave her some facts we didn't know before."

Marlene felt a headache coming on as Leo started talking about pictures of Meghan looking lovingly at Jeff, and then fighting with Amanda the very night she disappeared. She was close to a migraine by the time Leo got to Meghan's phone call to Amanda's lawyer and her connection to the girl who'd been killed at Colby.

"Where are you?" he asked. "Do you have a location on Jeff and Meghan right now?"

"I came home, but I'm sure everything's fine. Last I heard, they were at dinner with their friends. Let me call my lead guy on the scene now."

She hung up without saying good-bye, pulled up the number for Sergeant Jim Peters, and hit enter.

"Thought you were grabbing some shut-eye," he said.

"Me, too." No such luck, she thought.

"This sure is a beautiful place. I almost feel guilty collecting overtime for sitting here. Almost."

"You're still watching Hunter?"

"Yeah. He and the wife went to their room after dinner. If I see him leave, I'll duck into the stairwell and call Tanner downstairs. He's camped out near the elevators. We've been rotating for a change of scenery."

"So they're both there: Jeff and the wife?"

"No, just him. They had some kind of dustup and she stormed out of here a second ago. I went into the stairwell so she wouldn't spot me."

"Where'd she go? Is Tanner following her?"

"No, we're trailing the husband, I thought."

"We were. And are. Just call Tanner, okay? Tell him to keep his eyes on the wife, and you watch Jeff. Don't lose either one of them."

Marlene had changed into fresh work clothes and was putting on her shoes when Sergeant Peters called her back.

"You found Meghan?" she asked.

"No. I just talked to Tanner. He says she walked through the lobby, but he doesn't know where she went from there."

65

Jeremy looked at his watch, wondering how late he should stay at the hotel. He had gotten so distracted taking photographs of Laurie and her friends that he somehow lost track of the bridal party. By the time he walked back to the seafood restaurant, their table was empty.

He checked the other hotel bars, but no luck.

Now he was on the beach. A few couples passed him on moonlight strolls, but he didn't recognize anyone. The moon was beautiful tonight. It had been a long time since he practiced his nighttime photography skills.

He changed his camera to a long exposure, pointed the lens across the ocean, and snapped. He checked the digital image on the screen. Stunning. He hadn't lost his touch. At this time of night, most photographers would end up with either total blackness or a bright, harsh flash. But with a long exposure, he had managed to capture the pillows of waves across the ocean and the pepper of stars over the water. Not bad.

He was on his way back to the hotel when he spotted a woman walking toward him. She was alone, her long curly hair blowing in the wind. He was nearly certain it was Meghan.

He turned away as she passed. He gave her a hundred-foot lead, then began to follow. She'd never notice him from this distance.

66

Meghan sat at the edge of the hotel's private pier, her feet dangling from the side. She had walked past several beautiful boats on her way to this spot at the end of the pier. The moonlight across the deep blue ocean water was beautiful, but her eyes were focused on the screen of her cell phone. She was completely stumped about what to say to her own husband.

A new text message appeared. It was Jeff again. *Where are you? We need to talk.*

Maybe she shouldn't meet with Kate after all. She needed to smooth things over with Jeff. But Kate said she knew something about the TV show's plans to railroad Jeff. Meghan needed to find out the details.

She looked over at the three boats docked at the pier. In the darkness, she couldn't tell much about them except that they were large. She guessed they would be considered yachts, but she knew nothing about boats other than what she'd learned from the captain on their fishing excursion in the Bahamas.

What a perfect trip that was. She reminisced about their unofficial honeymoon. Jeff had organized every last detail, from champagne breakfasts to moonlit ocean swims. She shouldn't leave him waiting any longer. She could call Kate from her room. She was about to stand up when she saw a person in her peripheral vision stepping onto the pier.

She turned, expecting to see Kate.

Even though the person wasn't Kate, she began to smile. But as he came toward her, she realized that something was off. She'd known him for years, but this was an expression she'd never seen on his face before. She'd read somewhere that pregnant women develop a type of sixth sense to protect their unborn children from danger. Somehow she just knew. And he wasn't supposed to be here.

If this gut feeling turned out to be right, there was no way she could get past him and back to the hotel. He was blocking her path on this narrow pier. Pretending to be unconcerned, she waved and then started to call 911. But he was walking toward her too quickly. She could never place the call in time. And if she were right, he would never let her keep her phone. It could be used to track down her location.

On impulse, she changed plans. She slipped her phone gently between two wood slats of the pier. A crossbeam beneath the boards held it in place. She had to hope he wouldn't notice it there.

She stood up, deciding that she had a better chance of fighting back on her feet.

"Hey there," she said, praying with every fiber of her being that her instincts were wrong.

Then she saw the gun. There was no way to fight. She placed one hand protectively on her belly as he guided her along the pier and then shoved her onto the yacht. As she felt a sharp prick in the side of her neck, she prayed that someone would connect the dots between her phone and what was happening to her.

And then everything went black.

67

Jeff was pushing the elevator button as fast as he could. He never should have let Meghan run off like that. He should have chased her from the room and blocked the hallway if necessary.

The car seemed to descend impossibly slowly as he replayed their argument in his head. How could he have screamed at her that way? He had even accused her of not feeling anything about Amanda's death. He had been cruel. He knew Meghan didn't show her emotions the way most people did.

When the elevator doors parted, he rushed through the lobby, searching for any sign of her. I never should have doubted her, even for a second, was the drumbeat in his head. He, of all people, knew how hurtful it was to be suspected of harming Amanda. But how could Meghan possibly have run off this way? He had texted and called her repeatedly, and she wasn't responding. She has to know how terrified I'd be, he thought.

Jeff felt as though he was reliving a nightmare as he retraced all the same steps he'd taken when they first realized Amanda was missing. The pools. The shops. The promenade. No, he vowed silently, I won't let this happen again.

As he searched for his wife in all the same places he'd looked for Amanda, he realized how much the two women had in common, but only superficially. They were both smart and perfectionists, but their personalities were so different.

Jeff and Amanda had been together at just the right point in their lives for their relationship to make sense. When she was ill, she needed someone loyal and kind. And Jeff, who was struggling to figure out where a nice, easygoing guy like himself fit into the legal profession, sometimes needed a push from Amanda to be more assertive. Unlike Amanda, though, Meghan always accepted him just the way he was. She had never asked him to change, not even once. He was truly in love with her. They were meant to be together, not just at one phase of life, but forever.

How in the world could she leave me worrying this way? he wondered. He tried her cell again. No answer. Knowing Meghan, she had her phone on vibrate and might not even hear it.

As he was about to disconnect the call, an alert popped up on his screen inviting him to connect to one of the available wireless connections. He got an idea. Meghan always ran a "hotspot" from her cell phone because she didn't trust the security of hotel servers for her confidential client information. He was fairly certain that the range of a hotspot was about one hundred and fifty feet. If he kept searching for the name of her signal—"MeghanInBrooklyn"—he might be able to find her.

The network name popped up on the beach, just as Jeff was about to head back to the hotel. He scanned as far as his eyes permitted, searching for anyone who might possibly be Meghan. He felt a pang in his stomach as he spotted an elderly couple holding hands. They seemed very much in love. He wanted to be walking hand-in-hand with Meghan well into their eighties.

He kept walking, the light from the hotel growing dimmer. He stumbled across the uneven sand in the dark.

He continued to walk north, counting his steps until Meghan's wireless signal dropped. Forty-one steps, about a hundred and twenty-three feet. He returned to the spot where he had originally noticed the signal and walked south. Only eleven steps, or about thirty-three feet. He began again from that starting point and walked inland thirty steps before the signal dropped. No sign of Meghan anywhere.

There was only one direction left—the ocean. He felt a moment of panic until he realized that her phone wouldn't emit a signal from the bottom of the ocean. There was a pier, but he didn't see anyone on it. Still, he had to check. It was the only place left.

He walked the full length of the pier but saw nothing. Alone in the dark, he became so desperate he called out her name: "Meghan!" His phone was still getting her signal. Where was she?

He was about to turn back to the hotel when he saw the moonlight reflect off something between two wooden boards of the pier. He reached down and felt something metallic in the gap. It was the edge of a cell phone. It was Meghan's.

He'd found the signal, but his wife was gone.

68

Jeff knew instantly that the phone wasn't accidentally left behind. It had been deliberately placed between those boards, he was certain of it. The question was, why?

Her only recent text messages were the ones he'd sent her, asking her to come back to their room. No voice mails of interest. He pulled up her emails. The most recent message was from Kate. She thought the TV show was going to set him up as the prime suspect. No kidding, he thought. She wanted to meet Meghan on the pier.

Now where were they? His first instinct was that he didn't have Kate's cell phone number, but then he checked Meghan's contacts. Of course she had a perfectly updated address book. Typical Meghan.

Kate answered after two rings, but the wait felt like an eternity. He heard a television in the background.

"Kate, it's Jeff. Can I talk to Meghan?"

"Um, I thought this was going to be Meghan. You're calling from her number."

"I have her phone. Meghan's not still with you?"

"What are you talking about? I haven't seen her since dinner."

"You emailed her to meet you at the pier. I found her phone here, but not her."

Kate's voice was clearly worried as she said, "I hate to tell you this,

Jeff, but I didn't email Meghan, and I haven't left my room since I got back. If she was meeting someone at the pier, it wasn't me."

When Jeff hung up, he realized he had no one he could turn to. Kate may not have written that email, but whoever did was right: Jeff was the prime suspect. He could already picture the detectives' response once he reported his wife missing. They'd never believe him. They already thought he killed Amanda. Now they'd think he'd hurt Meghan, too.

Why had Meghan left her phone behind? What was he missing?

Jeff scrolled further back into her emails. Everything appeared to be about work. Then he saw one sent yesterday from a medical office. He opened it. It was signed Dr. Jane Montague, OB/GYN. He was about to close it when one particular word caught his attention.

"Hi Meghan, the nurse sent me your message inquiring about the effects of ultra-rapid metabolization on your pregnancy. Though it's good to know you metabolize drugs faster than most people, this only helps your doctors make sure you're on appropriate dosages when you require a prescription. It will not affect the baby one bit! Best, Dr. M."

Her pregnancy. The baby. They were having a child.

It all made sense now. That's why Meghan had been so eager to put this television show behind them. She didn't want to tell him while they were in the middle of an investigation.

He also understood now why Meghan called Amanda's attorney. Now that their family was growing, he and Meghan absolutely would need a larger apartment.

Jeff never wanted to take money from Amanda, but the fact that he was named in her will was exactly that—a fact. If Jeff would eventually inherit all that money from Amanda, wasn't Meghan's question to the lawyer reasonable, especially since they were now having a baby? The fact that Amanda's body was found only a few hours later was a horrible coincidence. But it looks really bad.

He felt tears burning his eyes. He couldn't believe he had ever doubted her.

He looked at the phone in his hand. Meghan must have left it for a reason.

He scanned the texts, phone calls, and emails one more time. He even looked through her photographs, hoping for some clue.

What else could it be?

The location. That was what she had wanted him to know. Not anything *in* the phone, but the location of the phone itself. Something terrible had happened on that pier.

He jerked when Meghan's phone rang in his hand. Please, let it be her. Let this nightmare be over.

"Hello?"

There was a pause on the other end of the line, followed by, "Is this Jeff? This is Laurie Moran. I'm sorry to call late, but I managed to lose the release Meghan signed for the show. My boss will go nuts. Would Meghan mind if I stopped by real quick? I'll sleep better knowing it's done."

"Meghan's not here. She's—gone. Please help me find her."

69

After her call ended, Laurie turned and faced the detective.

"He said she's '*gone*'?" Detective Henson was clearly unhappy about everything she'd learned in the last half hour. That Laurie had evidence she hadn't shared with the police. That her officers had watched Jeff, but not Meghan. And now, that their plan to find Meghan without scaring her off had failed.

Henson signaled to the officer next to her—she called him Tanner—to hand her his radio. "Peters, you still got eyes on Hunter?"

"Yeah, on the beach. Almost back to the hotel. He just got off the phone."

"Yeah, unfortunately that was us calling the wife. He said she's missing."

"What do you want me to do?"

"Bring him back here—we're in the lobby—so we can figure out what in God's name is going on."

Detective Henson made no attempt to mask her anger. "I can't believe you people didn't tell me all this hours ago," she said. "You should have given me those photographs the moment you had them."

Leo held up a palm. "Hold on a second. I backed Laurie up on that. We didn't think there was a rush. And we're able to do more as private individuals than the police. The minute we start working with you, the Constitution applies. We thought we were doing the right thing."

"We, huh? Funny, in my world, cops are a different breed than reporters and defense attorneys."

Leo was about to further defend himself when Alex interrupted. "I think it's safe to say we could have played things differently today. What can we do to help you now?"

"You can start by telling me what else you've been hiding from me."

Laurie started to say there was nothing else, but then she remembered there was one other thing. "Jeremy, the photography intern. I hired him to come to the hotel and take photographs of our subjects. His secret pictures from five years ago were helpful. I figured it was worth trying again."

"And you think he's here now?"

"I don't know. But I can find out." She called Jeremy's cell phone. He picked up right away and confirmed that he was at the hotel, in the courtyard. "Come to the lobby now. It's important," she told him.

They were still waiting for Jeremy when Jeff showed up with a man who Henson introduced as Sergeant Peters.

Jeff was speaking so quickly, it was hard to follow. An email to Meghan from Kate that wasn't really from Kate. The phone left at the pier. Meghan only called the lawyer because they were having a baby.

Detective Henson was unmoved. "We're going to sort through all that once you have a chance to explain it at the station. But, right now, Jeff, we need to find your wife. It doesn't look good that she's missing. We have some questions that we need to ask her. Running off like this makes her look guilty."

"Guilty? Wait, I was sure that you'd think I did something to her. You think Meghan—?"

"We just have questions," Henson said, "which means we need to find her. Now, we can start by you turning over that phone."

Jeff blinked in disbelief. "No." He placed the phone in his front pocket.

"That's a mistake, sir."

"It's called the Fourth Amendment. No searches without a warrant."

"It's going to look like the two of you killed Amanda together," she said.

"No, it's going to look like what it is. My wife is missing. Someone took her from that pier, and you clearly don't believe me. So if she calls this number for any reason, I want to be the one who answers it."

Laurie was about to try to intervene when she spotted Jeremy coming into the lobby, hurrying toward them. "Jeremy, please tell me you've seen Meghan."

70

Jeremy looked frightened, his eyes shifting between Henson and the other officers. "They look like police. They always turn everything around. They think the worst of me."

"It's okay," Laurie assured him. "I told them that I'm the one who asked you to be here. I hired you to photograph people from a distance. Do you know something about Meghan?"

"I saw her."

"Where? When?"

"About twenty minutes ago, maybe thirty. On the pier. But I don't want to get her in trouble."

"She's not in trouble, but we need to find her."

Now Jeremy was giving a nervous look to Jeff. "I don't think he's going to like what I have to say."

"I just want to find my wife," Jeff pleaded. "Tell us anything you know."

"I saw her with another man. At the pier."

"What man?" Jeff asked. "Where did they go?"

"I don't know who he was. I'm good at night photography, but it's impossible to make out faces. But she met him at the pier. Then they got on the boat."

"Jeremy," Laurie said, trying to sound calm, "we need as much information as you can give us. It's an emergency."

Jeremy covered his camera protectively. Laurie could tell he didn't trust them. They couldn't force him to talk or give them his camera. She thought about how she was able to connect with him earlier today at his house.

"This is your chance to help Amanda, Jeremy. Whatever you saw could help us find her killer. But we must act quickly."

His eyes brightened. "Meghan was sitting on the pier and a man came off the boat. I couldn't see everything, but she went away with him."

He lifted the camera from his neck and began scrolling through photographs on the digital screen. "You can't see his face, like I said, but he's taller than Meghan."

All Laurie could see were dark figures next to a boat. As Jeremy continued to flip through images, she asked him to go back to one that seemed to have a higher contrast than the others. "That one," she said. "I saw something that looked a little clearer."

When he reached the picture, he explained. "That bright spot is a white sign on the boat. The white metal catches the moonlight. It's a very good shot, isn't it? That's why I chose it for a close-up. You have a good eye."

But Laurie wasn't interested in the artistry of the shot. What mattered was the sign. LADIES FIRST.

"Ladies First," she said. "Why does that sound so familiar?"

Jeff was looking over her shoulder. "That's Nick's sign," he shouted. "He hangs it on every boat he charters. Meghan's with Nick? But he's in Boca with a client."

"No, he's not," Laurie said. "He was here, at least until this picture was taken."

"He texted me during dinner. He left hours ago."

"Then he never really left or must have come back," Laurie said. "Jeremy, are you certain Meghan got on that boat voluntarily?"

His brow wrinkled in confusion. "I can't be sure. I'm good at reading body language and facial expressions, but in the dark, from that distance? I just assumed—" He looked at Jeff, almost apologetically. He simply assumed Meghan was meeting up with another man, a guy with an impressive boat.

"I don't understand," Jeff said. "Nick's my friend."

"Or, he's not," Laurie said. She could feel all the pieces falling into place. She had been so focused on Jeff and Meghan, because they were the ones with a motive to kill Amanda. Jeff, for money. And Meghan, to be with Jeff. She was assuming that whoever killed Amanda—and Carly before her—was actually after them. But Laurie, of all people, should have realized that not all killers go after their actual targets. Some killers are willing to target people just to hurt someone else. A sociopath uses victims as pawns in a game no one else is playing.

Greg's killer had had nothing against Greg. He murdered him, and would have killed Laurie and Timmy, all for a personal vendetta against someone else.

She thought about Grace saying that Nick was much more appealing than Austin. But Jeff, unlike his friends, didn't even have to try. When Laurie first met Jeff, she'd thought of Greg. He'd had a natural ease that couldn't be learned or bought.

"He's doing this because he hates you, Jeff. He's jealous. You've found happiness with women who love you. All Nick has is loneliness and rage. Don't you see? Nick finds comfort around Austin, because he doesn't think Austin is as good as he is. But you're different. You're a threat. He wants what you have but he can't. Was Nick interested in Carly Romano at Colby?"

The mention of Carly's name seemed to spark a memory. "As I

said, she was one of the prettiest girls on campus. We were all interested. But no, there's no way Nick would do that. And a second ago, you acted as though Meghan was guilty."

"I don't think she is," Laurie said. "She's innocent, and she's in danger. Detective Henson, how can we find that boat? Nick told me it was the most impressive charter in the region."

71

Nick felt at home with his hands on the wheel, the ocean's air blowing against his face. He found himself smiling. LADIES FIRST. Normally that sign referred to his many female boating guests. He laughed out loud. Neither Carly nor Amanda had ever been at sea with him. Meghan would be the first.

Three different women, all distinct, but they all had one thing in common: they'd all rejected Nick's advances and fallen for that phony Jeff Hunter.

Taking Meghan had been much easier than forcing Carly into his car as she walked home from that party, or luring Amanda away from the hotel. One email from an untraceable, anonymous account, purporting to be from Kate, had done the trick.

With Amanda, he hadn't claimed to be someone else. He should have known she wouldn't want to talk to him alone. She was just like Carly. Women like them always raised their noses at him, like he was just a joke, a temporary flirtation. Amanda had rolled her eyes at him and Austin the entire trip at the Grand Victoria until he told her that Jeff was seeing another woman behind her back. That sure did get her attention! Suddenly he was the one in charge.

He took a look at Meghan splayed out on the cushions next to him. If only he'd known about the drug ketamine back in college.

He could have jabbed Carly in the neck with a needle. She had not gone into his car willingly.

He cut the engine on the boat. They were in deep water. Meghan was now conscious but, thanks to that injection, completely immobile. Based on what he'd read, she'd be in a dreamlike state, essentially paralyzed and living in an alternative universe. Soon, she'd be weighted down in the water, and he'd show up at his client's house, no one the wiser.

"How you doing over there, Meghan?"

She blinked, but he knew it was involuntary. She had no control over anything that was happening to her.

"I have to say, between Jeff's two great loves, I've always liked you better. Amanda was two-faced. She pretended to like me, but I could see the truth. I even heard her say to Jeff, 'I don't see how anybody who is as unlike you as Nick could be your best friend.' You should have seen her expression when I told her Jeff was seeing someone else. She immediately asked if it was you, by the way. Some friend, right? She was dying to know the details, no pun intended, but I made her wait."

He'd hinted that it was one of the girls in her bridal party, just to watch her squirm. He wanted to make sure everyone else had gone to bed before making his move. He told her to pick up her car after the dinner party and meet him at the turnoff at the end of the long driveway in front of the hotel. They could have a drink at the steak house across the street.

Even then, she protested, asking why they couldn't just meet at the hotel bar. But that night, she wasn't calling the shots. Nick replayed the conversation in his head. "What I have to tell you about Jeff could convince you to break it off. If that happens, I don't want anyone to trace it back to me. Jeff is my best friend. It's eating at me to tell you what I know, but in the end, it will be better for both of you. I won't tell you what I know unless you meet me away from the resort."

Meghan's eyes were now closed. "I played her like a fiddle," Nick said aloud. Even he could hear the satisfaction in his voice. "The rings were an especially smart touch. Jeff, the idiot who doesn't care about money, left his safe open. At first, I just slipped them out as a joke. But then I realized I could use Amanda's ring to frame Jeff. But, as with everything, I was a little too good at hiding her body. I thought it would take weeks or months to find her. But five years? Even then, it took my anonymous tip."

He felt a chill go up his spine in anticipation. He'd chartered the boat for his client meeting in Boca Raton, but now it was serving a second purpose. The police had found Amanda's body, just as he'd planned. Surely they found the ring, too. It was only a matter of time before they arrested Jeff. He'd weigh down Meghan's body, but she'd eventually wash to shore. It will take a little time, but they would have her remains, just as they now had Amanda's. And Jeff would spend the rest of his life in prison.

"I gave you enough of that drug to immobilize you for two or three hours," he told Meghan. "A bit wasteful, I suppose, because you have less than an hour to live." He chuckled at his own joke. "Don't worry, I won't strangle you like I did Carly. That won't be necessary. When I throw you overboard, you won't be able to move a muscle. You won't even be able to take a deep breath before you hit the water. You're going to sink like a stone."

Meghan White couldn't feel anything. Not physically. She felt terror, but her body was weightless, as if she were in a dream. She remembered a gun. The boat. A prick in her neck. Then she woke up, slumped on these leather cushions, her hands behind her back. She didn't think they were tied. They were just there, beneath her. She couldn't move.

She couldn't even control her eye movements, or she would look at Nick. She could barely see him in her peripheral vision. She could hear his voice and understand what he was saying, but wasn't sure if his words were real, or if she was hallucinating. Maybe she'd wake up any second in her bed at the Grand Victoria. But until then, she had to assume all of this was actually happening.

I have to save my baby, but how? she wondered frantically.

Nick sounded confident, as if he had plenty of time to enjoy his stupid boat and drone on about his evil deeds. That, she thought, will be your undoing, Nick Young. She remembered the email she got from her doctor yesterday. My baby is going to live, she vowed.

She just had to focus. Wake up, Meghan, wake up. Save yourself. Save your baby.

With every second, Nick's voice seemed clearer. She felt more focused. "I've thought about doing this so many times in New York, but I couldn't figure out a way to get you alone and unseen in the city. The email from Kate was easy. All I did was open one of those free accounts and write 'from Kate' in the subject line. And this boat is perfect. With Amanda, I had to jog the five miles back to the hotel after ditching the rental car so I didn't risk being seen. This time, I won't even break a sweat."

He looked at Meghan with a satisfied smile. He had no idea what she was thinking. Ten years ago, she had taken painkillers after having her wisdom teeth removed. She'd take one, feel better for half an hour, and then be in throbbing pain again. It turned out that the drug didn't work on her the way it was supposed to. Her doctor explained she had a gene variant that increased the liver enzymes that process certain drugs. She was what they called an ultra-rapid metabolizer.

Let that be the way it is now, she prayed. Please, please.

She wiggled her fingers against the cushions and was able to clasp them into a fist. She curled her toes and felt the muscles in her legs activate. And then she sensed that the engine of the boat was slowing down.

"Almost there," Nick said matter-of-factly.

72

Florida Fish and Wildlife Officer James Jackson had been eager to respond to the call about someone ghost surfing off Delray Beach. After eight years patrolling the beaches, he knew that speed on the water brought out the crazy in people, but he'd never actually seen ghost surfing in progress. According to rumors, some idiots out there thought it was a good idea to set a boat on throttle, then jump on a surfboard to ride the wake without a driver at the helm. Jackson was convinced the whole thing was a myth, but tonight there'd been a 911 call.

But when he arrived, there were no ghost surfers to be found, only a kid wakeboarding with his dad at the steering wheel and the extremely night-blind tourist who had called in the report.

Oh well, Jackson thought, just another night on the water. This job sure beat his old one with the Miami Police Department. Now the roughest criminals he dealt with were vacationers who underestimated the interactive effects of rum and sun. He warned the father and son about the dangers of water sports at night and suggested that they lower their speed and enjoy the stars.

Up ahead, he saw a good-sized yacht heading his way.

73

It had started with the wiggle of her fingers and then her toes, but Meghan could feel her entire body awakening. Her mind was clear. Her vision was absorbing every detail. She didn't dare move, but she was clenching and releasing her muscles to make sure she was ready.

Nick had stopped talking and was humming to himself. Meghan felt sick, and it wasn't because of the drug he'd given her; it was because of how happy he seemed. A wave of panic moved through her as she remembered the needle injecting her neck. Would it hurt the baby? She forced herself to push aside the question. She had to focus. Neither one of them stood a chance if she didn't get off this boat.

She felt Nick's eyes on her and continued to stare up into the stars, as though dazed.

Nick leaned back in his captain's chair, then shifted his weight. Still uncomfortable, he moved again. Then he reached into the back of his waistband, removed the gun, and set it next to the steering wheel.

As Nick turned his attention back to steering the boat, Meghan turned her head, her thoughts now totally clear, and took in her immediate surroundings. She saw the gun on the console to the right of the steering wheel but knew she could never reach it first. There was a hammer-like object in a slat on the railing just ahead of her.

A "priest," if she recalled correctly. On her fishing trip with Jeff last year, it was the object they would use to stun fish that were caught, brought aboard, and were wriggling on the deck. If she could use it to hit Nick, she might have a chance to grab the pistol. *I'll shoot him if I have to,* she vowed.

Seconds later, she saw what she believed would be her opportunity. Nick had his cell phone in his right hand and appeared to be trying to read a message while he steered the boat with his left hand.

She began to swing her legs up over the side of the deep leather chair. Stumbling, she took a few quiet steps to where the mallet was, bent over, and picked it up.

Her legs and arms struggled to obey her mental commands. She had only experienced this feeling once before. She had joined a group of students who were drinking tequila shots. Amanda and Kate half-carried her home as she had tried to will her legs to move forward.

Now, she needed that will again.

Nick cut the engine and slipped the phone into his pocket. This was as good a place as any. All he had to do was get the hand weights stored in the stateroom. He had slipped them into his duffel bag in the hotel gym, one more clue to lead police to Jeff.

As he got up to go to the cabin, he felt a glancing blow to his right temple. He stumbled to one side and fell back against his seat. Dazed, he looked up to see Meghan holding an object over her head, ready to hit him again.

Officer Jackson was admiring the yacht as it grew closer. It put the capital L in Luxury. He thought he recognized it as one of the higher-end charters available in the area.

The night silence was broken by the crackle of his radio, followed by an alert. A tracking device on a chartered luxury yacht placed the boat right in this area. The Coast Guard was on its way. The captain of the yacht was a man named Nick Young, presumed to be armed and dangerous, and believed to have a kidnap victim onboard.

Jackson cut the lights on his speedboat and accelerated toward the approaching yacht.

The second blow caught Nick on the side of his face, knocking him off the captain's chair. But as he fell, his hand grazed the gun, sending it to the deck beneath him. Horrified, Meghan watched him begin to recover and reach for the weapon.

She heard the engine of an approaching boat in the distance. Was it coming to help? But she couldn't wait. Nick would have the gun within seconds. He would shoot her instantly.

Nick's first shot came within inches of her neck. With one last desperate effort to save her baby's life, she hoisted herself onto the railing, held her arms protectively over her belly, and threw herself into the dark water below.

74

Officer Jackson saw the lights of the Coast Guard boats approaching. Just as he heard the sound of a gunshot, a figure jumped from the side of the yacht. He immediately turned on the handheld spotlight he had ready and pointed it into the water.

He saw someone leaning over the side and firing into the water.

Nick spotted the glare of a light from a nearby boat, and heard the sound of a voice through a megaphone, but all he could think about was killing Meghan.

He saw ripples in the dark waves. He fired a shot, then another, then another.

Meghan felt the dark, cold water wash over her, as she tried to stay submerged as long as her breath would allow. Everything now felt absolutely surreal. She hoped she would have enough strength in her arms and legs to paddle back to the surface. She could hear the dull echo of muffled bangs above her. Gunshots.

Nick was ready to fire again when a blinding light washed over the yacht's deck.

"Nick Young, you're under arrest. Drop the gun and put your hands over your head or you're a dead man."

Fearing her lungs would explode, Meghan flailed her arms and legs until her head was able to break the surface of the water. She gulped in a breath and saw Nick bathed in light with his head bowed and his hands raised. Another bright glare then covered her. She heard a voice yell, "Stay where you are. We're coming for you." I did it, she thought, placing a hand on her stomach in the water. We're okay. Me, you, and Jeff, we're all going to be okay.

Epilogue

One Month Later

Laurie looked out at the lights shimmering on the East River, thinking that she was going to miss this view. She was going to miss a lot of things.

"There you are," Alex said, appearing next to her. "Come into the den. The show's about to start."

"You know I've already seen it, right?" she said with a smile.

Alex had happily offered to host the viewing party at his apartment to accommodate the size of the audience. In addition to the production team and Laurie's family, Sandra and Walter Pierce were both in New York, visiting Charlotte, and had accepted the show's invitation to watch the episode with them. Alex's brother, Andrew, had also joined them. It seemed like the right time for Laurie to finally meet him.

After Ramon served cocktails, he came around with an impressive array of hors d'oeuvres.

Laurie followed Alex to the den, where Timmy and her father had saved a seat between them on the sofa. It had been exactly one month since the news of Nick Young's dramatic arrest shot across newspapers, televisions, and the Internet like a rocket. Brett was initially disappointed, convinced that traditional media had beat Laurie to the punch.

But thanks to Laurie's exclusive agreements with the show's participants, no other media outlet had the human stories behind the news. Jeff and Austin went back on camera to describe all those times they'd thought Nick was behaving more confidently than he really was. Laurie even managed to persuade Detective Henson to sit down for an interview.

"At first, he lawyered up," the detective said matter-of-factly. "He gloated that he could afford an entire team of the best lawyers in the country, ten times better than you, Mr. Buckley—his words, not mine. But I told him I didn't care how many lawyers he had; he'd be found guilty of at least Amanda's murder and the attempted murder of Meghan. I dared him to lawyer up. That was his best bet. Then he started to cry, blaming the victims."

Most riveting of all was Meghan's harrowing tale of being kidnapped from the pier behind the Grand Victoria. "I was so tempted to scream for help, but no one would have heard me over the sound of the ocean. And then I saw the gun. I had to decide in an instant what to do. All I could think about was our baby."

Just this afternoon, Jeff had sent Laurie an email to say they were expecting a girl. They planned to name her Laura. "Without you and your team I would have lived my whole life being under suspicion for Amanda's death," Jeff had told her.

Laurie had edited the show so many times, she knew every word by heart. She even knew that when Alex began his closing narrative, it would last exactly ninety-four seconds. "As one former FBI profiler told us, Nick Young was motivated by hate—a hatred for the romantic love he was sure he would never have. It seemed that the only women who rejected him were drawn to his friend Jeff Hunter. Tonight, Nick Young will sleep behind bars, charged with the murder of two different women and the attempted murder of another, in three states. And perhaps all women can sleep a little more safely."

The credits had just begun to roll when Laurie's phone started to buzz. Brett's, too, apparently, because he exclaimed, "Twitter's blowing up. We're trending. This is the biggest special yet."

The text messages on Laurie's screen meant more to her than any viral hype. The first note was from Kate Fulton: *I'm crying for Amanda, but am so glad you finally brought some peace for her family and friends. Thank you . . . for everything.* No one had found out about the time she spent with Henry Pierce years ago at the Grand Victoria. As far as Laurie was concerned, no one ever would.

Even Austin Pratt sent a note: *My engagement is being announced. She's a technological wiz, my kind of woman. Will change "Lonesome Dove" to "Lovebirds."*

The next one was from Jeff: *We're still in shock, but we're trying to move on. Thank God Meghan is doing well and we can't wait for the baby! Thanks to all of you for everything.*

The Pierce family had insisted that Jeff accept his inheritance from Amanda's trust. She would have wanted "Saint Jeffrey" to have it. Jeff had thanked them profusely and had told them that this money would allow him to remain at the Public Defender's office—where his heart was. He could support his family without going into private practice.

As Sandra and Walter rose from the sofa, Laurie couldn't help but notice that they'd held hands the entire night.

When the Pierce family left, Charlotte whispered a thank-you in Laurie's ear. "Still on for drinks Thursday?"

To Laurie's surprise, Charlotte had invited her to lunch when they returned from Palm Beach. She said she sensed that they were both busy women who could use some company outside the office. She'd been right. It was the first time Laurie had made a new female friend since Greg died.

"I wouldn't miss it," Laurie said.

• • •

Alex gave Timmy an especially long hug at the apartment door. Laurie tried to act as though everything was normal, but she felt the lump in her throat when she told her father she'd meet them in the lobby. When she was the last guest remaining, Alex give Ramon and Andrew a look that had them scrambling toward their respective bedrooms.

"So . . . ," Alex said sadly.

"It's not like you're moving thousands of miles away."

"No, but as I've told you, I have accepted a number of cases in federal courts, which will mean a lot of traveling in the coming months."

Laurie looked down at the floor. For the first time she noticed how beautiful this hallway rug was. Would she ever see it again?

It was just as she had told her father: if it's meant to be, it will happen naturally. They shouldn't have to overthink it. But deep down she knew that wasn't true. She wasn't letting it happen. And Alex wasn't leaving the show because of his law practice. He was leaving because he was in love with her. She was holding back and she knew why. She still missed Greg so much. She just wasn't ready to replace him.

"Did you see Walter and Sandra tonight?" She knew she was looking for something to talk about so she wouldn't need to say good-bye. "It looks as though they made it through. Some couples are soul mates, meant to be."

"And sometimes people have more than one," Alex said. "Look at Jeff. He loved Amanda, and now he loves Meghan. You see how happy they are."

His point wasn't lost on Laurie. "Good night, Alex." They held each other in the foyer, his only kiss a gentle one on her lips.

Laurie had no idea what Alex was thinking about as she walked out the door. It was a line from his favorite song: *God speed your love to me.*

• • •

Timmy was waiting in the lobby, trying to mask an involuntary grin. She couldn't imagine anything else that could have made her smile at that moment.

"Mom, I feel sorry for all my friends," he said mischievously.

"And why is that?" She looked to Leo for some hint of the punch line she sensed was coming, but he was sporting his poker face.

"Because their moms aren't nearly as cool as you are. You catch the bad guys."

When he hugged her, she thought it might be the best hug she'd ever had. She found herself looking forward to tomorrow. She had already found their next case. A young woman was in prison for a crime she didn't commit, and Laurie was going to prove it.

And Alex—when I'm able to open my heart again, please, God, let him be there.